The Caddis Man

Susan Slater

Books by Susan Slater
THE BEN PECOS MYSTERY SERIES

The Pumpkin Seed Massacre
Yellow Lies
Thunderbird
Firedancer
Under A Mulberry Moon
The Thaw
Ghost Dust
Paper Arrows
A Way to the Manger (a Christmas novella)

THE DAN MAHONEY MYSTERY SERIES
Flash Flood
Rollover
Hair of the Dog
Epiphany

STAND-ALONE NOVELS
Five O'Clock Shadow
0 to 60
The Caddis Man

The Caddis Man

Susan Slater

Secret Staircase Books

The Caddis Man
Published by Secret Staircase Books, an imprint of
Columbine Publishing Group LLC
PO Box 416, Angel Fire, NM 87710

Book layout and design by Secret Staircase Books
Illustrations © Ricardo Reitmeyer, Daniel Thornberg

First trade paperback edition: November, 2021
First e-book editions: November, 2021

Publisher's Cataloging-in-Publication Data

Slater, Susan
The Caddis Man / by Susan Slater
p. cm.
ISBN 978-1649140708 (paperback)
ISBN 978-1649140715 (e-book)

I. Title

BISAC : FICTION / Historical
813/.54

Author's Note
Caddis men, a slang term for the traveling salesmen of the 1800s, went door to door with their wares. Often bottles of condiments were carried in a myriad of pockets sewn into the lining of heavy overcoats. They literally carried their livelihood on their backs. Their namesakes, caddisflies, were a large order of insects that during the pupate stage, wove twigs, leaves, even sand and stone into portable housing that they wrapped around themselves, taking their belongings everywhere.

Part One

CONSTANCE WARKENTINE (1918)

CHAPTER ONE

Constance Warkentine buried her parents on a raw Kansas morning in March, 1918. Influenza, an epidemic among the elderly that early spring, claimed both within a week. Grief was stunning, but short-lived. Actually, she felt relief, then a sense of gaiety—illicit, irreverent, but persistent, and admonished herself for such callousness. But she was free without the fetters that pinioned others her age. And she was rich, elevated above the masses by fate and good fortune. It was her right to celebrate. She had been dutiful and loving all her twenty-nine years, but still an embarrassment—a late-in-life baby whose parents were shocked when she announced to the world their love was still carnal—a fact somehow scandalous.

The burial, delayed a week because of unyielding frozen ground, attracted a small group of church elders and their wives. Constance acknowledged murmured condolences, the doffing of a hat here and there, a peck on the cheek, but stood alone and willed herself not to fiddle with her dress. She tried to focus—"… pillars of the community, a brother and sister in God …"—and fought back thoughts of inheritance. All was hers that stretched as far as the eye could see beyond this family plot. She had been born to power and chafed to pick up the reins, to oversee, direct, build upon her father's already established fortune.

Had she loved her parents? Beyond honoring them as the Bible dictated? She wasn't certain. Her mother was standoffish and aloof—quick to criticize and slow to praise. There was no overt love—no show of affection by kissing or hugging and certainly no verbal follow up. Her father, on the other hand, seemed to appreciate her quickness, her accuracy with the books. He would often marvel that she had "a man's head on her shoulders," a rarity, if not a downright abomination.

Finally, the caskets were slipped below ground, and two men stepped forward to pepper their lids with dirt. "From ashes to ashes, dust to dust …" She bowed her head in brief prayer, then walked back across the brown, crusty grass to a semi-circle of carriages. Little blips of excitement put a spring in her step, and she imagined the singing of robins, so complete was her feeling of well-being. Would she travel? Perhaps, an entire summer in Europe? The opportunities were endless.

"I've arranged for the will to be read at the farm." The man touched her elbow, quickening his step to match hers.

She slowed and allowed Arthur Lloyd to take her arm.

"Arthur, how thoughtful to save me a trip to town." Still, a frown creased her brow. She couldn't help but wonder at his solicitousness. She could have easily met in his office.

"Friday might be a good day." He peered at her expectantly.

She nodded. Any day would be fine, the sooner, the better. She would like to get the formalities over with.

"Let's say eleven, then."

"Will you stay for lunch?" Perfunctory, a proffered kindness only, fingers-crossed that he would refuse.

The black mourning drape and wreath were to remain on the door for two more weeks, but that didn't preclude her from serving refreshments. Lunch for the bank president wasn't like entertaining, which was strictly forbidden under the circumstances.

"There will be three of us. I don't want to impose."

"Three? Who else will be coming?" This was a puzzle. She had no relatives.

"I've asked your pastor and a church deacon to attend."

She nodded, feigned an understanding and then dismissed the oddity. Maybe they were witnesses or, perhaps, he felt she needed some support—that she might dissolve into tears or shock or whatever young woman were thought to do under trying circumstances. That wouldn't be the case, but how was he to know?

* * *

They were prompt on Friday morning. Finally, the sun had coaxed a dozen crocus into full purple bloom beside the porch, making the day all the more momentous by their sudden beauty. She watched as the three elderly men climbed stiffly from a carriage pulled by a single, light draft horse, a mist of foam speckled across the breast pad of its patent leather harness. Hillsboro was a good two miles away, a taxing trot for even this youngster. There were horseless carriages in town but not many. Most folks preferred what they were used to—a dependable animal or two. But she admitted to curiosity. Perhaps, she should at least try one of the new-fangled things. She could afford to, now.

Deacon Peters handed the reins to her stable-hand, Clemetts, and the three climbed the front steps. She walked out on the porch. All had been to her parents' house before, but it seemed important to show this welcoming amenity herself and not appear so cold as to send a servant. They greeted her profusely, commenting on the flowers, on the beautiful day, on her own heightened color mistaken for good health and not the bursting-at-the-seams euphoria it truly was. As silence fell, there was some awkwardness, and she turned to lead them inside before Reverend Schmidt could dwarf her hand in his suffocatingly moist grip.

She'd rearranged the parlor earlier and dragged two armchairs to flank the reddish-brown horsehair sofa. At the apex of this horseshoe arrangement was a walnut table and chair. She preferred to meet in here and not her father's dark, cramped study now littered with stacks of farm papers—bills, receipts, orders—everything she needed to become familiar with quickly.

She took a seat on the sofa and absently smoothed the antimacassar, a piece of ecru tatting completed by a grandmother she'd never known. Arthur, nearing her father's age, appeared frail and drawn as he fidgeted and fumbled for his reading glasses. She turned to look at

Reverend Schmidt, a rotund, florid little man whose feet barely touched the floor. A born meddler if she'd ever met one. He took his ministry as God's nod of acceptance, giving him license to wantonly intervene where he wasn't wanted. She'd have little to do with him after today. He seemed nervous and glanced through her to the deacon sitting on her right.

"Well, I believe we're ready," Arthur cleared his throat and rattled the papers in front of him. In a drone he cited the date of execution and noted the fact that the will had been witnessed. He had been appointed as executor and was taking this opportunity to assure all parties involved that the courts had deemed this last testament legal and binding.

All preliminaries, she thought and let her gaze wander to the life-size photograph of her mother and father above the mantle. Such a severe looking couple in flat tones of sepia and black, their mouths drawn in tight lines of disapproval. Two people who took joy from their church and good deeds and little else. And, if their beliefs hadn't failed them, they were in heaven at this very instance continuing to serve their God.

"Let me begin by saying that the farm remains intact."

Constance loosely clasped her hands in her lap and faced Arthur.

Even though she knew what he would say, she must appear attentive.

"All machinery, animals, and equipment deemed necessary for the continued function of said property described as—"

Her thoughts leaped ahead of his ponderous drone. She knew the one thousand acres and their position in the county, the boundaries, the creek that crossed the southernmost pasture, the barns and sheds, carriage house and corrals—the list was lengthy.

"In addition to the residence at East Five Mile Road, assets include—"

Constance also knew them by heart. There were some two million in assets. Five hundred thousand dollars of railway stock among others, vacant property in town valued at one hundred thousand dollars, other holdings worth another half million including controlling interest in First National Bank, The Mercantile, and twenty rentals and, of course, the farm. There were several outstanding loans that Constance hadn't known about. All were current in their payments and seemed not to be a worry. She continued to give Arthur her sweet and attentive gaze.

"In summation, all of the above properties, as noted, free of encumbrance, owned by our brother in the faith, Galen Ezekiel Warkentine, loving husband of Anna Enns Warkentine, and beloved father of Constance Ann Warkentine, will be awarded in the following manner." Arthur took a sip from a cut glass tumbler of water. "There are a number of procedures that were to be followed if he had preceded your mother. Since that was not the case, let me just skip over to—ah, yes, here we are. Legal title to all properties and holdings and any monies collected from said properties and holdings will lie in trust to be administered under the leadership and guidance of my bank's president until the following conditions are met."

Arthur paused to nod benevolently and turn the page. "My only issue, my daughter Constance, is to remain on the farm and benefit from its largess until the age of thirty. If in that time she has not married, the farm and properties will be deeded wholly to the First Mennonite Church of Hillsboro, Kansas, to support their work done in the Lord's name. Constance will, at the age of thirty, find her life's calling in the ministry of the church's sisterhood and not remain a secular woman, but rather embrace the service of Christ and become a ward of the church for as long as she does live. In return, the church will provide for her every need both of a temporal and spiritual nature.

"If, however, she marries before her thirtieth birthday, the farm and holdings will be taken from trust and given over in their entirety to my daughter and her husband-to-be inherited upon their death by any sons that they might have, divided equally among them. If no male issue results from said union, the farm and holdings will revert to the First Mennonite Church upon my daughter's death with stipends for her daughter or daughters to be awarded upon their twenty-first birthday. May God bless and keep you dearest daughter, we are all one in Him."

Arthur placed the document on the table, slipped a handkerchief from his pocket and wiped his reading glasses. "Such a devoted father. He would have no peace if you were left uncared for."

Constance struggled to focus, but Arthur's benign smile blurred and faded. She braced her arms, pushing against the stiff sofa cushions and poking elbows into her sides to stay upright. If she was expected to speak, she could not. Nor could she cry out. All the anguish and unmitigated anger writhed in her middle and sent spasms of fear up her neck, down her arms and legs, and rendered her immobile. Terror, abject total terror, encompassed her. Trusts? Sisterhood? And the only way out had already eluded her for twelve long eligible years.

"Constance? My dear, this has been quite overwhelming. It often is like hearing the voice of the departed. We'll all miss your dear father. So well thought of. This community owes him so much." The deacon turned toward her, his hand not quite touching her arm.

Arthur stood beside her now, a hand on her shoulder, and the Reverend Schmidt leaned solicitously close to her face.

"Will you be coming by the deaconess home this week?" Specks of saliva spattered her cheek. "The facilities are really quite nice. You'll have a room of your own. Of course, the sisters take all meals together unless there is a reason, sickness, for example. You can bring a few pieces of furniture with you. Nothing too large. Perhaps, your bed with a nice dresser. If you're up to it, we could do an inventory today."

Without warning Constance pushed herself up from the couch and took a step forward nearly toppling the man. "I was twenty-nine in January. I don't believe my imprisonment begins for another nine months." Surprisingly, her voice was calm with hard, crisp edges.

"Oh. I thought … I mean I wanted to extend the invitation to have you join us as soon as you would like. There's really no need to wait. With the loss of your parents, staying out here by yourself could be—"

"I have the servants." The haughtiness hung from her words like icicles.

"Constance, dear, the three of us simply want you to give your life some thought. These decisions are not easy. You shouldn't be hasty, but you need to know that you have our support." Arthur moved as if to take her hand, but she recoiled.

"If you have nothing more, gentlemen, I ask that you excuse me." She walked to the door. Clearly not what they thought would happen, judging from the confusion as each looked to Arthur for explanation. Constance paid them no mind but pulled the bell rope for the housemaid to show them out as she walked across the foyer and started up the stairs. She ignored their hastily called good-byes and, using the railing to guide her, climbed one step at a time and fought the numbness that had settled in her limbs. To be cast out of her home, stripped of her inheritance—how could her father do this?

Hadn't he seen that she was truly his disciple? An able learner who had proved her worth by keeping his books? It was from Galen Ezekiel Warkentine that she inherited her mettle, her curiosity for life and her steadfast conviction that she could orchestrate his estate—her estate.

Finally, she didn't try to move forward anymore or keep back the tears and wracking sobs that rode one on top of the other, up from some center of her being to explode like sounds of the mortally wounded. She sank to her knees, clasping the banister, rocking and wailing until at last her breath came in raspy whispers and hiccupping gulps. Then she straightened, wiped her eyes and heard doors discreetly shut below. Curious servants, no doubt wondering at the unusual show of emotion.

Well, this would be the last display. Weakness was portrayed with tears, strength with action. And she hadn't lost yet. There was time to plan, to win, to beat these sniveling old men at their own greedy game. She could and would find a husband. She could not believe in a punitive God who wished her to serve Him on bended knee. No, her God would want her to have sons. Sons who would become pillars of the church, spread His word, build monuments to His goodness.

And her father? A poor, misguided individual governed by his times—women should be ornaments at best, not bother their pretty heads with numbers and money. Like children, to be seen and not heard. Have babies, raise a family, rule the kitchen—these were deemed womanly occupations.

She pulled herself up to her full height. She was tall, not an attribute but not a disadvantage either. If she took inventory, she'd list her thinness as a disadvantage, flat-chested as a boy, angular with bony elbows. But add her sapling strength and delicate wrists and ankles with the narrowest of feet—these were attributes that could arouse jealousy. Yes, her feet were truly her mark of beauty, the second toe longer than the first, a sign of royalty in ancient Egypt, she'd read.

And she was careful about her shoes, her instep always supported firmly by straps of richly finished leather. Her shoes were understated but expensive, brought from Italy by her father and made to specifications drawn on brown wrapping paper by chalk that tickled around the outline of her toes and clearly marked the height of her arch. Perhaps, as well, the height of her vanity, her mother once said.

She wore white, knew to play up the ethereal quality of her coloring. Her skin was the palest of ivory, her eyes, a clear grey. She bunched her thinning, ash-blond hair in a loose braid and twisted it into a circle at the nape of her neck. She neatly kept her blouses of organdy and tulle tucked into tailored black skirts. Over the years they'd swept her ankles then inched upward with the times to show off her well-turned ankle. And pearls—her father's gift from a mission to the Orient—no other jewelry except her mother's cameo. She was not plain. Older than most seeking a bridegroom, but not plain. Carriage and good skin kept her from being that. She could still catch the eye.

But looking at her left hand, she felt rather than saw the lack of a gold band. Her very life now depended upon righting that omission. Clearly marriage was her only salvation. So, who would it be? Quickly she inventoried the town eligibles. No. There was no one unspoken for who wasn't a drunk or feeble-minded or so old as to be ineffectual. No one. But she must find someone. Where would she look? But maybe, just maybe, it wouldn't be up to her. Wouldn't God provide, offer her the answer she sought? "Ask and ye shall be given." Hadn't she learned that in Sunday School?

As if a terrible weight had been lifted, she sank to her knees on the landing, her folded hands pressed against the banister and called upon Him to listen. She would have to have someone who would acquiesce, give her sons but never interfere with the running of the farm. Someone who could be trained, would look the part of a prosperous landowner, would be a Christian and devote his life to good works.

She gave God three months to answer her prayers. The time seemed appropriate. If, per chance, God chose not to answer, she still had six months to launch a search of her own. But so strong was her faith and so constant her prayer, she never for once thought God wouldn't act. Two months later when she found a likely man in her own kitchen, she was not surprised, but surmised that God had put him there.

* * *

"Miss Constance, come down here and help me with the choosing."

Mattie's voice carried up the back stairs, the servant's entry to the vast sleeping chambers above. A total of nine rooms included a nursery and play area built when her parents were young and hopeful of a family to fill them. Every room had high, embossed-tin ceilings and two wooden-cased windows that looked out over towering elms and drew in east to west breezes.

Constance yawned and pushed aside the filmy drape that surrounded her bed. How silly to sleep behind billowing, gossamer netting where there were few mosquitos, certainly none carrying life-threatening diseases. But when she had visited Africa as a child and slept in beds rigged like prairie schooners, she'd begged to have her own at home. Then she giggled. What would her bed—this great draped tower of white that took up quite a space—look like in the deaconess home? Would it even be allowed? She thought not.

"Miss Constance? You awake now?"

"Yes, Mattie. Give me a moment."

Whatever could be so urgent? Probably nothing. Mattie could be excitable. An African servant was unusual in Hillsboro, but Mattie had come home with her parents after a church mission to the Belgian Congo. The Congo was open to missionaries, welcoming even, and her parents had both gone several times to help with churches and schools and hospitals. Help with the building of them and the giving of money to see that they flourished after the missionaries left.

On one of those trips, it had been her parents' "assignment" to provide for Mattie and her brother, Clemetts. They had lived with the Warkentines in their homeland and then came with them to the States. The church in Hillsboro had been sponsors. It was deemed quite an honor by their village to be chosen, but Constance often wondered at the cost. Never to see their home again? Their relatives? The price was very high.

Another shout up the stairs. Hadn't the clock just struck seven-thirty? Mattie knew better than to call her before eight. Ah well, she was mistress of the house. Constance swept her hair up off her shoulders, then let it drop to swirl down her back as she grabbed her dressing gown. There would be no harm in running down the back stairs to the kitchen with her hair flying free and no shoes. If whatever it was could be so urgent, then she didn't have time for her toilette. But there was harm. She knew it the minute her foot hit the bottom step, and she was committed to entering the kitchen, that great, high-ceilinged, sun-drenched room with scrubbed oak counters and glass-faced cabinets. In fact, she'd already stepped over the threshold when she saw him—a caddis man, an itinerant salesman.

Turned slightly away from her, he leaned across the heavy plank table, intent on displaying his wares. He was arranging small brown glass bottles in a row, some with waxed corks, others with caps. All contained extracts or oils of cinnamon, clove, lemon, and almond. His shirt pulled tight over a muscular back as he dipped into the valise at his feet. His dark hair, much in need of a trim, crept over his stiff collar.

Constance stared as hazy illumination, emanating from a source that surely was divine, wavered about his head. If she'd needed a sign, God gave her one. The man's very presence quickened her breath.

She was jolted from her reverie by Mattie's stifled laugh. The mistress in her nightshirt about to entertain a gentleman in the kitchen was probably amusing. And then instead of doing what was no doubt expected of her—hightailing it back upstairs—Constance Warkentine pulled herself up to her towering five-foot eleven-inch height and advanced into the room. Wasn't this the miracle she'd prayed for? This dark, strangely irresistible man was surely providence at her own table.

"What exactly is it you're trying to decide, Mattie?" She willed her voice to stay calm.

"The quandary is whether to purchase the French vanilla or the plain, Miss," he said. His smile creased the skin around golden-brown eyes and pulled his wide mouth back to show perfect white teeth. He swung around easily, then got to his feet and offered her his chair—just as though it was his kitchen. But it was done so smoothly, never a hint that her attire was inappropriate, that she was doing at that very moment the most brazen thing she'd ever done in her life.

"What's the difference?" She kept her tone cool and even, as she sought the rungs of the chair with her toes and tucked her bare feet under the muslin that dragged the floor.

"This one's sweeter, a hint of sugar and less alcohol." He held out the long-necked bottle of French vanilla and easily let his hand brush hers, the slightest of contacts as he removed the cap. Intentional? She had no way of knowing but took a sniff of the pungent, heady natural perfume and kept her eyes lowered. He pulled out a chair and sat opposite before he reached across the table for the other bottle. "Whereas this one's still got the bean right here."

This time she took the bottle and peered at its contents. She tipped it to catch the sunlight that streamed through the etched glass panes that bordered the wide east window. What looked like a strip of withered brown bark floated in amber liquid, the finest bourbon whiskey from Kentucky or so the label claimed. Then she twisted the cap and brought the bottle to her nose. The aroma burst around her—whiskey and a cloying sweetness wrapped together that made her shiver at its strength.

"Did you call this a bean?"

"Actually the seed pod of an orchid found in Mexico and Central America."

"I never knew how vanilla was made." She thought of her wonder as a child when her father brought back a sack of nutmeg from East India—tough, acorn-hard nuts that when grated were aromatic but tasted bitter on the tongue. "Don't you ever ponder who discovered such a thing? How anyone could ever guess that this ugly shriveled thing could yield something so heavenly?"

"I imagine it took a little luck and imagination." He was smiling still, elbows on the table, relaxed, enjoying this tete-a-tete on a day that promised summer, in a room that captured light and held it captive. "I've always thought I sell as much vanilla for scent as for flavoring."

"You don't say." She'd never considered dabbing some behind her ears, but the idea had merit.

"It's the same principle as perfume, alcohol and a blend of essential oils."

"I suppose it is." She let her eyes stray to his and saw

a quickened interest, possibly admiration. Quickly she glanced at his left hand. Bare. Not even the indentation of having worn a ring recently, and a smile played around her lips as she looked down at the table and swallowed, forcing herself to breathe evenly.

"Do you have other flavorings?" Constance asked. She must keep him talking. Keep him in front of her so that she could look at him, get a feel for this wondrous being that God had so surely provided.

"My lemon is not to be bested. The oil is squeezed from the rind, not boiled down from the juice."

Once again a bottle found its way under her nose, then another, over and over. Pull the cork, offer the bottle for inspection, replace the cork, pick up the next. Almond mixed with orange and cinnamon and clove as bottle after bottle whirled beneath her nostrils. She felt lightheaded. She feigned interest in each and lingered, sometimes asking to be treated to a second whiff. And he seemed delighted, laughing as a pungent breath of peppermint brought tears to her eyes.

But their merriment had to end. She simply could not prolong it even another minute. She was the mistress of the house, and she was undressed almost—she had to think of what this must look like to Mattie.

"I'll take one of everything. Mattie will pay you."

Constance pushed back from the table and stood. Manners dictated that he stand, too.

"Harold Everett. Pleased to do business with you."

The grin said it all. He didn't hold out a hand, but nodded and with a slight bow turned back to sit at the table where Mattie was taking the lid off the lard tin. Household cash was always kept nearby for the traveling salesmen who sharpened knives, sold cookware and condiments, brushes and liniment and lingered in kitchens to flatter and cajole. The worn leather valise was proof of gainful employment. With his back to Constance, he bent over the task of writing a receipt.

Constance let her eyes rest on this handsome man who must be close to her age. There was a quietness about him that she liked but also an aptitude for conversation. And he seemed smart, knew his ciphers anyway. The minute she left the room she thanked God, who in His goodness, had sent this perfect being to lighten her burden.

* * *

At one o'clock that afternoon she'd taken her place on the porch. Mattie had trimmed her hair to frame her face in soft curls and brought the bun up to top her head at the crown. She wore a new pink, long-waisted dress of softest faille with puffy sleeves caught at her wrists in bands of white satin. She couldn't remember when she'd looked so pretty or so young.

The day was warm and beads of sweat dotted her upper lip. She pushed gently to keep the swing in motion. It wasn't a question of if he'd come, he'd be there. It was more a matter of what he would say to announce himself as God's chosen.

At three o'clock she watched Harold Everett walk up the half mile of herringbone-patterned, brick drive that made up the grand front entrance to her home. He'd gotten a haircut and now wore a jacket that was almost stylish although most probably second-hand.

But he looked glorious—clean-shaven, smelling of

cedar—his hat in his hand. His face was broad with dark, arched eyebrows over deep hazel eyes; thick brown hair parted in the center just brushed the tips of his ears. He was somewhat on the swarthy side—strong, thick of body but not fat—with a chest and shoulders that challenged the material of his coat.

"If you put these in water, they'll perk up quite nice."

She unwrapped the newspaper bundle he handed her. The flowers were peonies and white spirea, somewhat limp from the two-mile walk from town.

"Mattie will see to it." Constance pulled the bell rope she'd installed to the right of the swing.

"Don't you do anything yourself?"

He said it chiding, not mean but more to marvel at her status.

"Let's see. I tie my own shoes. And I choose what I want to eat." Her giggle seemed a bit unsteady.

"And suitors? Are you free to choose those?" Two dimples dotted his cheeks.

She caught her breath. His eyes sparkled, creasing into a smile at the corners. How brazen. He wasn't teasing; he wanted an answer. But wasn't he telling her that he already knew? Knew that he was the intended. She'd expected him to check in town. Only child of wealthy parents. Wayward girl. Stays out there to herself. An old maid now. Could he know that she had to have a husband? That whosoever betrothed himself to her inherited everything? No, she must remember her prayers. This was not some opportunist; this was God's doing.

"Is there someone around who wants to join the throngs?"

"Only if I'll be number one." His smile was sly, a

sideways glance to check her reaction.

She laughed and watched him relax, sliding down to sit on the top step, lean against the post and stretch short, muscular legs across the entrance. His trouser cuffs were frayed and pulled above his boots. But the gabardine was quality and well pressed, a crisp narrow pleat ran from thigh to ankle and hinted of boardinghouse laundry service. And the audacity, beyond self-confidence like a garment he'd slipped on and wore with aplomb. His cockiness took her breath away and intrigued her and charmed her all at once. So, this was what it was like to be pursued, courted actually. There had been no others—not at eighteen, or nineteen, or now. None could have gotten past her father.

"What makes you think that position is available?"

"Intuition."

"And gossip?"

He shrugged but didn't look away, just that same sly smile pulled at a corner of his mouth. "You could use a good man."

"And I suppose I'm looking at one?"

"The best."

They both laughed. She gazed out at the fields of wheat, tall and green, showing a blaze of gold in laden heads—it was still two months before harvest. The first that she would bring in alone. "What exactly is it that you want from life, Mr. Harold Everett?"

"To make my own way. To earn the respect of my fellow men. To leave my mark."

"And just how are you going to do all that?"

"I'm going to marry the richest girl in Hillsboro."

His eyes met hers, offering some sort of irresistible pact. An agreement between two people who knew beyond words how much the one needed the other. It was a communion blessed by God—of that, Constance was certain.

They stayed seated on the porch, talking, sometimes sitting in silence. At the end of an hour, he rose to go. Constance walked with him a quarter mile down the front drive.

"Will you come tomorrow?"

He nodded. Then he took her hand and kissed it above the knuckles. A long lingering press of lips to pale skin. "Your hands are beautiful." He slowly turned her hand supine and kissed the palm. That one gesture was the most intimate thing she had ever shared with a man. It left her breathless and tingling, the pink creeping up her neck. Lost on her was the jagged scar that peeked out from a raised cuff. A broken white line stretched across the underside of his wrist, wide and puckered along the edges from being clumsily sewn.

"Tomorrow then." Her voice sounded breathy.

He caught her left hand and kissed her fingertips before she could pull away.

CHAPTER TWO

He knew when fortune smiled on him, and she was fairly beaming at him right now. Hadn't he known it? Known that he'd find good pickings someday? He skipped a flat stone across the road and stood a moment to admire this Miss Constance's home. It was grander than most, set back as it was a quarter mile from the road. And trees, not only windbreaks planted solidly to the north, but big old elms and maples snugged up close to the house offering shade to the upper story. The gingerbread trim, painted a contrasting brown and yellow-gold, set off the smooth cream of the wrap-around porch. Red brick chimneys, one for every fireplace in the house, tallied at five, shot up into the blue Kansas sky like beckoning hands in welcome.

The house reeked of money. Good old comfortable established power—and a woman was at the helm. He shook his head. That by itself was reason enough for him to step in. The situation was ripe for change, if he had any sense of things. He knew the signs. She'd practically put a noose around his neck. Well, if she wanted him that badly, maybe she could just have him. A smile sneaked around his mouth. He wanted what was in front of him. All of it. And if that came with a breathless, skinny spinster, so be it. He could accept that.

Townspeople hinted at a will that left everything to the church unless—he laughed out loud. He'd never been the answer to anyone's prayers, least of all some woman's. But he had a feeling just maybe that was changing. It was about time he looked good fortune in the eye.

He'd gotten into town last night. Rode a flatbed on the eastbound train as it rattled its way up through Tonkawa and Ponca City crossing into Kansas south of Winfield. The fifty-car freight had labored past small communities, stopping now and then to take water from a tilted tower with a swinging spout. He helped with that, walked upright across the tops of cars to the engine, steadied the spout, then swung it back to be caught by a yard-man. And there'd been other odd jobs like sweeping out the boxcars after a load of grain had been delivered. In pay, the brakeman looked the other way, turned a blind eye to a free ride. But he was tired of free rides.

Harry Evans deserved better. He was a man of nineteen, just this side of twenty. He used to love the danger, the exhilaration of defying death. Once he'd caught freights clear across the United States—one ocean to the other, spent a whole six months just riding ... and running. But that had been more than a year ago. He was safe now. But maybe not safe enough to use his real name. Safer to be Harold Everett. But he could settle; there was time for that—especially if the paycheck was a tidy one.

He frowned as he felt the plain yellow gold band he'd slipped into his pocket—it'd spent a lot more time there than on his finger. Still, a problem, a hitch in his plans. But even now his mind was working on how that might not be an obstacle. Because nothing, nobody, should stand in his way. Flat and simple, opportunity beckoned and he wasn't going to miss the call. Once this spinster found out who she'd married, well, then there would be a good-sized settlement for him to disappear. And he'd do just that, never to be heard from again. Still, the size of this fortune might keep him around extra long.

* * *

He came early the next morning, walking up the long driveway, coat slung over his shoulder, and sat in the kitchen poking good-natured fun at Mattie while Constance dressed. When she finally came down and had a cup of tea and sat with him at the table, he suggested a picnic. He asked that she show him all of her land, saddle some horses and ride the boundaries, then find a spot to spread a blanket and lunch.

Mattie helped her cut thick slices of bread, cheese, and ham and make fresh potato salad, then tucked her best custard tarts into the basket for dessert. Constance hummed while she prepared the food and glanced over her shoulder often, getting the shivers every time she looked at this wondrous creature.

Clemetts brought two horses to the back door around ten. A matched pair of bays that took her to town in the carriage once a week. But now, Constance wore trousers and sat astride. Both mounts were skittish and didn't settle until they'd cleared the barns and loped across the pasture behind the house. Then, out of sight of their stable-mates, they were amenable to trotting and eventually slowed to a walk when asked.

"This is the best day of my life." Harold reached over and grabbed her hand and held it, keeping his horse alongside.

She giggled. How could she admit that she couldn't remember having a better one herself? Wasn't it better to pretend there had been other suitors?

She skirted the cemetery with its two fresh mounds. Taking him there would seem like flaunting, tempting fate somehow, even though she knew her father couldn't reach beyond the casket to yank away this happiness. But he would if he could. Of that, she was certain.

Harold was quiet during most of the ride, stopping only to remark on the fields, their progress before harvest or an acre that needed clearing along the creek. He chose the picnic spot, a grassy knoll shaded by hundred-year-old cottonwoods all dipping forward some thirty feet above the ground to form a canopy.

"I'm going to walk some before I eat." He unsaddled his horse and replaced the bridle with a leather halter, then did the same to her horse and deftly hobbled the two so that they could graze but not wander far.

There wasn't an invitation to join him, so Constance busied herself with spreading the blanket and putting out the luncheon items. When he returned, he fell to eating and remained silent so long that Constance felt the stirrings of worry. Was he having second thoughts? Would he take back his promise of yesterday? What was worse, she could think of nothing to say, but she watched as he stared out across the creek chewing bites of ham sandwich and changing his posture only to pick up a glass of iced tea.

"This here's a lot of land." He waved in a 180 degree arc that took in the creek and all beyond. "It'll take a lot of men to harvest."

"And someone to lead them."

"You think I'm that someone?" He looked at her full on and she met his gaze.

"Yes." It was a simple answer, too brief, perhaps. But what did he want her to say?

"There's those that would laugh, thinking of me leading others."

"Who?"

"Just some people. I've tipped over a couple outhouses in my time." He was joking now, hazel eyes crinkled at the edges. He put his sandwich down and lay back on the blanket, arms beneath his head. "You know, you're my good luck charm. If you could sprout four green leaves, you couldn't be more lucky." He shaded his eyes to look at her, and she felt herself blushing. "The sun on your hair, like it is right now, makes it turn gold." He squinted up at her, scrutinizing her face until she turned away. "Hey, cat got your tongue? How 'bout a thank you for a couple fine compliments?"

She giggled as he pulled her down beside him and she rested on her elbows gazing into his eyes.

"Do you believe in destiny?" he asked.

Her heart skipped a beat. Of course, she believed. Why ever else would he even be here? "I believe my meeting you was destined."

"Yeah. Me, too. I can't believe no one else had come along and swept you away."

"My father was strict. No one would have been quite good enough."

"I know what you mean. My pa beat the daylights out of me just for good measure—whether I needed it or not."

"Where's your father now?" She was curious; it was important that she knew his family.

"The same place yours is."

"Dead?"

"One and the same. Along with my ma."

"Have they been gone a long time?"

"You could say that."

"I'm sorry."

"No need to be. I grew up in spite of 'em. And I didn't do a half bad job, if I do say so myself." The grin again as he lifted his head, thrust his chin out and turned right and then left for her to admire. They both laughed and she turned over onto her back, her arm just grazing his. The warmth of his skin burned to the touch and she shivered and moved away.

"Where are they buried?"

"Who?"

"Your parents, silly. Weren't we just talking about them?"

"Yeah." But his mind wasn't on his parents. She could see that as he raised on one elbow and leaned over her to trace an index finger along her nose, outline her lips, then start down her neck to the hollow above the breast bone.

"So where?" She wiggled out of reach mostly because she thought she better and a bit because she was afraid. Nothing would happen, she assured herself of that, but the way he made her feel. It was difficult getting her breath.

"Iowa. Now, can I come kiss you?"

She nodded and closed her eyes but opened them again when she heard him pull away. He was sitting up, his back to her, going through his pockets finally pulling something from his shirt.

"Damn. Thought I'd lost it. Close your eyes and don't open them until I say to."

She sensed him inching closer, his breath warm on her cheek. But he didn't kiss her, instead he took her hand and slipped something on her finger.

"There. What do you think?"

She sat straight up, the fingers of her left hand splayed out in front of her. On her ring finger was a narrow-twisted band of gold with a pin-point ruby nestled in a cup of green-gold leaves.

"With this ring I promise to make you Mrs. Harold Everett, just as soon as I can." He rocked back on his heels, all the time watching her. "Well, come on girl, say something. Do I need to take it back?"

But there was nothing to say. Nothing that the tears didn't shout out all on their own. So he pulled her to him, smoothed her hair back away from her face and then offered a clean white handkerchief.

"I take it all this wet stuff means a 'yes'?"

She could only nod and dab at her eyes.

"So, when's it gonna be?"

"August."

"That's the end of the summer. I was thinking you'd make about the prettiest June bride old Hillsboro has ever seen."

"June is one month away."

"So?"

"That's too soon."

"Too soon for what? We both agree that this is our destiny."

"I need time to plan."

"You buy a dress and bake a cake. What more?"

"I want to design my dress, have it made. I'll have to send off for the lace. And I need engraved invitations. I want to invite the whole town. There needs to be food and music. All these things take time. August is only three and a half months away. Maybe that's too soon even."

"So August it is?" He sighed and turned away.

She nodded, mesmerized by the twinkle of the ruby on her finger and didn't notice that he seemed upset. The ring was a size big but she'd have it cut smaller. She never wondered how he could have possibly come up with a ring at all in less than twenty-four hours—how he knew so suddenly that he'd need one. She was too busy thanking God and turning the ring to catch the light.

Then he kissed her, pulled her chin up and bent forward, placing his lips over hers. And she was afraid that she'd stop breathing. With a little gasp she pulled away, took a gulp of air, but he quickly leaned forward and placed his hands around the back of her neck, pulled her to him and pressed his lips to hers again, hard. She felt his body stiffen before he roughly nipped her lip, and fell on top of her bringing a hand up to caress a breast.

"No." She squirmed away and struggled to her feet.

She held her hands crisscrossed over her chest.

He rolled onto his back and glared up at her.

What had she done? Said no? Why was that so bad? She wasn't idiot enough to sleep with someone before she married. No one did that unless she was a total fool or received money. She fit in neither category.

"I don't want this. Not yet. I'm not that kind of girl."

"You got a ring on your finger."

"What's that supposed to mean?"

"It means I just got through making promises. Some girls would be a little appreciative."

"Shouldn't we first see if you keep them?" She wanted to grab the words back, shred them when she saw the look on his face, a squinty hardness around the eyes before he turned away. She couldn't afford to be choosy right now. She needed this man and if she ran him off, God might think her ungrateful and not provide another.

"Please, Harold, listen to me. This is all so sudden. I'm not used to, I mean …" She couldn't finish; her heart was in her throat. What if he ran? Just up and bolted? She watched as he stared out over the creek. What was he thinking? He took a couple breaths and sucked on his lower lip, then turned to her.

"Connie, come here. There are just some things that a man can't turn off as quickly." His anger mastered, he beckoned for her to sit beside him again.

"Maybe we should go back." Still, she wasn't ready to just go to him. Did they have an understanding or would he try the same thing again?

"All right. Have it your way." Abruptly, he stood, looked at her as if he wanted to say something, then strode quickly to ready the horses.

She dusted her breeches, hanging back until he brought the horses forward and offered cupped hands to help her mount. He was silent, not meeting her eye. They rode in silence until he stopped to inspect more fields of wheat—red turkey wheat brought from Russia by her grandparents—but mostly the strain between them hung like a pall. With the barn in sight, Constance reined in her horse.

"Harold, I've made you mad. I never meant to. It's just that I ... I have to be married before ... before I can do what you wanted back there. I need to make that perfectly clear. I want to be your wife."

"Look at me, Connie. Do I look mad? Forget it. I don't think the physical part is all that important to us, anyway."

Before she could ask what he meant, he'd urged his horse into a gallop.

* * *

The days that followed were a blur. There was so much to do. She was the happiest she'd ever been, but she was not so smitten that she didn't realize—gift from God or not—he had his shortcomings. For starters, he was three inches shorter than she and not quite twenty, not her age after all. Yet, he seemed worldly wise. She found out from gossiping townspeople that he'd arrived the day before they met on the flatbed of a freight, wearing a great flowing wool coat, his possessions rolled in a blanket, and his wares tucked neatly into an aging leather case. One good pair of shoes, slung around his neck, dangled from knotted laces.

And he readily admitted to being a traveling salesman—nothing more, nothing less, and there didn't seem to be any history other than that. None that he wanted to share. She'd nudge and prod, but the bits and pieces didn't add up to much. A farm boy from Iowa who supported his widowed mother until she died, releasing him to seek his fortune elsewhere at the age of sixteen. There didn't seem to be siblings—at least none that could be discussed. The topic put such a strain on any conversation that she stopped asking. Wasn't it enough that he was with her now?

Even with these unknowns, all would have been bliss had it not been for an unfortunate incident involving Mattie. Some five years her junior, Mattie had never seemed a sexual being, as having any wants whatsoever past serving her family and certainly no physical needs. But she'd been wrong.

It started with Harold's asking to stay at the farm. Why should he pay boardinghouse rent when he could be of use to Clemetts? Sleep in the barn, get up with the roosters and work until sundown? There was a lot to learn before harvest. If he lived there, he could familiarize himself with what had to be done.

It did make sense. And she wasn't one to be worried about talk, townsfolk passing judgment. After all, she wasn't alone with Harold and if people couldn't give her the benefit of the doubt, trust in her good judgment and upbringing, then let them think the worst. There was something just a wee bit titillating about Constance Warkentine being discussed as a "fallen woman."

So, he moved in, brought his possessions to the barn and accepted the handout of a couple blankets. Bathing was a dip in the stock tank, and she assumed other matters of his toilette meant the stand of poplar directly behind the house. When she protested, he said the outdoors built character. If he could be comfortable with this, then so could she. But she had an outdoor privy put in anyway.

All went smoothly at first. Constance reveled in the fact that they saw each other every day. She took to getting up at dawn to meet him in the kitchen for breakfast, sitting over a cup of tea or coffee, sometimes two, laughing at his ribald good humor, basking in the attention of her very own man. She was smitten and hung on his every word. She'd gathered a pinch of loose hair left on his brush in the barn and folded it into her mother's cameo locket. She wore it over her heart.

She could tell that Clemetts liked him, started to defer questions about the machinery to him which denoted a trust he'd always reserved for her father. And Harold worked hard. She had to give him that. This husband-to-be was no shirker, even if he seemed more comfortable doing than giving directions to others.

By the second week in June the weather had turned so unseasonably hot and muggy that, as a topic of conversation for the townsfolk, it surely must have edged out her situation. Without a breeze, it became too stifling to sleep in the upstairs bedroom, and she would sit on the porch swing stirring the still air and drying the perspiration that streaked between her breasts and prickled around her neck.

On a certain Wednesday evening, she'd even brought down a comforter and quilt, intent on spreading the bedding on the porch's wooden slats and spending the night. She'd just stretched out on her temporary bed when a sound caught her attention. At first it was difficult to pinpoint just where the laughter was coming from. The garden? The barn? Faint, but unmistakable, Mattie's shrieks cut through the heat.

Whatever could be the matter? It sounded good natured, no one was getting killed, anyway. But if the sound was coming from the barn ... she didn't need to think further but wrapped a quilt around her and ran down the porch steps to follow the sound across the back lawn.

There was a light in the barn, which in itself was unusual. Electricity was not to be wasted. The huge dull red structure loomed before her, now bleached of color by a three-quarter moon but glowing from within with wavering light. She raced to the double front doors but pulled up, panting. One side was open, giving a panoramic view of the breezeway between the stalls. And there was Harold with Mattie thrown over his shoulder turning in dizzying circles, a hand clutching her ample rear, the other too close to her breasts for Constance's liking.

"What's going on?" She shouted to be heard.

"Your turn's next." Without missing a beat, Harold deposited the shame-faced Mattie feet first on the ground, then steadied her, keeping an arm around her shoulders.

Constance pushed the door open and walked toward them. "I asked what's going on. I want an explanation."

"Hey, a little fun, that's all. Keep your shirt on."

Mattie squirmed out from under his arm and stood looking at the ground. "I jus' brought the Mister some late supper. He's a been working like a mule."

Constance could see the tray covered by a gingham cloth but she wasn't a fool, and she could see in Mattie's eyes that there was more to all this than delivering supper. Did they think she was blind? She'd seen Mattie turn away to button the top two buttons of her bodice. And in that instance Constance felt a flush of emotion unknown to her before. It was all she could do to keep from smacking Mattie sharply across the cheek. Instead she muttered,

"Looks like more than errands to me." Constance bit her lip to keep from saying more and felt her cheeks flame crimson with anger.

"So, she got fresh with me, and I was teaching her a lesson. No crime in that unless you make it one."

He stood before her in a belligerent stance, legs apart, arms akimbo, sweat glistening on his forehead in the muted light of the meager wattage of the single overhead bulb. Mattie was forgotten. Now it had become some struggle of pride and dominance between the two of them like that morning beside the creek.

"If you say so." She raised her eyes to stare him down. She could have said more, but didn't. She didn't exactly win the tussle but neither of them lost, and that was important. Intuitively she knew the importance of that. This was not a man to be bested by a woman. Even a woman who could make him incredibly rich. No, appearances were everything. She'd have to remember that.

She reached out to take Mattie's arm. "Let's the two of us leave Mr. Everett to get some rest and enjoy his dinner in peace."

Without another word, she steered Mattie toward the door and the two of them crossed the lawn without looking back. But vaguely, the incident bothered her. She supposed all would be well after their marriage when he would bring his needs to her bed. And that was all it was. She was sure of that. A deprivation that drove him to lust after the flesh of women. But a husband with a willing wife wouldn't wander. She'd overheard her father discussing the needs of men with Arthur Lloyd when she'd been all of sixteen.

He'd excused a fellow parishioner some dalliance because his wife was sickly and known to sleep alone. Even then she'd caught the implication that turning your husband down just invited trouble. And wasn't that what was happening here? Harold had mistaken her rebuff and without outlet for his desires was tempted elsewhere. She'd have to keep a careful watch.

* * *

She took Mattie into Hillsboro to shop for her wedding, more to keep an eye on her than anything else. Constance still smarted from what had almost taken place. But she put it from her mind and kept the two of them busy with almost daily trips to the milliner, the dressmaker, the bakery. The lace alone would take two full months to arrive from Belgium, via New York. And Harold had wanted to get married next month. Men simply did not understand the planning, what had to be done.

The community expected it of her. They would want to celebrate this joyous day with her, see her in her finery, sample the pastries and meats fixed especially for them. She would spare no expense. The party was for her friends, her parent's friends. No one would forget the day that Constance Warkentine became an Everett.

But it was not to be. Barely a week after the incident with Mattie, she was awakened sometime past midnight by the insistent whinnying of a horse. The sound mingled with angry voices and pushed into her consciousness. Afraid that some animals had slipped the confines of their corrals, she hurriedly dressed and, careful not to wake Mattie in her alcove behind the kitchen, let herself out the back door.

The night was calm, sticky, and close so that just the exertion of hurrying out onto the lawn left her breathless. At first she didn't see them, the two figures under a giant elm one holding the reins of a skittish roan. But at the sight of her, they jumped apart, Harold taking a few steps in her direction.

"Did we wake you?" He seemed solicitous and all apologies.

"I heard the horse."

By now she was abreast and could see the other man, small in girth, shorter than she, jacketless in the heat, thinning hair plastered to his scalp with a pomade that left a hint of wilting roses in the air. He looked at the ground and seemed bent upon not meeting her eye. He wasn't familiar, not from around Hillsboro anyway.

"I don't believe we've met." She waited a beat but no name seemed forthcoming.

"I, ah, we were just talking business. Nothing to worry yourself about. You just go on back to bed now." Harold wasn't meeting her eye.

"You the missus?" Finally, something from the taciturn visitor.

"This is my betrothed." Harold moved to put an arm around her shoulders. This in itself was a rare display of affection that Constance marveled at.

"Then I reckon it's just about all in the family. If you're fixing to marry this gent, you might want to know why I'm here."

"Shut up." Harold's arm slipped to his side. Constance could see the flexing of his jaw muscles.

"Suit yourself. Pay now or pay later." The visitor seemed to be enjoying himself and wrapped and unwrapped his horse's reins around his fingers. The horse, having already called out a greeting to those in the barn, stood quietly.

"Pay for what?" Constance found her tongue.

"You gonna tell her or should I?"

Suddenly, Harold grabbed her arm and, almost jerking her off her feet, propelled her toward the porch.

"What's going on?" she instinctively whispered.

"Something I needed to take care of a long time ago."

"What?"

"Connie, I killed a man. It was mostly an accident, but the judge said I should pay restitution to the widow, send money each month until I'd paid her one thousand dollars."

"And that kept you out of jail?"

"Something like that. It was a fight—"

"Over what?"

Wife or not, Constance sensed it had something to do with a woman. "Over what?" she repeated.

"The reason isn't important."

He wasn't going to tell her. All the more reason to suspect something he wasn't proud of. "Have you kept up on your payments?"

"Best I could."

"Then why is this man here?"

"He's the wife's brother. He wants more money."

"The balance that's owing?"

"Yeah."

"And that sum is?"

Harold studied the toe of his shoe. "Nine hundred and seventy-five dollars."

"Seems you've paid off precious little."

"I've done the best I could a dollar at a time."

Did she believe that? Did it matter? It appeared that she would need to buy off this man, her much-needed husband. But it rankled. How much more was there that she didn't know? How much more that God would test her with.

"I'm not saying I won't rest your debt but I, *we*, need assurances that this is the last we'll see of this man. I'll send the exact amount to the judge who presided over the case. Is there something in writing, a judgment?"

Harold nodded.

"I'll expect a court-ordered release. So, you go tell your visitor now and get on it in the morning."

"You're a marvel, Miss Constance Warkentine, an absolute marvel." Grinning all the while, he bowed from the waist then turned on his heel, taking long strides toward the man by the tree.

Had she done the right thing? A killing. Should she have pressed for more information? Of course, young men with hot tempers could get into trouble. If only she didn't need this man. With a pang she added half out loud, "If only I didn't care so much."

By the time she reached her bed, she was wide awake, and it was nearly dawn when she fell into a fitful sleep that wasn't to last long.

There was no warning this time when Arthur Lloyd and the pious Reverend Schmidt came to call. Seven a.m. and the two angry men in crow-black coats stormed into her house, demanding she listen to them, waving Mattie aside, calling to her up the stairs. It was little consolation but she made them wait a full thirty minutes while she dressed.

Constance stepped into the drawing room and Arthur started immediately. "I will not allow you to marry a vagabond." He paced across the bright flowered pattern of the African Kilim, coming to a stop beneath her parent's photo. "Think of these dear people and the disrespect you do them—if you don't think of yourself."

"This is criminal. You've lost your senses," the Reverend broke in, his voice strident and angry. She couldn't prove it but his mood must reflect the fact that she'd kept them waiting.

"You've lost a fortune." Constance was the only calm one. She brushed past them and perched on the edge of the piano bench that jutted out from the baby Steinway. She lightly rested her left hand on the closed keyboard so that her ruby ring caught the sunlight. "Your concern is admirable but all the more understandable when one realizes the stakes."

The Reverend gaped at her. Brazen talk coming from this woman. "I offered spiritual guidance to your father. His life was my church. His good deeds were done in the Lord's name and the Lord demands his due. It is fitting and right that your father's money goes to furthering missions to the poor. This ... this wedding is a mockery done by an errant daughter who spits on her parent's grave."

"Such strong rhetoric." Constance was amused. There was nothing they could do. She was certainly of age and didn't need their blessing. But why were they here this morning? After the visitor last night? Had the miserable little man with the rose-scented pomade gone to them?

"Constance, listen to us." Arthur shushed the Reverend and tried another tactic. "We have your interests at heart. What do you know about this man? He could be anything. He could murder you in your own bed." Aha. Maybe they had some information. But, then again, why would anyone bite the hand that feeds it? No, this visit was purely happenstance. They knew nothing. She relaxed.

"Is all this necessary? Do you really hope to gain

anything other than my ill will with your ranting?"

Arthur slumped heavily onto the sofa across from her. "You're as good as prey for any unsavory type that comes down the road. And he's living here, I understand. Constance, you're behaving like some hussy. Yes, I'll use that word with you. I've known you since you were born, but never did I think that you would take leave of your senses. Well, I won't see this marriage take place. I won't see some fortune-hunter take advantage—"

"Arthur, please. Let's not be melodramatic. I think I'm a good judge of character."

"Is he a Christian? Do you even know that?" The Reverend was getting a second wind. "You don't know, do you? Well, I'll tell you one thing. The two of you will not be married in my church. This is the way the Devil works. I would not be surprised if the religious community decides to shun the both of you." With a look of utter satisfaction, he pulled himself up to his five-foot five-inch height and stood in front of her.

"It doesn't matter." She hadn't thought of this before, but she didn't need this miserable little man. And suddenly she saw what she had to do—under the circumstances—it was imperative that she do. "We will be married here in our home by a Justice of the Peace. The marriage will take place one week from today."

"But your religious commitment?" The Reverend was fairly sputtering now. Had he suddenly realized what he had done? Severed the church from the inheritance? Because the church was still in the playing if there were no sons. Constance watched him squirm and look to Arthur for help.

"I don't want our conversation to end this way." Arthur,

always the placator, reached out as if to take her hand, but she withdrew and moved to stand by the stunning expanse of glass that looked out over the drive, a window bordered by etchings of local birds.

She smiled but kept her back to them. This was a moment to savor. She was almost giddy with the heady power of winning. And she had won. No one could deny that. Now, she could have a little fun. Sternly, she turned to survey her visitors.

"Arthur, if you're concerned about your position at the bank, you can put your mind at ease. I will not make any changes for the next six months. I will, however, attend a thorough audit of the books—no, no, not that I anticipate finding anything out of the ordinary—this is just a precautionary step."

Arthur looked as if he'd been slapped.

"I like to think of it as my own inventory of my inheritance. When I return from my honeymoon, I'll contact you. Now, gentlemen, I really must get busy. There are so many plans, you know."

There was nothing else to say. She stood as the two of them hemmed and hawed, determined to find something to stop her. But there was nothing they could do. So finally, she ushered the grim-faced men to the door and watched them wait in stony silence for Clemetts to bring the buggy. They had tried and failed. There was nothing else anyone could do. Constance Warkentine would become an Everett.

CHAPTER THREE

The wedding took place on the twentieth of June, just one month from the day they met. Mattie and Clemetts attended. Mattie, giggling and ill at ease, wore a smock embroidered with scarlet birds and flowers on black with strings of horn, shell and bone draped across the bodice. Her hair, tethered by wooden beads in blues and yellows, bounced out from her head like tentacles. Clemetts looked fine in one of Mr. Warkentine's black suits, although the cuffs of the coat pulled above his wrists.

The ceremony was brief that late morning in the parlor under her parent's picture. Officiated by a Justice of the Peace who obviously longed to be elsewhere and seemed uneasy with the odd gathering in front of him. There had been no music or baskets of flowers or time for a dress.

She wore an ivory blouse and skirt. The only color, a simple nosegay of violets pinned to her blouse had gone limp within an hour.

A wedding luncheon of cold potatoes and side-pork was eaten alone, just the two of them at the great oak dining room table. The austere man who'd supervised their vows bolted at the first opportunity. The two-dollar payment only slowed his escape long enough to share a cup of chilled cider.

Still, they were married. Harold had purchased two plain gold bands most likely with the money she'd paid him for the condiments. But that didn't matter. Their vows were clear and binding. She'd wanted a honeymoon, had been prepared to spend upwards of five hundred dollars to travel for a month or more—revisit all the exotic places of her youth. But Harold had been appalled. Spend that kind of money and be gone from the farm right before harvest? That would invite disaster. He'd upbraided her for thinking like a woman.

Reluctantly, she admitted he was right. It was only that she wanted what all brides want—the ceremony to be special, different, unforgettable—and a trip to leisurely become one with her beloved, sailing beneath the stars on moonlit nights. But she chided herself at her childishness. Useless romanticism, her mother would call it. She must count her blessings. Harold had promised to love, honor and obey, hadn't he?

But love? It was a word that hadn't been said between them. Not in all the afternoons on the porch, not in the privacy of their walks or the picnics. And Constance didn't question the lack of this endearment. She had never asked God to send her someone to love, only a man to save her life and give her sons.

Since there wasn't to be a honeymoon, Harold had followed Clemetts to the barn after lunch to continue work on the horse-drawn machinery that needed to be in tip-top shape in barely three weeks. The thrashers would perform twenty hours at a time until the last of the wheat was cut and stacked; teams of horses or mules, changed often, were kept fresh and willing. At the height of it all, some thirty men would take up residence in the large room attached to the barn. Harold had much to keep him busy.

So she sat that first long afternoon as Mrs. Harold Everett in her father's office studying the deeds and trusts and miscellany that was her heritage. There was only one last thing to do and that was consummate this union that made everything possible. And she felt a twinge of eagerness, unladylike curiosity at what, exactly, it was going to be like to beget her sons.

Earlier in the day she had made room for Harold's clothes in the cupboard in the master bedroom, her parent's room, now freshly papered to match new curtains, blue flowered sheers that swirled easily in the slightest of breezes. He'd had precious few things to put away—two shirts, a change of drawers, a good coat. She'd see that this meager store expanded. He was of modest means but that didn't mean he wasn't a good man. God simply wouldn't have sent her someone unworthy.

She felt they took overly long at supper. It was almost eight before he'd come in, washed up and met her in the dining room. And he seemed preoccupied, eating in silence and barely acknowledging she was there. Finally, the meal was over. She'd hardly touched the roast chicken and dumplings, but rose to follow as he pushed back from the table.

"Shall we go up now?"

"I'd rather read the paper for a bit. It's early yet. But you go on."

Her heart banged against her ribs. Why was he stalling? He'd been eager enough a month ago and then again that night with Mattie. But he had said he didn't think the physical part would be that important to them. What had he meant by that? Some inclination that might keep him from her bed? She didn't know that much about men but weren't they supposed to be lusty sorts—at least in the beginning? He had surely proved to have normal appetites.

"I do have a piece of cross-stitch that I started. I think I'll sit awhile." She followed him into the parlor. But she was too agitated to sit still and soon excused herself to go upstairs.

She spent an elaborate amount of time on dressing for bed, brushed her hair a hundred strokes, chose between three lightweight cotton gowns all with ribbons or mother-of-pearl buttons, washed the parts of her body that she knew would come into contact with that part of him designed to give him pleasure. And all the time kept an ear on the chiming of the grandfather clock.

The clock had just struck eleven when he came to bed. Had he hoped she'd be asleep? She thought so.

"Connie, we don't have to rush this act if you'd rather not." He sat on the edge of the bed with his back to her, easing his arms out of his suspenders, slowly unbuttoning his shirt.

"This part is important. I'm ready to accept my duties as your wife."

"I thought that day on the picnic that this wasn't something you looked forward to."

"Now, I'm married."

"I don't want to do it if it's something you think you have to do."

"I want to." She almost echoed *have to* but caught herself in time.

She was sitting up now, hugging a pillow to her chest. What was he trying to say? That he didn't want her in this way? But he must. This was the part that was important. She was almost thirty, well past the childbearing age of most women. Time was running out.

Was it some embarrassment? Some reluctance for her to see him naked? She lay back and turned toward the wall and listened as he put his clothes away—opening and closing the cupboard doors, turning off the light, walking to the window to pull closed the drapes—all done in maddening slowness before he returned to bed.

The mattress tilted sharply, then righted with his weight as he stretched out. She stayed turned away and waited for him to do something. At last, he laid a hand on her shoulder.

"The first time can be painful. I could spare you that."

"I don't care. I'm your wife. I'll be able to bear the pain."

She sat up and slowly pulled the gown over her head then turned to kneel in front of him rocking back on her heels and keeping her eyes closed. The room was dark, illuminated only by a first quarter moon peeking through a crack where the drapes barely touched. He was silent. She felt his eyes roam over her breasts, her stomach, the part between her legs. She opened her eyes when she felt him leave the bed, then watched as he stood with his back to her and slipped off a pair of long flappy drawers.

"I wasn't sure our marriage needed to be more than an agreement on paper. That you would want more …" He sat on the edge of the bed, facing away but she could hear his breath coming faster now.

"There must be children—sons to inherit when we die." She threw her arms around his neck and buried her face in his hair. "Please, give me sons."

"Children can wait, Connie." He unclasped her hands that hugged his neck.

"No." She clung to him. "I can't wait."

Still there were a few moments before he turned to her. And then he simply looked at her before he eased her onto her back. It was a perfunctory mating, a little rough as he kneaded her breasts and dragged the stubble of a beard across her chin. His kisses hurt, her lips were pressed so tightly against her teeth. And then he squatted between her knees and guiding his member, thrust inside with a suddenness that made her recoil in blinding pain.

And that was the end of it. A few forward motions and then he withdrew, simply deposited seed that dripped down her thigh, and moved on—in this case fell to the side and began to snore.

She lay awake and wondered about it all. Wondered at how her body tingled at remembering him inside her and how quickly she had forgotten the pain. She put a hand between her legs and felt the warmth and wetness. She should wash but she reveled in the novelty, the suddenness with which she had become a woman. She pushed up to prop herself on one elbow, then fell back. The house servant would change the sheets in the morning.

This was her husband—and the beginnings of sons. There was no need to wonder about love. Had her parents been in love? She honestly didn't know. Two people bound by the same hopes and dreams would be enough.

Sunlight broke across the horizon and tumbled through the window before she fell into an untroubled slumber.

As the days after the wedding night unfolded, Constance found herself infatuated with her new husband. The pleasures of the bed drove her through the day in anticipation. There was no pain now only the headiness of belonging to another human being in this intimate way.

She'd follow him to the barn, sit and moon over him as he worked, clutch him to her in the middle of the night until she felt him grow hard and then ripping at his night clothes taking him into her, into the center of her being, panting in haste and with a need that didn't make him recoil until—three weeks after the wedding.

"I don't like someone coming at me all the time. Women aren't supposed to ... to want it like a man."

Constance sat up in bed watching him undress. "So what am I supposed to do, pretend I'm not interested? Lie back and just wait?"

"What you're not supposed to do is rip my clothes off. Connie, I excuse all this because you want sons so badly and you're gonna be a bit old to start having them. Your body has made you desperate."

"Desperate? My body?"

"Yes. Nothing says we have to have a child right away. I'd hope we'd wait awhile."

"I don't want to wait."

"Connie, I can't work fifteen hours in the fields and be expected to perform every night. I need my sleep, my energy. We're facing a harvest in one week." He sat down heavily on the bed and stretched out on his side. Before she could think of anything to say, he was snoring.

She let him be after that. Not because of their talk but because of the good news, the news that would awaken her in the middle of the night and make her hug herself in joy—two weeks after their wedding night, she had missed her period.

It had happened just as she knew it would. She was pregnant carrying the son that would seal her destiny as the inheritor of all her father's riches and give distance to the greediness of the church. The tiny being assured her she would never grace the halls of the sisters' dormitory. She'd told no one. She wouldn't risk ridicule at knowing so soon. Besides, who would she tell? For now, it was her secret, but she found herself, on occasion, laughing out loud and bore the curious stares of the help in silence.

Her life was so full and rich. Still, she longed to stop the vicious gossip. When she and Harold would shop in town, their visits to the hardware store or clothiers seemed of unending interest and a report would get back to her through Mattie who heard it from a domestic at the Condons, or McCandless, or Supernois that—

"The new mister spent ten dollars on clothes."

"That opportunist thinks he knows about farming, just let him bring a crop in, then we'll see his colors."

"You'd think Miss Warkentine would have thought of her position first—to think she married outside her own church—didn't even have a church wedding."

That part still rankled. She'd been cheated out of what every girl dreamed of, swirls of white and lilies of the valley and baby's breath. But that paled in comparison to the insinuation that she had lost position—something she'd been born to, had never questioned—now did she detect less reverence when she passed on the street, fewer doors held open for her to pass?

Constance became obsessed by her need to silence the townspeople. But how? Then, thanks in part to a conversation with Harold, a plan took form. One evening when she had settled to her embroidery in the parlor after supper, Harold put down the evening paper and sat staring into space.

"A penny."

He looked up startled.

"For your thoughts."

"That'd be a waste, I think."

"No, out with it. You've seemed preoccupied for some time. Is there some problem with the farm?"

"None I won't be able to remedy."

"So there is a problem." She hated his reluctance to share with her. She had to pull things from him.

"I'm going to have to go into Marion, or even Strong City, to get harvest hands."

"Why? Why wouldn't you use the able-bodied men around here?"

"Because they won't help us. The church has seen to that. We're lepers in this community. There are rumors … I'm sure you've heard them. People are saying I'm using you, taking advantage, that I married you for your money."

"Did you?" She kept her voice light, but as always, he took a long time to answer.

"What do you think?" He squarely faced her but there was no hint of merriment in his eyes. This verbal sparring had taken on a deadly earnestness of late.

"You're my husband. No one can change that." She met his stare. "No one needs concern himself beyond that point. With time people will come around."

"Maybe." He'd turned away from her, pensive, withdrawn into some private world of thought that she wasn't privy to.

It was the church that needed to initiate the acceptance, be the first to embrace her husband as one of its own. Why hadn't she thought of it before? If she could turn this powerful entity around, somehow put Harold in good stead . . .

"In the meantime, we don't have any hands except Clemetts and the two older men who work the stock."

"Then get help from neighboring towns. Be generous, if you have to. We must have a successful harvest. I hear the Stuckeys over by Marion have six strapping boys. They'll hire out as a unit including their mother. I could use some help in the kitchen."

He nodded, folded his paper, tucked it under his arm and rose to go out into the foyer—without a good night, a touch, a kiss—the small affirmations a man should be expected to show his new wife. It crossed her mind to tell him he would be a father in the spring. But she needed to be certain. It was too early yet. She let him go. He often spent his evenings in her father's study sleeping on a rollaway that was left made up in the corner. And strangely, she didn't mind. He'd given her a child and for the time being that was all that mattered.

* * *

The harvest was over in seven days. The same time it took God to create the world, her father used to say. But what a seven days! Even with the Stuckey family there weren't enough hands. Harold went down to the freight yards and gathered up those down on their luck. When he brought the first motley crew home, Constance was infuriated.

"They're beggars. Maybe running from the law. Not a one has had a bath in who knows how long."

"Most are good men, Connie. Bathing don't make a person more honest than the next. Give 'em a chance to earn their keep."

She fumed and swore she wouldn't sleep at night and used their presence to get him back to her bed. But the men did work out. Too tired at the end of a sixteen hour day to do anything but eat and go to sleep, they kept to themselves and her worries dissipated.

And she soon became too busy to care. Up at three to prepare a breakfast by five, then clean up, do the laundry from the bunk house, prepare lunch, clean up the kitchen, do the baking that was needed for the next day or shopping, or butchering, then back in the kitchen by six to prepare the big meal of the day. The routine was exhausting.

Every evening Mattie and the two maids helped her carry two wide multi-leafed tables out on the lawn. The heat that July was unbearable.

There was no feeding the crew indoors. Sometimes she thought she couldn't spend another minute in the kitchen herself with all its boiling kettles, the oven eating log after log.

After the first couple days, she'd gotten rid of the linen tablecloths as simply being something that was not needed. To wash and dry and iron them every day was overburdening her already overworked staff. She served the same thing twice, then three times and didn't think anyone noticed. It was enough if food was simply warm, abundant, and served on time. There were no other demands. But it took a bushel of fresh corn, a peck of tomatoes, beans and greens, a dozen chickens, a side of hog, fifteen pounds of flour and ten dozen eggs to just get through a day.

On Thursday the skies were overcast. By ten in the morning, intermittent drops of rain splashed down the kitchen windows. The crew worked feverishly, driven by this turn in the weather. There was nothing worse than wet harvest years with machinery stuck in the fields and grain going moldy. But after a brief shower the sun came out, and the humidity rose, keeping pace with the temperature until everyone prayed for sundown. But even then, the heat didn't slacken.

After the dishes were washed, Constance walked down past the barns to get some air. The night was stifling. Her blouse stuck to her, absorbing the perspiration between her shoulder blades, her breasts, at her waist.

When she came to the pond, she didn't hesitate but took off her shoes and then her skirt and blouse, spreading them carefully on the grass. In slip and bloomers, she waded out, sinking into the silt-bottom, relaxing in its coolness, not minding the squish between her toes. Dabbling her fingers in the water, she walked waist-deep and watched the moonlight ripple a path in front of her. It was the first time that day she'd been comfortable.

"Race you to the dock."

She jumped. She'd been so absorbed in thought she hadn't seen Harold until he dove into the water and took an obvious head start. But she was a good swimmer and caught up with him, then passed him, touching the flat wooden structure first.

"Ha." She was out of breath but feeling victorious as he pulled himself up to sit beside her. She turned to the side so as not to stare at his nakedness.

"You're good." He shook his mop of hair like a dog, then slicked it back from his face with both hands.

"As a child I wanted to be a mermaid."

"You would have made a good one." His laugh sounded good, natural, and relaxed as he stretched out, flexing his toes. The harvest was going well. He should be proud.

She leaned back on the narrow pier, hands clasped under her head and closed her eyes as a breeze skipped across wet skin. Her husband was beside her, naked as God had made him, triumphant in his newfound calling as proprietor of Warkentine farm. This felt so good to be here with him; she wanted to hug the moment to her, never let it go.

"It's like you were born to this work. I watch you with the men. They'd follow you anywhere; they respect you so much."

He was turned toward her, propped on an elbow, water glistening across his abdomen.

"You think?"

"I know."

"Maybe some of them. The ones I've given a chance."

She heard the pride in his voice. "This harvest is every bit as good as any I remember my father having. People were afraid of him. They're not of you. That makes all the difference."

If she was surprised when he ran a hand up under her slip, she didn't let on. Then suddenly he was on top of her pulling at the wet material, tearing her underpants, ripping the bodice of the slip to expose her breasts. His ardor overwhelmed her. She thought to caution him that someone might see but didn't. For the first time in their love-making, he sought her mouth and kissed her gently, thrusting a tongue between her lips as he entered her.

"Connie, I …"

The sentence went unfinished. If he'd been about to say "I love you," he'd thought better of it. A series of grunts and a stifled cry brought the act to an end. And he slipped from her, rolled off the side of the dock and splashed heavily into the water. She sat up, hugging her knees and watched his dark muscled arms slice air, then cut the pond's surface, his head turning left, back right, carrying him to shore.

He had meant to say that he loved her. She was certain of it. And that, she knew, would make her life complete. The success of the harvest would shut up most of the dissenters. And if it didn't, then she'd just play her ace.

She'd given it lots of thought recently—how the most powerful, the entity that could reinstate them to a position of power within the community, was the church. And it was safe now. She was married, and there was a child coming. She could afford to court the Church. And if she could position Harold as a deacon or maybe someday as a lay minister, she would dare those to defy God's chosen with their tongues.

Picturing the fat Reverend Schmidt, she could just imagine how he would relish a generous sum of money, a gift large enough to build the new west wing of the sanctuary or even a college in her father's name. No, the money wouldn't be turned away. It would assure Harold's future—and hers.

And then she laughed out loud. Sitting in torn underwear on a dock in the middle of the stock pond having been ravished by her husband wasn't the most reverent time to be thinking of God. But He'd understand. She put a hand on her stomach. Was it her imagination or was there already a pronounced roundness? Could this son of hers be making his whereabouts known this early? Silently, she thanked God in all His goodness.

* * *

She waited until the end of the harvest to approach Harold with her idea. They shared a late supper of cornbread, boiled potatoes and roast beef the first night after all the extra help had left. At last something other than chicken. She'd relieved Mattie early and sliced the cucumbers and tomatoes and peppers herself, arranging them in layers with peeled baby onions in a bowl filled with vinegar and sugar. She spent two to three hours every morning in the garden, now depleted after the harvest, but it would come back and she'd help with the canning in the fall.

"You know," she said as she watched him spear three slices of roast at once and pile his plate, "the success of the harvest has made people give us second thoughts."

"Yeah?" He never seemed bothered by talking with his mouth full.

"Ours was possibly the best organized harvest and went off with the fewest hitches. I mean not once did our machinery go down. That's thanks to you. People see that. I think they're ready to give you your due."

"I don't care what people think, Connie."

"I do. My family has been important to this town. We've had their respect for years. I'm not going to give that up."

"Even though you married a caddis man?" He was teasing now.

"It wasn't the caddis man who got over three hundred bushels to an acre."

He shrugged and cut a thick slice of bread. But he liked her compliments, she could see that.

"Harold, I think I know how to get everyone to forget your beginnings."

"I don't see how there's much to forget."

"You know what I mean. We need to give you respect. A position of honor in the community."

"So you've got some pill I can swallow?" Again, that grin.

"No, silly, we're going to position you in the church."

"The church?" He put his fork down.

"Reverend Schmidt won't turn away someone who's willing to work for God."

"How much is this going to cost?"

"Maybe a college."

"A whole college just to make me legit?"

"My father always wanted something like that done in his memory."

"I can't see you romancin' that old fool Schmidt just to buy me some respect. I thought the church was out of it once you married."

"And had a son." This was probably as good a time as any, she thought and took his hand. "I'm pregnant. Our son will be an April fool."

He didn't smile at her joke but simply looked at her. "You sure?"

"Yes."

He pulled his hand away and pushed back from the table. "I didn't think it'd happen so soon."

"Aren't you happy? Isn't it what you wanted?"

"It's what you wanted, Connie. I never thought I had much say in it."

She was tongue-tied. Didn't he want the baby? What was he trying to tell her? Before she could answer, he'd slammed out the kitchen door.

The next morning she was late coming down for breakfast. The first queasiness had kept her lying flat until the spasms passed and so she was surprised to find him waiting in the kitchen.

"Connie, I'd like to talk about the church, your plans, the things you mentioned last night."

No apology, but had she expected one? At least he seemed eager to discuss becoming a part of the church. And surprisingly, he'd seemed amenable, anxious even to do what she suggested. He accepted her gift of a leather-bound King James Bible and kept it with him during the day, placing it on the floor beside him when he retired. She doubted he ever opened the book. It seemed more for carrying around—it was often on the seat of the buggy when he went to town. That struck her as odd. But it was the principle of the thing. At least, he wasn't shutting God out.

What was most surprising, he grew a beard. Even her father, devout in his faith as he was, abhorred facial hair. But Harold reveled in it, only trimming his mustache when it curled over his upper lip and threatened to obscure his mouth. And it changed his appearance—made him appear squat and square, a stolid *little* man. But maybe that was just Constance's preoccupation with her own height. She'd catch their reflection in a plate glass store front—the willow and the stump. And yet this man who adopted the round-crowned, straight-brimmed black hat of his new-found faith was her husband. And that very word never ceased to thrill her. She never questioned why he might embrace the church so willingly or quickly.

She chose a Tuesday for her visit to the church's rectory and went by herself, not telling Harold of her mission. She dressed carefully, giving special attention to her hair and drawing it back away from her face. She wanted to look mature and not fanciful. The longer skirt, longer than was currently the fashion, and crisp white long-sleeved blouse gave her a no-nonsense air that was exactly right. Recently, she'd taken to wearing wrappers around the house, loose, flowered house-dresses with kimono sleeves that allowed air to circulate around her body, a body thickening ever so slightly through the waist.

The good reverend was out when she first knocked. His secretary, a woman Constance had gone to high school with, said that he would be back in an hour. She thanked the woman and said that she'd wait, almost forcing her way in when the woman didn't understand that she meant there.

"Constance, what a pleasant surprise."

She'd heard the hurried whispers in the hall before the minister walked into his study. She bet he was surprised.

"I won't take up too much of your time. I have a proposition that might interest you."

"Could you bring us some iced tea, Mrs. Hall?"

He hesitated to take her hand, started forward then detoured behind his desk. Wanted to, if she was any judge, but thought better of it until he found out why she was there.

"I believe it is time to put things behind us. My husband is proving himself to be a good member of the community, and it is my wish that he also become a good member of the church."

"Yes." He drew out the *s* overly long but didn't say anything more, just squinted his eyes in concentration. He wasn't going to comment until he'd heard her out, but that was all right.

"I believe you could use someone in his position, someone who is eager to learn the ways of our Lord, someone who could carry on the missions started by my father—support them with his own money and actual physical presence."

At this she thought his eyes flickered with interest.

"Harold would need your tutoring, your acceptance. I have thought it was time to carry out my father's wishes of building a college bearing his name. I own a five-acre tract at the north edge of town that would do nicely. I can certainly understand your concern over my marriage but, surely, now you can see that the choice was a right one for me. We should put our differences behind us, wouldn't you say?"

"Perhaps, that is, I mean to say it does appear in all likelihood that Mr. Everett is a fine upstanding young man, a sterling addition to the community."

"And a college? Surely you cannot be opposed to something I know you and my father talked about often."

"No, of course not. The college is a fine idea. But so are the missions. We could accept a helping hand with spreading the word of the Lord. Harold would be willing to travel? Spend time away from home for the ministry?"

"He would consider it an honor, Reverend Schmidt."

She'd approached the subject, and Harold had seemed taken with the idea of traveling. Maybe too eager, she'd thought at the time. But it was the center of the church's work. A new college, a mission, perhaps to Africa, and all would be well in the community. Yet, she was still somewhat shocked that Harold had been so eager to follow her suggestions.

"Have you thought of a sum that would be comfortable in starting the college?"

"One hundred thousand should get us started," she said.

The little man nearly fell over himself thanking her. They sat for another few minutes discussing architects and then Rev. Schmidt saw her to the door. They also set up a schedule for Harold's visits—first there would be lessons in church history, then a founding in ritual and beliefs— Reverend Schmidt assured her he looked forward to it, and she left, knowing that she'd regained any ground that had been lost. Her position was intact. And she could pat herself on the back for coming up with the right solution.

A trip to the Congo—her parent's oft-traveled destination was perfect for a first-time missionary. After a bloody start, the country had established a system of government referred to as the "colony trinity" made up of three entities: the state, missionary, and private company interests. The country, according to her father, was poised for industrial expansion—a railroad was being built to connect its commercial center with revenue producing, outlying regions. How exciting for Harold to be involved with this ground-floor capitalism. And how important that he carry on her parents' work in guiding, perhaps, the establishment of other missions.

* * *

He had to get away. It wasn't like what he'd thought. This wasn't some soft young woman who'd yearned for his masculinity, his strength to run the farm. No, this was someone who fought him for control—would always fight him for that. He was an outsider—yes, the provider of her home but never one to be let in.

The harvest was a success. Even she acknowledged that. But she was the one to do up the books, go to the bank, plan next year's planting. He wasn't much better than hired help. And now a baby. That was a complication.

He didn't want a child. A child could get him into real trouble. A man could run out on his wife but never a child. No man worth his salt would desert his family. But if he left now, long before the baby was born ... masquerading as the church's chosen might keep him from being recognized and allow him to travel.

On a Friday evening some three months after the wedding, Harold came up from the fields and washed for supper. He used the pump in the kitchen and filled a bucket to overflowing, then carried it and a towel and a bar of scented lye soap out to the porch. Here he stripped off his shirt and undershirt, threw both over the railing, tied the towel around his waist and dunked his head in the cold water. Standing upright and sputtering for breath, he shook his head sending a shower of droplets across the porch.

"This is a dangerous place to sit."

He startled. He hadn't seen her sitting cross-legged, leaning against the house, picking through a crock of apples.

"I wish you'd let Mattie or Clemetts draw you a bath. Hired help bathe like this. We use bathing chambers, warm water and scents." Her father had added a bathing room upstairs just a few years back. A cast iron enameled tub from France graced a dais and water was pumped to the second story from a cistern in the root cellar.

"And do you get any cleaner?" A hint of laughter, poking fun and avoiding an argument.

"Probably." Petulant, her lower lip protruding, she added, "People would wonder at how you were raised."

"And just what people would these be?"

"The people you have to be better than. The people in this town."

The bar of homemade soap was glycerin clear but offered little lather even when worked against the roughness of the straight-bristled hand brush he used to scrub his neck. He finished with a vigorous buffing of cuticles and nails.

"Do I have to remind you, I don't care much for what people think, Connie." He rinsed by leaning over and splashing handfuls of water onto his neck, turning first left and then right before patting his chest dry. "Waste of time if you ask me."

"Well, nobody asked you. I know this town and I'm telling you how it is. You married a Warkentine. That comes with certain responsibilities."

"Responsibility?"

"You owe the community. They look up to you, to the money. It's your duty."

"D-u-t-y ... That's a big word for only four letters."

He was silent and towel-dried his hair before he threw the bucket of water out beyond the porch and spread the towel over the railing. There were more of these spats now. Her will meeting his unwillingness. Yet, she hated the fact that they had words. Her life would be perfect if it wasn't for the arguments. And he never said he was sorry for provoking her. She watched as he stared out at the fields. Finally, he turned to face her.

"Connie, I need to be gone for awhile. I'm leaving in the morning."

The apples spilled noisily from her lap, bouncing across the wooden planks, bumping and thumping their way over the porch's edge.

"Gone?"

"Just for awhile."

"You can't go." She slipped, getting to her feet, dropping more apples from the cup of her skirt. A wave of nausea brought bile to the back of her tongue. He couldn't leave. He'd never come back. She'd lose him. He was meeting with Reverend Schmidt. His lessons were going well. They were accepted in the community. *Please, God, no, don't take him away.*

"Why would you go?" She fought to keep her voice calm by taking shallow breaths.

"I've got reasons. I'll be back, Connie."

"When?"

"I don't know that. Maybe two weeks, maybe a month."

"A month?" The word was a wail of disbelief.

"I hope it's not that long."

"What will happen to things around here?"

"The fields are turned and seeded. I've hired two new helpers for odd jobs. Clemetts will tell them what to do. Connie, you'll be all right."

"Take me with you."

"I can't."

"I'm your wife."

"This doesn't concern you. Besides, travel wouldn't be good for the baby. You can't travel, not now."

"Then don't go."

"I must."

"Who could you owe more allegiance to, than me? And your child? This is your home; I'm your family."

He was silent but had turned away to lean out over the porch railing, arms locked to brace his barrel chest. She couldn't see his expression but saw his shoulders tense, corded muscles standing up along his neck. He was angry with her. But he had brought this on. Couldn't he see that?

"You're being unreasonable, Connie. I'm a grown man. You're my wife, not my mother."

"I wonder that you ever had a mother." She spat at him in her anger.

Whirling, he grabbed her by the upper arms, hairy fists digging into her flesh.

"Don't talk about something you know nothing about."

"And why do I know nothing? Is your mother's memory too precious to share?" She leaned into his face.

He shoved her backwards, not roughly but merely to rid himself of the scrutiny, the carping. But her heel caught the edge of a skittery apple, and he grabbed her before she sprawled among the red MacIntosh and upturned crock. She was mindful that she'd struck a nerve, and let him crush her to his chest, bending her head so that the difference in height wasn't noticeable.

"Connie, why do you do this? I would never hurt you."

"Then don't go."

"I must."

"Take Clemetts."

"You need Clemetts here."

"I will not let you go alone."

"You have no choice." He stepped back and took her by the shoulders, gently this time and lowered his voice. "I will say this once. I have honored my marriage vows. I am the father of your child, but you do not own me. I will always be free to come and go—*without question*. Do you understand?"

"I have given you all this." She pulled away and moved to lean against the porch rail. "As far as you can see, the land is yours. How can you be so ungrateful?"

"And I have given you, in return, exactly what you wanted, no, *needed* to have."

She didn't say anything. He spoke the truth. How much more he knew of her situation, he'd never said. A breeze lifted the wisps of hair that had pulled loose from the chignon at the base of her neck. She absently wiped them away as they stuck to her flushed face. Why couldn't he be happy here with her?

"I love you." She said it softly, not without pain, and didn't turn to face him.

"That wasn't necessarily part of the bargain. I never asked for that."

If she'd thought to comment, she waited too long. The screen door thudded softly behind him as he entered the kitchen, the sting of his words fresh and painful. And it was true, this love part. She felt an emotion that nearly rocked her to the core when she thought of losing him. He was bound to her now, in marriage and through their son, and this belonging to another gave her life a dimension she'd never go without again. He would not leave her. At whatever cost she would keep him.

When she did go in, he was already at the table, loading his plate with chops and potatoes and greens. Nothing ever seemed to dampen his appetite. She took her place at the head of the table and didn't speak. There was nothing to say, but the silence was unbearable. Mattie outdid herself on a peach cobbler that went uneaten.

Constance moved a chop around her plate but didn't take a bite, then pushed back from the table, made excuses about being tired and went to the study. In the front northwest corner of the house, the room benefitted from breezes when the wide casement windows were opened. Even the heavy rose damask drapes swayed behind her as she sat at the desk on this early fall evening. Fresh air or not, the space reeked of a maleness that was unsettling. Almost every evening that she could remember, her father had finished the day in this same room.

But what was more unsettling was the fact that Harold was right. There had been no promise of love. Was she schoolgirl enough to think he'd become smitten with his new wife? They had a clear and easily understood agreement—he would give her children and assure the success of the farm; in turn, she gave him the opportunity to become respectable and "leave his mark," as he put it.

Nothing could be simpler and just this morning she'd felt the kick of the child. But if he left, what would become of her? What rights did the church have if she lost the child or if it were a girl? But wouldn't it be bad enough to be deserted? Could she face the townspeople? Most thought something like this would happen. She'd be ruined. And a child without a father … that had not been her plan and wouldn't be now.

He didn't knock a half hour later when he joined her in the study. Nor did he sit. He simply stood in front of her in the middle of the floor and asked for money.

"There will be traveling expenses. I'll go by train."

"It's my understanding that you're quite familiar with train travel, but I don't recall that you ever paid your way before."

He ignored the taunt. His mouth moved as if to say something, but he remained silent and unflinching, his feet planted solidly in the middle of the Persian carpet. And his handsomeness wasn't lost on her in the dusky light. His heavy dark hair as always parted in the center was still damp from its cleansing. His beard had a ruddy cast in the waning light and bristled fully one inch around his chin. Dark chest hair curled above his collarless shirt. The sight of him always affected her physically. She swallowed and turned away.

She loved the smell of him and felt the faintest of stirrings in the pit of her stomach as she fleetingly thought of nights that first month when they'd coupled and then the night on the dock. She would never let this man go. But what could she do if money and pregnancy couldn't hold him? What else was there? Hysteria skipped within her and made her short of breath.

"If this were farm business, I'd feel differently. But I don't even know where you're going. That's my only concern. That I'm being kept from knowing the truth."

He didn't answer. She switched on a desk lamp whose green glass shade muted the low wattage light. The hooded light cast gray circles around his eyes, and she rose to face him. It was his turn. There had to be an explanation.

Finally, after a deep breath, "I don't want to go

through all this again. It's not necessary to know where I'm going. It's enough to know that as your husband, I'm saying that I have to. You have my word that I'll return. I've given you that."

Could she ask more? Wouldn't it be better just to trust him? Did she even *owe* him that trust? Still that panicky feeling seemed to close around her heart.

"How much do you need?"

"Fifty dollars."

If she thought this was exorbitant, she didn't show it.

"I don't keep that kind of money at the farm. I'll need to go into town this evening. I'll make arrangements for you to pick up a bank draft at First National in the morning."

He didn't try to stop her, didn't say that he'd postpone his trip. That her going into town would be easier in the morning. And he didn't ask to go with her. He simply nodded, then turned and left the room, with not so much as a thank you.

Tears pushed against her lids as she squeezed her eyes shut. She'd been forced to give in, but she wouldn't give up. And she wouldn't sit and wait for him to return, either. No one could make her. She was her own person and if she felt she needed to take action, then she'd do it. Not her father, not Arthur Lloyd, not this man she called her husband could stop her.

She sat up straight, tears forgotten. Of course. Why hadn't she thought of this before? She'd follow him. She'd make arrangements for the money and stay overnight in town. No one would question her need to rest her horse or do her shopping in the morning. She could take the same train and stay in a compartment. The ticket master would know his destination.

Constance couldn't suppress the excitement that bubbled inside her—made her giddy with anticipation. Not once did it occur to her that spying might yield more than she bargained for, even more than she was prepared to face. Her mother had always chosen solace in not knowing. "What I don't know won't hurt me." But not Constance. He was her husband; she had every right to know.

CHAPTER FOUR

He sat on the porch a long time. As far as he could see was land that belonged to his wife. Only to her. In little ways she never let him forget that he was secondary and that he would never be master. He'd been given an allowance and had to earn it. Oddly, he didn't care anymore. His freedom was more important than the luxury of being taken care of. He'd never imagined he would think that way. Everything he ever wanted, and then some, was before him at this very minute. And he'd learned to hate it and the shackles of bondage it represented.

He would run the rest of his life. If he put his mind to it, she wouldn't find him. And pride would keep her from trying. Of that he was certain. To tell anyone that she'd erred in judgment? Been taken by a man? Never. There'd be some story. Some premature death—maybe, a graveside memorial for a husband who lost his life doing good deeds. He laughed. It'd suit her, his death would. That's all she needed, a husband in name and a baby on the way. Her life was complete. He was the odd man out.

* * *

The town was laid out north to south with a one-mile main street cluttered by opposing rows of one and two story businesses. Most clapboard facades had been replaced by solid brick, some like the bank, with ornate cornices and window sills of thick gray slate. Gold leaf printing adorned plate glass and announced a drug store, law offices of William L. and William T. Brown, Esquires, two banks and a healthy smattering of stores necessary to the town's survival—a mercantile, hat shop, dress shop, hardware and feed store. Avenues with churches and elaborate homes stretched east and west running like spokes behind this hub of commerce.

Constance knew that Arthur would be at the office, a single large room on the second floor above the bank. He seldom went home before ten, but took Monday as an additional day of rest. He was elderly; he'd earned it. He barely hid his surprise at her late night visit and pulled a chair up to the desk.

"This travel seems sudden."

"It is. Harold's aunt isn't expected to live much past Thanksgiving. He hopes to spend some time with her now before her condition worsens."

"I thought it was his mother who was ill."

"Mother?"

"The one he's been sending money to."

She shivered as if an icy finger had skipped down her back. "What do you mean?"

"Well, I'm sure you're aware of the monthly withdrawals, fifty to one hundred dollars at a time. Let's see, I was just looking at the account earlier, overdrawn again, I must say ... here it is." He pushed a ledger across the desk. "The first withdrawal was made just two days after your wedding, June 21, then another July 6—"

"I can read." She hadn't meant to snap. But all this money, over five hundred dollars. For what? Yes, she'd set up the account, felt he should have money of his own, but to withdraw this amount and not tell her? Withdraw far more than was allotted.

"He is your husband, Constance, I didn't feel it was necessary to discuss it with you." A hint of triumph? There was a definite edge of something in his voice just this side of "I told you so," and he was watching her intently. She hated this man sitting across the desk, a reminder of her father. Maybe she would replace him.

"I see nothing out of the ordinary. There have been some family ... difficulties. See that the last amount is covered."

The sum of one hundred dollars, leaping from the ledger's lined page in stark red, had been issued just two days ago.

"Of course." Smugness, that's what it was.

Arthur sensed she knew nothing about Harold's need for money and reveled in the fact. Well, he could just continue to wonder. She wouldn't give him the satisfaction of an explanation. And there probably was a good one, she just wished she felt more certain about that.

She hurriedly finished her business. Fifty dollars would be waiting for Harold when the bank opened, and she withdrew one hundred dollars for herself. She had no idea where she would be going, or how long she would stay but more than ever, she knew she must follow. A man who could be deceitful about money could lie about other things, too. Somewhere deep in her being, she knew Harold intended to leave her. He'd amassed a tidy nest-egg at her expense and obviously made plans that didn't include her.

* * *

The room gradually lightened with daybreak bringing the bold, brown pattern of the wallpaper into focus. But Constance had been awake for hours, lying fully clothed on the lumpy bed of Hillsboro's best hotel. Was she being stupid? She didn't know, but she'd lost a bit of her resolve.

She was haunted by the money. Wasn't it like stealing? Taking behind her back, lying to the banker? And why? Harold could have come to her. If the reason was on the up-and-up, he could have asked for money, been open about his need. She'd never begrudge his family. She wasn't stingy.

Had she said too much to Arthur Lloyd last night? Going on as she did on her way out, reiterating about the Everetts traveling to visit a sick relative, how they were taking advantage of beautiful fall weather to go back East because the aunt might not last another month and, of course, at Thanksgiving with the possibility of snow and all, they couldn't plan on being able to travel. Iowa could be miserable in November.

Since Iowa was the only home Harold had ever

mentioned, Constance assumed that this was where they were going. She wasn't certain Arthur believed her, but she didn't care. She'd come to look on him as a hired hand, she could only hope he wouldn't jeopardize his job with gossip.

By six a.m. she had changed clothes, slipping into a gray drop-waisted dress of heavy linen with a darker gray duster. She pulled a black cloche hat well down her forehead and tucked every golden strand of hair out of sight, completing the disguise by pulling on black gloves. Harold wasn't looking for her and that would help.

She quickly packed the wicker valise, snugly buckling the straps. No passenger trains were due before seven thirty, east or west bound. If Harold picked up the money when the bank opened, he wouldn't be at the station before nine-thirty. But she wouldn't take chances. She'd go directly to the station, have breakfast in the Fred Harvey restaurant, then wait where she could eye those buying tickets.

The wooden bench, one of twenty-five or so in the waiting area of the station, grew unbearably hard after the first hour, and Constance walked out on the platform to stretch her legs. In front of her, eight tracks spidered their way across Main Street, past the station, a roundhouse, and the rail workers' shanties. Two blocks beyond was the Carnegie Library on land sold to the philanthropist cheaply because it once housed the town's red-light establishment.

The sudden whistle of a freight gave her an uneasy thought. What if Harold planned on saving all of the fifty dollars and took his usual mode of transportation? She hadn't thought of that. She watched as the train slowed and finally stopped, blocking Main. If he hopped the freight, he'd do it about fifty cars to the south, behind the roundhouse, and she'd have no way of knowing. And her being there would have been a wild goose-chase. But she wasn't ready to give up yet. She'd wait and watch. She walked back inside and took a seat on the dreaded benches some thirty feet from the ticket counter.

By ten, several passenger trains were being serviced in the yards but still no Harold. She'd been waiting three hours, and her body ached. Her shoulders slumped away from the slab-hardness of the bench's wooden back and her knees, left unsupported by the narrowness of the seat, suffered cramps that necessitated her standing at regular intervals. Her breakfast of greasy eggs and bacon hadn't set well, and she'd lost it in the cool green tile of the ladies room some time earlier. But the station was filling up, and she didn't want to lose her spot in the back. Better to agonize than risk running into Harold. So she stood in place, stretched, rubbed her lower back, and sat down again.

This time the wait was short. Barely had she thought she couldn't endure another minute and there he was, his back to her, rounded hat solidly on his head, the condiment case on the floor at his feet as he counted out money for a ticket.

The case. His livelihood. That clinched it. He wasn't planning on coming back.

Her heart hammered and she feared she couldn't stand. She willed herself to rise, turn sideways and walk toward the windows on the opposite wall. A vantage point. But he mustn't see her. Now came the tricky part. She'd have to wait until he boarded, then rush to the counter. He wasn't sitting. That must mean that his train was in. She shaded her eyes as Harold walked out the double doors onto the platform. After checking his ticket he headed briskly for a train on Track 2.

This was her chance. There were three people at the ticket window, one a young woman with two children. Constance nervously watched the door. But he didn't return, Harold must have boarded. Finally, it was her turn.

"I'm surprising my husband, Mr. Harold Everett. He's traveling on business and begged me to make arrangements to go with him, but I said that I couldn't. But when I thought about it, what better time to travel than now. Our weather has been so good. Usually I get motion-sickness if the windows can't be opened. But with all this sunshine and warm weather, I'll be fine." Constance stopped. Had she said too much? Too fast? Did he wonder at her agitated state?

But the agent simply smiled and gave her an understanding nod, "Let's see here, Mrs. Everett was it?"

"Yes. I need a ticket on the same train that Mr. Harold Everett is taking."

"Well then, that'd be to Kansas City. A business trip, did you say?"

"Yes, my husband is in household goods." Had she covered her surprise? Kansas City? Not even a full day's ride. This wasn't Iowa. "I'll want a compartment, too. Lying down often helps my queasiness."

"Good choice and I expect you'll want a one-way just like your mister."

"Yes, of course." She tried to block out the words, *one-way*. He wasn't coming back. Hadn't she known it?

"You'll be leaving from Track 2 in about ten minutes. The conductor will give a call but you might want to go on out now. Compartments board to the rear. You go ahead and get settled. The porter will bring Mr. Everett back to find you. Pleasant trip now, to the both of you."

She thanked him and hurried out. Harold was nowhere to be seen but she kept her head down. A porter showed her to the compartment, a fold-down bed, and fold-down table, sparse but comfortable. And she wouldn't be there long. Kansas City was only six hours away.

In exactly ten minutes the train lurched, the couplings banged together, a whistle sounded and the train inched forward. She didn't even take her gloves off but sat, primly watching the countryside lurch and clackety-clack by. Train travel was dirty and loud and uncomfortable. But she dozed anyway, waking once to remove her hat and shoes, tuck her feet under her and settle into sound sleep.

The knock of the porter startled her. How could they be coming into Kansas City so soon? But they were. She must have slept more soundly than she thought. Quickly, she forced her shoes onto slightly swollen feet and again tucked every strand of her hair under the bucket-like hat, then gathered her belongings and stepped into the aisle. Coach seating was some two or three cars in front of her and she made her way forward pushing the heavy doors open between the cars trying not to look at the ground rushing past lest her stomach begin to churn.

She had lumbered unevenly down the aisles of two cars before she found him. Thanks to his black hat, Harold was easy to spot seated halfway down on the right side. The car was filled with boisterous children and he was turned away looking out the window. So far, so good. She slipped into an empty seat and waited for the train to pull into the station.

She knew at once that she couldn't lose sight of him or she might not find him again. The station was enormous. But her height kept the bobbing black hat in view as he walked through the crowds and out the front entrance. There she hung back as he pushed his way to the curb and looked up the street. He and about twenty others waited in a cluster. She feigned interest in a newsstand. Would he take a cab? A number of horse drawn hansoms were lined up to the right.

But, no. The minute the streetcar rounded the corner two blocks up and the heavy draft horses pulled abreast with the station, he quickly walked in that direction. Harold was one of the first to board and sat in the back. She moved with a group of eight or ten who crowded around the streetcar's entry. She kept her head averted as she stepped into the car.

"Will you be getting off before Wyandotte?"

My God. Was the driver speaking to her? She looked at him blankly.

"I said, will ya be needin' a transfer?"

"If she don't, I will." A voice boomed out behind her.

"Let's get a move on if you please, Miss." The driver was kindly but anxious to board and get moving.

"Yes. I need a transfer." She dared not look at Harold but dug in the pocket of her coat for coins. Surely her exchange with the driver hadn't caught his attention. She slipped down onto the wooden plank seating behind the driver and dragged her valise up on her lap, half expecting Harold to take her shoulder from behind and demand an explanation. But he didn't. No one paid her any attention. Another fifteen people boarded and the car was packed, many crowded into the aisle. With a gloved hand covering half her face, she twisted to her right and glanced back at Harold. He was turned away from the passengers and stared out the window about ten rows behind her on the opposite side.

With a lurch the car glided back into the middle of the street. The driver would slow at every corner but not stop unless someone called out. Occasionally, passengers jingled the bells tethered at intervals to ropes strung above their heads. But most often it was a voice that yelled a street and then that individual would go to the rear and wait for the car to stop.

It seemed as if they had traveled over a good part of the city before she heard Harold's call. The car had emptied by half and she couldn't turn around. They must be close to the business district because the buildings had gotten taller—and dirtier. There was debris in the street—manure and bits of paper. And the sidewalks weren't even bricked in front of every business, simply unevenly planked over.

When the car stopped, she looked over her shoulder and watched Harold slip from the car and head up the street. She rose quickly but not before the car had lurched forward.

"I need to get out here." She yelled louder than she intended and got several curious stares.

"Only at designated stops. And that means the corners, Miss. We'll be coming up to the next one pretty quick like."

"No!" She screamed the word and bolted for the back. "Stop. You have to stop."

But he wasn't going to. This was unthinkable. She'd lose Harold. After coming this far, he'd be swallowed up by the city and she'd have to go home never to see him again. She took a deep breath, closed her eyes, muttered a prayer, and stepped off. The valise broke her fall but still she sprawled full length across the brick paving before quickly struggling to her feet. Luckily, she hadn't turned her ankle or worse yet, broken something. She'd have some bruises but those would heal.

She hadn't given a thought to the baby. He was in God's hands and God wouldn't take away what He'd given her. She'd done the right thing because a block ahead, Harold was walking up the steps of a three-story building on the corner. Another couple minutes and she would have lost him.

He was well inside by the time she stopped in a doorway directly across from the Rose O'Sharon boardinghouse. The name in four-foot-high scroll curved over double doors. She waited what she thought must have been ten full minutes, but Harold didn't return. He must have taken a room. And if this was where he was staying, then she'd stay there too. Picking her way around a steaming pile of manure and dodging two horseless carriages, Constance crossed the street.

Up close the building didn't look as shabby as it had from a distance. At one time, it must have been grand with gilded knockers and etched glass transoms, solid deep red brick patterned into spreading fans above each window. The steps were now devoid of paint, worn smooth, roundly indented in the center from years of use.

The high-ceilinged foyer appeared empty when Constance pushed the thick front door open. The place smelled like a mausoleum, musty with an overlying scent of flowers. The bouquet was on a table by the baluster of an intricately carved staircase that wound upward to the second and third floors. Dozens of red carnations spilled over the sides of a tin bucket. Odd vase, Constance mused as she walked past the flowers toward the back where a sign that said Office swung from a wooden arm above a counter.

No one was around. Constance put the valise down on the emerald carpeting and inched the register around so that she could read the names. Harold had just been there. He hadn't come out again, but the last entry was one Harry Everson. Harry, Harold, Everson, Everett—of course, Harold's labored penmanship—he was using an alias. But why?

"And what might I do for you my dear?"

Constance barely kept the shriek from pushing past her lips. The woman had walked up behind her as stealthily as a predator. And what an odd woman. Overweight in a coarse, paunchy sort of way, pendulous breasts strapped flat under layers of beads that cascaded down the front of a pale pink pintucked bodice. A cigarette dangled from a jeweled holder clenched between even, yellowed teeth, the mouth outlined in scarlet against powder-white pockmarked skin. This was a woman who had never been pretty.

"A room. You do rent rooms?"

"Yesssss. And might this be for just one? Or will you be expecting company?" The wink was outlandish.

"One."

"And for how many days?"

She had no idea.

"A week, I think."

"And will you be taking your food with the others in the dining hall? We offer three squares, nothing fancy." She had moved past Constance by now and was standing behind the counter in the office, her head bent over the register, bobbed henna-red hair falling forward onto rouged cheeks.

"I'd like to have meals brought to my room."

"My, my, we don't spare the expense, now do we?"

The sarcasm was lost on Constance whose eyes had wandered to a set of three gilded cherubs intertwined above double doors marked Dining Hall. The building was far too ornate for her taste.

"I prefer to be alone. Oh yes, I'd like a room on the front." She'd almost forgotten. She must have a room that overlooked the street so that she could follow Harold when he went out.

"Well, that we have. First floor, even. Would you like to see it first?"

"No. I'm not particular."

"Well, then, two dollars and fifty cents and you're set."

Constance knew the price was exorbitant. A dollar would buy meat for a family for a week and good cuts, too. But she felt caught. This wasn't a place of her choosing.

"I'm Rose. If you have any questions, address them to me. I'll give you one key. If you need another there's a deposit."

Rose pushed the register toward her and scooped the money off the counter.

"May I ask what business brings you to the city?"

Constance looked up blankly. She'd almost signed Constance before she caught herself and wrote Carrie Walker.

"It's personal."

"Well then, my dear, if you'll follow me."

Rose's shoes were badly runover at the heels by bunioned feet that were too big for the cheap, high-heeled pumps, and she waddled, it seemed to Constance, instead of actually taking steps. Constance followed at a discreet distance.

She had no expectations of the room and was pleasantly

surprised when Rose threw open the door. Paisley print wallpaper, forest green on cream, looked new. The bed had a white coverlet and, in this area, the emerald carpet wasn't worn. The room was large with a freshly painted, pressed tin ceiling whose squares met at the corners in curlicues and bows. And the furniture was good. A sturdy parlor chair and ornate cherry night stand were to the right of the bed, itself a giant of oppressive walnut with carved pineapple bedposts.

"It's quite nice."

"Glad you like it, deary. Supper's at six. The boy will bring a tray at six fifteen. Wash basin's over there. Set the pitcher out in the morning for fresh. Tub and commode two doors down the hall on your left."

"Thank you."

Constance waited until the door closed before putting her things on the bed. That woman gave her the willies. But the room was clean and would catch the morning sun through a large bay window flanked by heavy green satin drapes. A padded seat curved under the wood sill and offered the perfect vantage point to view the street.

Supper was two hard boiled eggs in cream sauce, two pieces of unbuttered toast, and tepid tea with lemon. Not the hearty meals that Mattie fixed. Constance pushed at the eggs with a fork and in that moment, felt tears well up and the last of her resolve fade. A wave of homesickness took her breath away, so acute was it in intensity. What was she doing here? Where was her husband who had promised to protect her and keep her?

The cry felt good and so did the exhausted sleep that followed. She awoke to the room bathed in light, hurriedly splashed water on her face, and slipped the supper tray into the hall. Breakfast was already there. If anyone had knocked, she hadn't heard. Lifting the cloth she gazed at three pieces of fried cornmeal mush in sorghum molasses. The mug of tea was already cold. She dropped the cloth and left the tray in the hall, fighting to keep her queasy stomach in check. There were downsides to having a baby, and the smell of food early in the morning was one of them. She breathed out a few times to clear her head of the cloying molasses odor and walked down to the bathroom.

Back in her room, she quickly changed into a skirt and blouse and took up a place of surveillance on the window seat. The three-sided glass protrusion over the street was a perfect lookout.

The first hour passed quickly. A number of gentlemen left the Rose O'Sharon heading in the direction of what must be downtown. But not Harold. There was no sign of him coming or going. She tried not to leave her post even to go to the bathroom and then, with bladder bursting, she'd rush the two doors down and spend hardly two minutes before she was back, gazing out at the street again.

Lunch was vegetable stew and she ate everything on the tray, crackers, the butter pat, and apple—tray and all balanced precariously on her lap as she scanned the street below for the familiar black hat.

By dusk, she was faintly worried. Had he checked in and then left? Had she missed him altogether? But she couldn't let herself think that way. He was here, maybe too tired to go out the first day or sick ... maybe he was under the weather and chose to stay in. That was plausible. She was probably worrying for nothing.

She kept up her post until well past midnight and began the second day in exactly the same way, a quick splash of water to her face, a few nibbles of cinnamon toast and then the vigil by the window. By late afternoon her faint worries had grown to panicking fear. He wasn't here. She was sitting by a window like some idiot sentinel, and Harold was God knew where.

By six she knew she had to act. When she'd looked at the register, there were names marked through in pencil; obviously, those who had departed. If she could sneak another look at the book without encountering Rose, she'd know in an instant whether or not she was being foolish.

She waited another thirty minutes until she knew everyone would be in the dining hall then carefully stepped over her own dinner tray and continued toward the office. Her timing was perfect. She passed no one and reached the office undetected. Sliding the register toward her, she scanned the page. There were the signatures of three new boarders, but Harry Everson was still at the Rose O'Sharon; furthermore, he was in room 212.

Now what? She made her way back to her room. He was here but seemingly as cloistered as she was. She was certain beyond a shadow of a doubt that he'd not left his room in two whole days. Of course, he could be ill. Seriously ill. There could be no other explanation. If he came here on business, he wouldn't be staying in his room day after day.

She had to help. A quick prayer thanked God for placing her at the side of her husband in his time of need. Sick as he was, he wouldn't be in the dining room. Without another thought, she flew up the stairs to the second floor.

Here the building was dark, lighted even in the day by glass-globed electric lights that flickered from wall mountings beside each door. The maroon carpet, a runner that stretched down the middle of the hall showed the wear of twenty years' footsteps. Room 212 was halfway down but before she'd reached it, the door opened and a tall, tweed-suited man emerged carrying a black leather bag by its two round handles. He bowed slightly and touched his hat as he passed.

The doctor. Oh no. This wasn't good. Not good at all. Constance fairly ran to the door and turning the knob burst into the room.

"Harold?"

Barely had his name left her lips than she was able to focus on the bed. A big austere thing like the one downstairs but here the sheets were mussed, covers thrown on the floor, and in the center was a woman—no, girl was more like it, a young girl with large-breasts and thick blond hair, pencil-dark eyebrows, painted lips forming a large O in surprise—and nothing more, not one stitch of clothing.

"Who are you?" It was all Constance could think to say.

"I think I should be askin' you that." The blond pulled a sheet up to her neck.

"I'm looking for my husband, Harold Everett. He's registered to this room."

"Well, he musta switched with somebody, 'cause this room belongs to Harry Everson."

"The man I passed in the hall?"

"I don't think so." The girl looked confused, then added, "You mean the doctor. I got the runs. Been up here for two whole days now. Doc gave me something, though. He says that I'll be good as new by the morning."

"And your husband?" Constance realized her voice was barely audible, and she steadied herself by grasping the high back of a chair.

"Cleaning up. He's in the bath down the hall."

The girl was staring at her, wary-like, hugging her knees, white arms on the outside of the sheet, but her eyes never left Constance's face. This wasn't going to be easy, but Constance had to know.

"What does your husband look like?"

"And just why would you want to know?"

Constance shrugged. She could think of no good reason, at least, not one that she could share just yet.

"Unless, you're one of those women." The blond squinted, brow furrowed, spreading a frown across her forehead.

"One of what women?"

"Can't say, forget it." The girl, who was probably all of seventeen, flounced back on the bed to lie prone, the sheet discreetly pulled to her neck.

Constance took a deep breath. It was now or never. "Listen, I have reason to believe that my husband is staying in this room. I don't intend to leave until you give me some answers."

At this the girl sat up again. "You followed 'em, didn't you?" She gaped at Constance in disbelief. "You have some nerve. But he ain't your husband. Don't lie to me about that. You's are engaged, but there's no way he married you."

Constance suddenly didn't trust her legs to hold her upright. "Why don't we start by discussing just who this *he* is, and why I'd be engaged to him." She sank into a gaudy, clipped-plush arm chair.

"Because you're a fool, some desperate old maid who wants a man. You're all alike. And you or your father paid him handsome to disappear, save your reputation, once you found out he could never be yours. It's because of your kind he's had to disguise himself. So why'd you follow him?"

Constance felt the words like a slap. Paid to disappear? Disguise?

"Not only am I married, but I'm carrying my husband's child."

"Then we ain't talking about the same him. My husband might have tricked a woman or two into giving him some money and maybe he had to lie to do it, lead 'em along, promise marriage, but he never, never married nobody, and he never got nobody with a baby."

Constance sat up straight and clutched the arms of the chair. "My husband, Harold Everett, is about five foot eight and thick-set ... about this tall." Constance rose and held her hand out at the level of her cheek-bone. "He was wearing the black suit and hat of his religion or his disguise as you call it. He wears his hair parted in the middle, his eyes are hazel—"

"Stop." The girl looked like she was going to be sick.

"Harold and Harry are one and the same?"

She nodded. "The bastard. He promised. Said there was no hanky-panky. It was just a way to make some money quick, get ahead, ya see? Even told me this religious stuff wasn't for real. It'd just throw them women off iffen they tried to find him. He's been running this scam for a couple years now."

Constance sank onto the edge of the bed. "Scam?"

"He'd check out some small town for eligible women, someone older, who might not have a beau and then let their fathers pay to have him disappear when it looked like they was getting serious."

"We haven't been too smart, have we?"

The girl shook her head. There were no tears, but two bright spots of pink colored the girl's cheeks.

"I'm Constance. I guess I don't know my last name." The laugh was rueful, and hard-edged, but she held out her hand. Strangely, she felt strong. "And you're?"

"Nettie. Pleased, I think." She shook Constance's hand.

"You know, Nettie, we need to talk."

Constance started with her father's will and how she could have lost everything without Harry/Harold. Nettie listened with eyes round, stopping her to comment on a father so mean as to do that to his only child. The sympathy was there as Constance counted on because once again, she wasn't about to let some man get the best of her. All of what she'd uncovered didn't alter the fact that she needed a husband, preferably the one she had.

She ended by saying that their baby was due in April.

"He's scum."

"I don't disagree. But how about the two of us calling his bluff?"

"How do we do that?"

"How long have you been married?"

"One year come next month."

"Nettie, this is what I'll do. I'll send you fifty dollars every month so long as you live, if you have your marriage annulled."

"Fifty dollars? Every month?" Nettie moistened her lips. "That's a lot of money."

"You could do anything you ever wanted. You'd be free."

"And Harry?"

"Harold will be my husband and father to my children. If he refuses, I'll have him thrown in jail. No judge will be lenient with a man who tricks a woman and then deserts her in the family way." She didn't add that he'd stolen from her.

"He deserves jail."

"I don't disagree. So, what do you say? Is it a deal?"

They were in the process of shaking hands when Harold walked in. The look of panic made Constance laugh. He stood in the doorway, uncertain, his face drained of color.

"Harold, or is it, Harry?" She walked toward him. Her breathing was shallow, as wave after wave of anger washed over her. She was furious with this man who thought he could dupe her, make a fool out of her. She didn't even have a name anymore. It certainly wasn't Everett, and it couldn't be Everson because he already had a wife by that name.

"Connie …"

He hung his head. And that made her angrier.

"Tell me what your name is, what *my* name is. Am I an Everett? Or should my name be Everson? Or maybe neither one if you already had a wife when you married me."

"Is that what she told you?" He motioned toward the bed.

"You bastard." Forgetting the sheet, Nettie flew out of the bed. "You know I'm your wife. Don't try any of your lies on me." Harold caught her wrists and held her.

"Put some clothes on, Nettie."

"I don't need you telling me what to do. Not today. Not ever again." But she twisted away from Harold, dragged the sheet off the bed, and wound it around her slight frame.

"Nettie and I have just finished having a little talk. I

think you'll be interested in what we have to say." Constance outlined the plan. "We'll see a solicitor in the morning."

"Don't I have some say?"

"No, I don't think you do. You're a bigamist, one who's gone so far as to get me pregnant—" He started to disagree but apparently thought better of it. "And you've stolen money from me. I set up an account that allowed you ten dollars a month and you took hundreds. Either charge is a felony but the two together, what judge wouldn't throw you in jail?"

"And if I don't want to go back to Hillsboro?"

"I don't see that you have a choice, do you? I think for the rest of your life you're going to be doing those good deeds that will leave your mark on your fellow man." She didn't disguise the snideness.

"I say you're getting off too easy," Nettie added her two cents. "I say Constance here is being too kind. If it was me, you'd be in jail. All the promises, the lies. When was me an' you goin' to have babies? You always said we couldn't, that you didn't want any. But you didn't have no trouble getting her pregnant. You don't deserve nothing good." Nettie fell onto the bed and buried her face in a pillow. Her sobs rattled around the walls of the small room.

Harold moved to the window, hands deep in his pockets. He'd exchanged the black suit for brown serge trousers, red suspenders, and a blue checked collarless shirt. Casual dress suited him. Coats made him look bulky and squat. His hair was wet from a bath, and the beard was gone. He looked exactly as he had that morning four months ago in her kitchen, only maybe the cockiness was missing.

But Constance felt herself softening and more than a

little pleased at the control the situation gave her. If love and pregnancy weren't enough, the threat of ruining him would be. He'd be hers now, never to stray.

"Just like that, you can stop loving me? After all we've had, Nettie?" Harold turned from the window. When there was no answer, he pushed past Constance and sat on the edge of the bed. Constance watched, strangely at ease. For the first time since she'd met him, she had nothing to worry about. This man would not risk jail. He was not one to overlook which side of the bread his butter was on.

At first Nettie ignored him then, pulling the sheet around her, sat up. "For fifty smackers every month? I'm no fool. Constance and me know a loser when we see one. But if she needs you and is willing to pay ... well, I guess I'll go along. A girl has to look out for herself."

"Then, you've won." Harold turned to Constance. He looked at her long, a hint of defiance as well as defeat.

"For today and tomorrow and all the time we will be together. We will be remarried before we leave Kansas City. If your name needs to be legally changed to Harold Everett, we'll do that, too."

"Thought of everything haven't you? Haven't I always said you were a marvel?" It was said with indifference as much as resignation. He rose, took her by the elbow and moved to the window. "Do you even want to know that I'd come to care for you?" He said this last softly, and reached for her hand.

"It'll make going back all the easier then, won't it?" She pulled her hand out of reach. Could she believe him? Ever again? Wasn't he just a little too clever? Charismatic when it was needed? "And there won't be any more of these little trips."

"It gives you the upper hand. I know how you like that."

"Safe-guarding my future? My child's future? I think I could be excused my preoccupation with that."

"So you didn't love me anyway?" Nettie wailed.

Both turned to look at her. It was as though they had forgotten she was even in the room.

"You've done all right by yourself. Let it be," Harold said.

* * *

Harold moved downstairs with Constance, and Nettie left for her home in Walnut Grove. Rose issued an extra key and acted nosy, but otherwise kept her distance. At least she didn't ask questions. Once they were moved into the first floor room, Constance collapsed on the bed. Her strength lasted until she was sure she'd won, and then she felt as though someone had squished the air right out of her. Harold brought up a cup of hot tea from the dining room then sat by the window and read while she napped.

She watched him for awhile out of half-closed eyes. How, after everything that had happened, could she still want him to be her husband? But she did. Stronger than ever. And wasn't it possible that this was just one of God's tests? He had given her so much. There must be an explanation for this turn of events. Did He need proof that she was worthy? Prepared to fight for her gifts? Wasn't it true that answers to prayers were seldom given without some trial, some test? And this is what God had given her to bear.

And it did seem like God wanted Harold to have a

clean slate, change his name and start anew. Certainly He'd challenged the man during his young life. And then brought Constance in to save him. She thought of it that way, that she was his savior. What Harold thought, she never knew. He was now her husband, completely, totally hers and that was all that mattered. She owned his soul.

When she awoke, he was still in the chair by the window.

"Am I still to believe that home is in Iowa?"

He started not realizing she was awake, then came over to sit on the bed.

"I'm curious. There's been so much lying." She looked up at him.

"I was born here in Kansas City in an unwed mother's home and ended up in an orphanage until I was thirteen, then I traveled around doing odd jobs where I could find them. Life wasn't easy." He pointed to the scar across his wrist. "I botched the only attempt to make it better."

Constance believed him. The pain in his voice was real.

"Connie, I want you to know that I didn't want to leave the farm. I just got scared. There was too much you could have found out, and I figured that with the baby and all, you didn't need me anymore. I've never had a chance like the one you gave me. Not to really make something of myself. And I knew that sooner or later you'd find out about Nettie. But I want to try, Connie, I want to take the chance that you're giving me."

* * *

When they left the court house that next morning, Constance was indeed the wife of one Harold Everett, and her happiness was restored. She knew what she wanted, what she would have now no matter what—a wedding in a church. She thought Reverend Schmidt would gladly officiate. She'd wheedle and coax him into agreeing that the town *should* participate in their happiness. If the weather held, they could hold the reception outdoors. It would be a glorious beginning to the rest of her life. And, of course, the new college would have an Alfred Dunston Schmidt chapel. She'd pledge extra money for that.

The Santa Fe Railway delivered Mr. and Mrs. Everett and ten parcels of finery to Hillsboro on the fifteenth—a mere five days since their departure. One huge dress box held the ivory satin dress that fell straight to her ankles and whose jacket was covered with seed pearls and cut crystal beads. The straight, loose cut kept her growing stomach concealed. The veil was anchored by a wide band of matching satin, a crown with a single teardrop crystal hung in the center and puffs of netting billowing from all sides. A new suit for Harold and the wedding was set to take place—once again.

Indian summer in all its red and gold glory offered the backdrop for the event. This time Arthur Lloyd and his wife, Pearl, stood as witnesses. The church ceremony was brief but played to a packed house. No one wanted to miss seeing what was reported to be a three hundred dollar dress. And the food was rich and plentiful. No one went away hungry. It did, in fact, change things, Constance thought—made the townsfolk come around.

In retrospect, the day was always the happiest of Constance's life. And in the months following, she and Harold settled into a routine. No more was ever mentioned about what had taken place in Kansas City. Harry Everson truly did not exist. But the knowing was security. Nettie was never heard from again. And if ever she was called upon to play it, Constance held the trump.

CHAPTER FIVE

The winter was horrendous. Christmas passed in snowbound isolation, and Constance grew large and uncomfortable. Even Mattie wondered at the enormous protrusion that made her mistress's legs appear like sticks. "Jus' like a grandaddy spider," she'd mutter to herself, then fret over Constance and worry that this pregnancy was somehow unhealthy.

Instead of growing close, Constance and Harold seemed at odds. He was taciturn, possibly resentful, and staying inside made him irritable. There were just some animals you couldn't cage, she'd recall her mother saying. But Constance was cross herself, carrying such a lump on her slight frame. Only knowing that it was the first of many sons kept her spirits from flagging completely.

Sometime in late January she awoke in the night to such pain that the doctor was called. At first, he detected an irregular heartbeat on one side of the purplish-veined mound of her stomach, then upon more careful examination decided it was two—the heartbeats of two separate beings. Constance was ecstatic. Sons. God had bestowed his blessings in plural.

The doctor prescribed bed rest and fussed about the pain. Often twins were not carried full term and they must eke out every additional day that they could until the due-date. The last two months must be uneventful. Constance was to give up the running of the house to Mattie and take all her meals in the sitting room adjoining her bedroom upstairs.

She overheard the doctor admonishing Harold to make up a bed elsewhere so's not to disturb his wife's rest. She strained to hear Harold's answer, but couldn't. He seldom visited the bedroom upstairs and certainly not to sleep with her. They'd had separate rooms for some time.

She finished a quilt for the crib in blues and yellows, then started on another one. Clemetts was ordered to drop everything and build another crib. Booties and caps and sweaters were next. The mercantile soon ran out of blue yarn.

The thaw began in March, leaving soggy reminders of what can happen if two feet of snow melts quickly. Getting feed to the stock mired wagons to the hubs, and it took days to extricate them. But the neighbors helped. The community offered one big collective effort—you scratch my back, I'll scratch yours.

Constance wasn't opposed to this neighborliness. Harold was gone from dawn to dusk and the activity made him less sour. He was accepted. There was no longer a problem. Memories could be so short, Constance mused. Be generous with time and money, and all is forgotten.

He remained clean-shaven and refused to receive any more lessons from Reverend Schmidt. But Harold had petitioned the church to go on mission the first of the summer. Constance refused to release him. It was too soon. Wait another year after the babies were older and Harold had proved that he wouldn't just disappear. It wasn't that Constance didn't trust him; she was simply being careful.

Just when she thought she couldn't endure another skein of blue yarn, she felt a ripple of movement, a surge that started somewhere under her chin and crawled in peristalsis perfection across her stomach. March thirty-first. As if the calendar had been consulted, Constance went into labor.

Mattie was in attendance, but Harold rode into town to fetch the doctor at eight, when it seemed the children were being somewhat reluctant to make their appearance.

While the doctor was directing the help in the kitchen, Harold had come up to sit awhile. What appeared to be husbandly concern turned out to be something more when he asked, "What happens to me, to the farm, if you die?"

"I won't die."

"None of us know what God has in store."

Harold's pretense to righteousness infuriated her. If anyone in the family had God's ear, it was she.

"Women have babies all the time."

"Your age is against you, Connie. And twins …"

"Really? Since when are you the expert?"

He ignored this and waited until another contraction racked her body before continuing.

"I think I have a right to be concerned about my future."

"About money, don't you mean?" She wadded the bedclothes in her fists and rode out yet another spasm without screaming, but this one left her panting. "Don't you just want to know how much you'll get?"

"Have it your way. Yes, how much will I get?"

"Nothing. Nothing in your own right, that is. Everything goes to the children with you as trustee. You'll have a roof over your head until they reach age." This last was hissed between clenched teeth.

"And if they die? If I lose all of you?"

"Nothing. A train ticket back to Nettie."

"Let me get to work now." The elderly doctor, the one who had delivered her, stood in the doorway. "Mr. Everett, I suggest you go down to the study and pour yourself a good strong shot of whiskey. Now, now don't protest. If you don't keep a bottle in the house, you'll find one under the seat of my buggy. The church will look the other way on such an occasion. I've never lost a father and don't plan to start now."

Constance only dimly remembered Harold lingering in the doorway until Mattie shooed him away. Did he *want* her to die? What a terrible thought. She had to concentrate on the task ahead, not dwell on some utterly fanciful, macabre—this time she didn't hold the scream back. The pain was unbearable, her insides were being shredded, sucked with a dizzying force down between her legs.

At twelve fifteen in the morning of April first, the first baby came screaming and kicking into the world.

"Oh, Missy Constance, she's beautiful."

She? Constance didn't have the strength to talk quite

yet, but a girl? She had endured that pain for a girl?

"She's a little beauty, all right. Healthy, ten fingers, ten toes and hungry, to boot. But we're not through yet. I need another mighty push from my girl to get that little one's sister or brother on the way."

The lull in the pain quickly vanished and Constance had no time to wonder about the girl child swaddled in blue blankets and held by a kitchen servant.

"More pressure, more pressure. That's it."

The doctor was once again busy between her legs and she felt another great squishy release. This time a wail thanked him for his work.

"Well, I'll be. Your first youngun' has a baby sister."

Sister? Girl? Another girl? Constance tried to raise to her elbows.

The doctor was rolling down his shirt sleeves and looked quite pleased with himself. Mattie was showing the housemaid how the babies should be washed. Both newborns were squalling lustily and waving crepey pink limbs in the air. Constance covered her eyes but there was no energy left for tears. Girls. Her father's will provided allowances for girl-children until they reached twenty-one. But his precious farm without a grandson would become church property eventually. At least she had been saved the sisterhood.

Mattie, with the housemaid close behind, was leaning over the bed. Two blue bundles. Blue. What a waste.

"Here's your mama, little ones. They's just the spitting image of you, Missy Constance, long and thin with fluffy golden hair. Look at these pretty little toes—"

"Take them away." Constance turned to face the wall.

"But Missy, you're their mama. They needs their mama."

Constance refused to turn back.

"Pay no mind, Mattie. I've seen this time and time again. The woman can get too exhausted to respond normally at first. Give it some time. Nature will win out. When someone's breasts fill up and get to aching, we'll see who does what." With a broad wink, the doctor went down to the study.

But her breasts didn't fill, and it became clear that she couldn't have fed even one baby let alone two. So a wet nurse was brought in, and baby Ella and baby Emma flourished even if their mother acted as if they didn't exist.

* * *

Constance waited three months until the bloody aftermath of giving birth was no longer evident and her body was slim and taut again. Then she went to the study to confront him. He was sleeping there full time now on the rollaway pulled out from the west wall. The place smelled musty with a maleness that was unnerving. She sat on the makeshift bed and tried to plan her approach. But when he'd walked in, she simply blurted out. "It's time to begin another child."

She could see his surprise, maybe shock even.

"Connie, you almost died."

"Nonsense. It was a normal birth. A woman can't escape the pain. There were just two of them. That added to the difficulty."

"The doctor suggested that we not try again."

"What?" This was the first she'd heard about that. "Why not?"

"He feels you're just not made for child-bearing. You're narrow in places that should be wide. Yes, that's the way he put it. He fears for your life if we have another."

"Hogwash."

"Connie, be reasonable."

"I am reasonable. I'm past thirty. I must have more children, soon."

"I don't want to be a part of killing you."

"Yet, you want me dead."

"I've never said that."

"You've thought it. God punishes thought as much as deed."

"Connie, listen to what you're saying. You're crazy."

Slowly she stood and pulled the strings on the kimono, letting it fly open, then fall from her shoulders. She was naked underneath. And the flicker of Harold's eyes as they sought first her breasts and then the light fluff of a triangle between her legs weren't lost on her. He was a man, wasn't he? And even all they'd gone through couldn't have shut down his animal urges.

He took her roughly, exploding inside her almost before her back reached the cot's spongy mattress. Then he pushed off of her, stood, dressed, and walked out. All without one word. But she lay there luxuriating in the feeling of promise. Another child would be on the way.

She'd consulted a specialist and warned as she was that it was more theory than proven reality, she followed his advice. She needed to establish her fertile times, that day or so midway between her periods and then only have sex then. She'd waited until she was regular after the birth of the twins before she'd approached Harold. And this child would be the boy she wanted. She felt it. Having girls first wasn't all so bad. The oldest girl was committed to caring for her parents as they aged—putting their needs first, before hers. The twins were such good babies. At least Ella was—no doubt this would be her mission in life.

* * *

Constance allowed Harold to name the next baby, another daughter but this one dark and feisty with a head full of hair and long-lashed brown eyes. He was besotted and carried the child on his shoulder as she grew into a pixie version of himself. He called her Eve. Later, Constance was to wonder at using a name known for seduction. How could an Eve not get into trouble?

Eve was followed by what the doctors called a nervous breakdown for Constance. Brought on by repeated childbirth, depleting the body of its resources was their opinion. Let them think what they would, but Constance knew what was wrong. She had been abandoned by her God. There were to be sons, not sniveling girls, but there they were everyday—at breakfast, lunch and dinner—Ella, Emma and Evy prattling away.

The house smelled of starch, and petticoats flapped from lines behind the kitchen or worse yet dripped across the kitchen floor on inclement days. The laughter and shrieking irritated Constance. Like fingernails on a blackboard, it set her nerves on edge. By the time they were five and six the household was always in some kind of uproar. A toy broken, a kitten lost—Constance took to her room and left the day-to-day running of the household to a nurse, a housemaid, a cook and the ever-faithful Mattie.

But in all the turmoil, Harold blossomed. There was never any question about his being gone. He reveled in his family and took them everywhere—there were endless rides in his new car for ice cream in town, ponies to be purchased, new dresses to be ordered. He spoiled them unmercifully. And they adored him. If Constance admitted to anything, she would say to herself that she envied Harold's closeness to the girls, his easy way with them—then she'd pray even harder for a son.

Five years had passed since Evy's birth and Constance was soon to be thirty-six. Old. But she was beginning to think again of having another child. Hadn't her mother given birth at forty-one? It wasn't impossible. The doctor would be incensed. He'd gone through the same life-threatening warning every time she even mentioned her interest. "You will surely be tempting fate if you try again." She knew what he'd say by heart.

But she did try again. By accident, actually. Harold was to go on mission. At last, she acquiesced. She couldn't see that there would be any harm. She'd kept him long enough at her side. He begged for a chance to travel. It always seemed secondary, but he aspired to spread the word of God. Or so he proclaimed. She sometimes doubted he was even a Christian. But over the years his act was convincing and Reverend Schmidt even put in a plea for his services.

That last evening before he was to take the train to New York, they dismissed the nurse and put the girls to bed themselves, at Harold's urging. She was reluctant but went along. She really found no pleasure in her raucous daughters. But that night, the two of them opened the hot stuffy room together, now a dormitory made to order by tearing out dividing walls and filling the space with three single beds.

The early summer was hot and muggy, oppressive in this room above the kitchen. Already the girls fussed about wearing nightclothes. But gowns were put on and all three crowded into one bed to hear their mother read to them. She'd chosen various passages from the Bible—those that had special meaning for her. It was a concession on Constance's part. She really was trying to make Harold's last evening at home a good one. But it was their father who bent over the three damp foreheads and kissed each good night before closing the hallway door.

"Connie, I have a grand idea. Let's you and me go for a swim."

If she was surprised, she tried to hide it. The pond still brought back wistful memories of a happier time.

"You're on."

No one had said the word "race", that was simply understood. At the edge of the water, Harold struggled out of his clothing while she shrugged her kimono off and was in the pond and on her way to the dock before she heard his splashing come up behind her.

"It's not fair." He said it laughingly between huffing and pulling himself up beside her. "You wear less clothing."

She'd turned on her back and stared up at the moon and felt in that instant a warmth toward Harold that she thought had been long dead.

"The girls adore you. You're good with them."

"They're little beauties, aren't they?"

"One of them is," she said matter-of-factly. Ella was a stringbean and homely; Emma, chubby and squat with squirrel cheeks and squinty eyes. There would be very few suitors for those two. But Evy. Even at five she dazzled; thick dark hair refusing to be tamed burst from braids to swirl down her back. And eyes, doleful, surrounded by thick lashes, pulling you into their depths. Constance never understood where this creature had come from.

"Don't be so hard on Ella or Emma. They'll grow into beauties."

"Let's hope, or we'll be supporting extra mouths for a long time to come."

He fell silent and after awhile, put an arm around her waist and pulled closer.

"I hate to leave you—you and the girls. But you know I have to do this. I'm being called to do this. There are so many others in the world who are not as fortunate."

"It was something my father did. I have fond memories of Africa. I'd like to take the girls when they get older."

"I'd like that, too."

His hand found a breast and he began a circular motion that made the nipple stand upright and her breath quicken. Then he was on top of her. The fullness of him slapped against her stomach before he slipped back and guided his penis between her legs. Constance arched upward and met his body with arms clasped around his neck. He rode her, thrusting, pulling back, thrusting again until she cried out at the burst of joyous pain. And this time he stayed with her after the release shook his body and made him groan. He rolled onto his back and the two of them counted the stars in the Milky Way.

* * *

Edward Galen Everett was born on Valentines Day. His father wasn't there to see his birth, having been detained in the Congo due to a quarantine after an epidemic of cholera. But nothing could have dimmed the joy of that moment—the moment of holding her son in her arms.

And he was perfect. He would inherit her height and coloring and strength. Already his lungs sent the household scurrying to meet his needs.

She nursed him as best she could, reluctantly handing him to the wet nurse when it was apparent she couldn't do the job. But she continued to try, knew it was important for him to bond to her and to no other. And she never left his side. She moved a cot into his room and stayed beside the canopied crib, covering him, uncovering him, offering him a bottle of honeyed goat's milk, fussing until she was exhausted.

Constance took her meals on a tray and hardly went downstairs. The girls would tiptoe into the nursery decorated with trains and toy soldiers and hung with mobiles of dancing nursery rhyme characters—a little Miss Muffet, sans spider, spun dizzyingly in front of the window next to Old King Cole and Mary with her lamb.

The girls would line up solemnly and stare at their new brother until they were shooed out the door and admonished to be quiet. There was never any doubt as to the importance of this newest family member.

Harold returned in March and marveled at the tiny being who had invaded the household while he was gone and turned it upside down. The baby was strong and vigorous—of that he was thankful—but he was concerned about his wife. Not her health, she seemed to have blossomed, put on weight that filled out cheekbones and rounded her hips. No, it was more her attitude. Some mental change that was frightening in its intensity.

On his first evening back he'd slipped up to the nursery while Constance was bathing and picked up his son. The tiny boy was sinewy-strong—exactly like Constance—and

had her pale eyes and hair. He wasn't a judge of babies—
he knew his Evy was beautiful—but he thought this baby
plain. But did it matter for a boy? The child wouldn't
want. He stood to inherit a fortune.

"Put that child down."

Harold started. Not so much from surprise as from the
tone of Constance's voice. The woman who rushed toward
him looked wild in the dim light, hair tangled and wet from
her bath, eyes wide. He handed her the baby, marveling
at the intensity of emotion. She placed baby Edward in
the crib and immediately opened his blanket and checked
his little body, cooing and running fingers lightly over his
stomach, legs, arms.

"Connie, for God's sake, I'm his father. What are you
doing? Surely, you don't think I'd harm our son?"

As if sensing the drama of the moment, Edward began
to whimper.

"See what you've done?" The look bordered on
hatred. "Oh, Mother's precious. Did the big man scare
you? Mother's here, you mustn't cry. There, there, dear little
man." Constance had sunk to her knees beside the crib and
rocked it gently, not turning around.

Harold started to say something but was shushed
immediately. There was nothing left to do but leave the
room.

The family saw little of Constance that spring and
summer. She'd elaborately dress Edward for an outing
and then push his buggy up and down the front drive, not
allowing anyone near. At other times she'd pack picnic
lunches and push the carriage into the wooded area behind
the house. They would be gone for hours but always return
just as Harold would be ready to send someone after them.

Edward became a finicky baby. If he cried and pushed away his carrots, he'd be coaxed to eat them with honey coating the spoon. He drank goat's milk until he was three, sucking on the great rubber nipple on the bottle and throwing it across the floor when angry—which was anytime he didn't get his way. But the baby did no wrong. Constance would lash out at anyone who said differently.

Once, Dr. Baxter approached Harold about what he called, "Mrs. Everett's constitution" and prescribed a tonic. But by then Harold wasn't sure he cared. He was relieved, if the truth were known, that he didn't have to interact with this odd woman who was his wife. He'd found it easy to withdraw; his pleasure was watching the growing beauty of Evy, in her cheerfulness and ready smile. But he was careful to give time to Ella and Emma. Constance certainly wasn't going to acknowledge she had other children. He took the girls into town, bought them dresses and bonnets and baubles. The dormitory became stacked with dolls and doll houses.

He had planned to return to Africa. Reverend Schmidt had suggested a mission in the spring—a mission that would pledge raw wheat to overpopulated, drought-ravaged areas—and Harold was to be the spokesperson. But the trip had to be postponed—Edward developed asthma.

Constance would later rant and rave and blame Evy. It was her cold and cough that she'd given to the baby. There was no reasoning with her that Edward had a condition, something independent of germs. And that was just the start of his spells.

By four Edward developed symptoms of being fragile. At first Harold thought it was Constance's imagination but later, after two particularly virulent bouts of asthma less than two months apart, he knew better. Each had necessitated hospitalization, placing the skinny child in an oxygen tent to relieve the wheezing, and Harold sought the advice of specialists.

Constance went with him to the meeting. They had paid to have two pulmonary experts come to the Hillsboro hospital. Stuffy men, Harold thought, researchers almost displaced in the sterile surroundings of Edward's room. And they were of little comfort. The child shrieked when they touched him, coming at him as they did wearing white gauze masks, poking, prodding, and listening to his chest.

"I'll die if anything happens to Edward." Constance was sitting outside Edward's room on a straight-backed chair that allowed little comfort in one of the rare times she had left his side.

"No, you won't. Sometimes things happen. It's in God's hands. You must take strength in your faith." Harold leaned against the wall.

"Edward is everything to me. I'd have no life without him."

Harold looked down at her upturned face, the dark circles under the eyes, the thinning hair now almost gray. Constance hadn't aged well. Now in her late thirties, she seemed old, prematurely withered as if four children had sapped her youth.

"Of course, you have a life. There are the girls—"

"I know it's a sin, but I only care about my son. I can't help myself. Even more than you, he's my salvation, God's promise. He can't take him. He can't."

Harold was at a loss to soothe her. What could he

say? He watched as she got up slowly and returned to Edward's room.

Part Two

EVY 1929-1950

Tea leaves, or cards or the stars? Why can't there be some way of knowing in advance what life will bring? Give us a choice of whether to carry on, take what's coming up in stride, or refuse to even get involved. Sometimes I wish I had known.

CHAPTER SIX

August 1929

Evy's screaming brought the kitchen help out onto the wide, white wooden porch shaded by a dozen towering elm. Mattie and the two girls, who came on Saturdays, leaned over the railing as Evy barrelled around the side of the house.

"He killed him!" Evy sobbed. "I can't look."

She threw herself on the ground and covered her eyes, hands flat, fingers full length pressing into her face leaving the skin white around each indentation to her forehead.

"Who died? Evy, look here. What you talking about?" Mattie knelt beside the child.

"The puppy. My birthday puppy from Da. Edward threw him out the window!" Evy's sobbing threatened to reach hysteria.

"Oh no." Mattie quickly ran to the grassy spot below Edward's second story bedroom. Evy hadn't lied; Mattie knew the tiny thing was dead before she picked it up. She looked up at the window and saw the lacey sheer waver then fall still. In bed with an asthma attack, sick all night, yet well enough to crush the very joy out of his sister. What could have happened to a four-year-old to make him cause such sorrow?

She scooped the puppy up, wrapped him in her apron and started for the barn. Clemetts could handle this. The puppy had barely been six weeks old. Too young to leave the litter if they'd asked her. But they hadn't. Would an older puppy have survived the fall? That wasn't the point, and she knew it. She handed off her bundle, shook her head in answer to Clemetts' questioning gaze, and walked back to the house.

"He ruins everything. I hate him. I hate him."

Mattie found herself wanting to agree. But she said nothing, just cradled Evy's head in her lap and pushed the porch swing to rock gently.

Finally, she offered, "Edward's still a baby, honey. I don't think he realized what he was doing. That puppy could have been a stuffed toy. He don't know the difference."

"Couldn't you have saved it?"

"It was hurt too badly, Evy. This here's a farm. Everything has to earn its right to live. The sick and the weak don't have no place."

"Me? Even me, Mattie? Do I have a place?"

"Hush. Course you do. Your mother and father love you. Now, no more silliness. We'll find another puppy."

But Evy didn't want another puppy. Even at nine she knew she'd fret and worry herself sick, never wanting to leave it alone—sick unto death that Edward would do the same thing. Tomorrow was her birthday and Edward had already ruined it. Twice. The first time by having an asthma attack and making Mama disinvite all her friends.

Da had ordered the pony rides before he left on the missionary trip to Africa. Nothing was to spoil her special day. Not his being gone, not the rainy summer—if there was rain, then they were to ride in the barn, go in circles under the rafters after Clemetts cleared the hay.

Only Da hadn't counted on Mama. Evy didn't ever think he realized the extent of her devotion to Edward. Edward made himself come down with an asthma attack—Evy was sure of it. Out of spite—out of pure nastiness, knowing better than anyone how she'd dreamed about that party.

He'd followed her around for days whining, "I want a party." And she'd hush him and tell him again when his birthday was and that he'd have to wait. But he didn't want to wait and wailed and clung to his mother until she said that Evy would just have to share her party.

But Evy wasn't going to do that—invite only the girls she knew who had brothers worthy enough to play with Edward. No, this was her party. Hers. He wasn't going to get his way. Her mother said she was spiteful and promised Edward his favorite ice cream. But Evy saw in Edward's eyes, peeking out from his mother's skirt, that he would ruin her day.

And that night in her room, she lay listening to the screams and the running back and forth, up and down the stairs. She didn't have to go out in the hall to know that Mattie was carrying pots of steaming water, setting them around Edward's bed underneath a canopy to relieve his breathing as her mother yelled orders. He had done it—

managed to get sick and she knew there would be no party in the morning.

Quietly, she slipped out of bed. There were so few things that brought her happiness, but her room was one of them. By nine she'd outgrown the dormitory and begged to be given one of the small east rooms at the end of the hall. Her father was on her side, and Ella didn't seem to mind staying with Emma in the big open dormitory that had no privacy. They were twins. They did a lot of things together. But there was a fight just the same. She overheard her father pleading with her mother.

"Connie, why let the rooms go to waste? No one uses them."

"It's the principle."

"There are enough rooms to go around if Ella wants her own someday or Emma."

"A coddled girl makes an impossible wife."

"The child is nine. We're talking about a little privacy."

So, her mother gave in. The room was wonderful, small but with a high ceiling and two dormer windows. New wallpaper with tiny yellow flowers matched the starched, ruffled chintz curtains that Da had ordered just for her birthday. Evy had even been allowed to decorate her room. And it was the cut-outs that she loved the most.

One night Da had brought up a stack of French magazines and the two of them carefully cut out flowers and animals and women with straight, bobbed hair and men in suits and tennis whites and tacked them to the walls. Everything just five feet off the ground, as high as she could reach. Some of the women she placed so that they could talk with each other and she made up what they said, lying in her bed at night she'd slip into her crowd and flit along the walls in her imagination.

"Hello."

"Well, hello to you, Miss."

"Do you like my new curtains?"

"Yes. Yes. We all do."

"I got them for my birthday. It's tomorrow."

"Aren't you a lucky little girl."

"I am, aren't I?"

A knock on the bedroom door, "Evy? Who are you talking to?"

"No one, Mama."

"Well, you get to bed, hear? I don't want you sick, too."

"Yes, Mama."

But there was light enough, a moon sending streams of pale silver across her bed, and she stayed up a little longer whispering her conversations with the wall people. She didn't know why but she knew that her mama would be displeased with her talking to them. Mama hadn't wanted her to tack them up over the nice new wallpaper and had yelled at Da. But he'd just laughed and said it was Evy's room and her decision. Evy thought the room looked glorious.

* * *

By the time Evy came down for breakfast, all her school friends had been called and, with regrets, told the party had been postponed. Edward was a little better and her mother bustled around the kitchen fixing a tray. A tray for the two of them because she would stay with her son for most of the day.

She made this announcement to Evy and Ella and

Emma as they waited for Mattie to place bowls of oatmeal in front of them at the big plank table. And then, just as their mother ascended the back stairs, she turned and asked that they try to be quiet and stay out of the house.

"If it rains, go to the barn. Edward must nap. He got very little sleep last night." And with that she was gone, tray balanced above her head as she went up the stairs.

And the barn it was. Soon after breakfast the rains started. At first a light drizzle and then a full-fledged shower came down in sheets. But the barn was warm and smelled of animals and hay. Evy loved the stalls and loft. Only Ella had brought a book to read and perched in a corner, oblivious to her sisters.

Evy never tried to get Ella to play. She was so stuffy and better than anyone else. Even now, ten year old Ella's high pitched voice sought her out.

"You shouldn't wear your Sunday best dress out here in the barn."

"It's my birthday. I can do as I want."

"Mama will be mad."

"I don't care 'cause she don't care. I'm not Edward so she'll never notice."

"Doesn't, Evy."

"Huh?"

"She *doesn't* care. Oh, never mind. But don't say I didn't try to get you to change."

Evy flounced away to find Emma. Ella was so tiresome. She was always quiet; she could've stayed in the house. Just then a cloud of straw floated over Evy.

"There you are." Evy looked up at the mischievous missing-tooth grin that beamed down at her from the loft.

Leave it to Emma to want to play. Evy loved her round,

fun-loving older sister who was always up for a game, no matter what. Later, Evy would try to remember whose idea it was to play swords and pirates. Hers, she was afraid. She had been the one to find two sticks behind a corn bin and, remembering the one movie she'd seen in her life—before her parents found out a friend had taken her one day after school—she talked Emma into helping her recreate Wallace Beery, swashbuckling his way up a gangplank.

They'd chosen to play in the loft because it gave an air of authenticity to their imaginary scene—high up above the water, in this case the barn floor. Evy pushed a box squarely in the center of two overhanging rafters, plopped a foot-wide board against it. It made a pretty real-looking gangplank, if she did say so herself.

Then she struggled out of her dress—her prettiest with a pleated organdy skirt in lightest yellow with ribbons and bows instead of buttons—and smoothed it out across a bale of hay in the corner. Her petticoat was white and starched stiff so she struggled out of it, too and stood only in a camisole and bloomers. Much better, she could move now.

She recreated the story for Emma who listened to her, wide-eyed, hanging on every word. If their parents had anything to say about it, Emma would never go to a moving picture show. They were evil, a "ruination," her mother called them. But Evy could tell that Emma was already thinking how she could see this make-believe world that played out across a screen in a dark room with a piano player.

Then out of kindness, she told Emma she could go first—try the gangplank and sword. But Evy had to demonstrate the act of trying to balance and fight off the evil pirate all at the same time. Evy was lithe and quick and darted up and down the board and back brandishing the make-believe sword, her bare arms flashing above her head, then down and across before a thrust forward.

Emma couldn't wait to try it but couldn't master wielding her play sword and running up and down the tilting board. Finally, she just positioned herself on the box and continued to wave the long stick around her head in circles, stabbing in the air, letting it fall, then heaving it aloft again. Evy was hysterical with laughter.

"Emma, stop. You won't kill anyone that way, silly. Here let me show you again."

Emma's screams were so loud and sudden that Evy who was right in front of her didn't see at once what had happened. Not until the angry buzzing, the cloud of yellow jackets had swarmed over Emma's face, stinging again and again, first her temples, along her hairline, her lips.

"Clemetts!" Evy's shriek was one of pure terror.

She stood rooted to the spot adding her screams to Emma's and covering her eyes. She didn't see Clemetts until he had smothered Emma's head with his shirt, pulling the cloth back to pick the hornets off and smash them with his fingers. Then he grabbed both girls about the waist and, leaning into the ladder, carried them down from the loft and ran through the rain toward the house.

Mattie ran out on the porch and took Emma in her arms and yelled directions for Clemetts to gather mud, a tub of mud and get back there "right quick" and not to forget to chip some ice from the block in the cold chest. No one noticed at first that Emma had slumped limp and lifeless against Mattie's broad shoulder. Mattie just headed up the back stairs for the dormitory and laid Emma across the bed.

"There, there little one. You's gonna be just fine. Emma,

you hear me now? We's gonna make all this hurt jus' go away." Then suddenly Mattie jumped back and started to scream. Evy who was hanging over the headboard thought she'd been stung, too.

"Oh, Missus, oh, Missus … Missus come here quick!"

What was wrong? Mattie would never scream for their mother like that. Then Mattie threw herself down on her knees beside the cot and began to move Emma's arms, then slap her face. A face that was no longer Emma's, swollen as it was so that her eyes couldn't open. Evy looked closely at the red, pulpy mass and felt sick.

"Shut up this screaming. Whatever is the matter with you?"

Evy's mother swept into the room and swooped down upon them.

"Look at you, Evy. In your undies. Have you no shame?"

"Our Miss Emma's dead." Mattie sat on the floor and began to rock, holding herself with arms wrapped tight across her front, mussing her dress.

"Don't be melodramatic." But her mother caught her breath when she bent over Emma. "My God. Oh my God, what happened?" Then she straightened and backed away.

"Stings. Poor thing was attacked by them yellow jackets."

"Here's the mud. I gots plenty of it." Clemetts pushed into the room and plopped a wash basin down beside the bed.

"Too late. You're too late. The child is dead."

"What's 'dead' mean?"

Everyone turned to see the frail boy in the doorway.

"Edward. You must go back to your room. My darling,

you mustn't be out of bed. Come with Mama, now."

If Evy remembered correctly in that blur of an afternoon on the day that she turned nine, her mother left all the arrangements to Mattie. Her mother went back to Edward's room and didn't come out until supper.

Mattie called the doctor, left a message at the church, placed a long-distance call for Da before washing Emma's body and dressing her in the red velvet dress that had been her favorite. Mattie pulled her best shoes out of the closet and lace-edged stockings from a drawer. She was tender and loving, crooning a song that Evy hadn't heard since they were babies. At last, she tucked Emma's hands, also puffy and swollen from stings, in a fur muff and tacked a veil on Emma's most treasured possession, a white rabbit fur hat, and pulled the hat well down over her forehead. The angry redness was hardly noticeable.

"There now, she look almost pretty."

"Will Da come home?"

"I reckon he will. He won't get here tomorrow, but he get here all right."

"I want Da."

"I knows you do, sweetheart. I knows you do."

Evy had to go downstairs when the doctor came. Later, after he'd been with Emma for awhile, he came down to the kitchen and talked about allergic reaction—hadn't they known before? Hadn't she been stung before? All kids get sideways with hornets or bees. He sat in the kitchen and sipped a cup of hot tea after administering to Clemetts' hands, puffy and red from stings when he picked the hornets off Emma's head. The doctor made Clemetts keep his hands in a dishpan of ice water.

"Coroner will be here within the hour."

The coroner was coming? Then it dawned on Evy that they would take Emma.

"You can't take her away." Evy grabbed the doctor's sleeve.

"Hush. They has to." Mattie poured Evy a glass of cold milk and put it in front of her. "How'd you like to share a piece of your birthday cake with Dr. Elders? It's chocolate and I bet that's his favorite."

"Well, how'd you guess? I sure would like a piece of that birthday cake." The doctor beamed and patted Evy's arm. Evy recoiled and slumped against the high back of the chair.

"No, no, no. I won't let you take her!" Evy pushed away from the table knocking her chair to the floor and spilling her milk. Then she rushed up the stairs, burst into the dormitory half expecting Emma to be playing with her dolls, and threw herself on the bed and hugged her sister.

"You won't go. I won't let them take you. If Da were here, he'd stop them."

But they did take her. After all, Evy couldn't stop them. Mattie held her, kicking and screaming, crying as if her life had ended then sobbing until she slept from exhaustion. And not once did her mother leave her brother's room.

* * *

The funeral was held in town on the following Sunday. Her mother didn't want Emma's body in the parlor and people with germs parading through their house to gawk. She had to think of Edward's delicate condition.

Evy wished with all her heart that it had been Edward who was placed below the ground in the cemetery, five miles from home. Emma was laid to rest beside two old people she didn't know, grandparents she'd never met. And Evy worried that there would be no one to play with.

The Reverend Schmidt talked a lot about God calling his own back to rest with Him on that bright, sunny morning. And now our young Emma, as he called her, would do God's bidding as a member of His family. The service took place at graveside beside the small opening in the ground that gaped ominously. Evy tried not to look at the hole but concentrated on a flock of chickadees that darted around the base of a large pine.

But when they began to lower the casket into the ground, she screamed without stopping until Mattie carried her away from the crowd and, sitting on the grass, held her, smoothed her hair back from her forehead and hummed softly, rocking back and forth until she quieted.

On Monday morning her mother brought Edward to the kitchen table, propped him up on pillows and personally made him a mush of cornmeal and ground barley while Mattie bustled around making toast and scrambled eggs, pausing to yell up the back stairs, "Breakfast's goin' cold, you hurry down now."

Of course, the only person not at the table was Evy. Ella sat in silence sipping her juice.

"Oh, good Lord, what was that? Sounded jus' like someone threw a bag of oats down those stairs." Mattie rushed to the landing but not before Evy had staggered upright and, holding the banister, continued her descent into the kitchen. Her arms were in front of her feeling her way into the room.

"I can't see. Mama, I can't see." Terror leaked through her voice.

"Evy, I'm sick and tired of your theatrics. Take your

place at the table."

But Evy stood in the center of the big room and began to cry, a puddle of urine forming on the floor beneath her nightgown.

"I can't find the bathroom. Help me."

"Evy." This time her mother's voice was strident and threatening.

"No, Missus, Evy's sick. Don't you fret. I'll take care of my girl." And in one swoop, Mattie picked Evy up and carried her back upstairs.

The doctor found nothing out of the ordinary. He poked and tapped and looked into ears, eyes, and nose and returned to the kitchen with his diagnosis. Evy was suffering what he supposed would prove to be a temporary blindness. No less real and frightening to the victim, it was, however, a symptom of hysteria brought on by the trauma of losing her sister. The mind was a powerful thing.

He suggested that they not rely on just his say-so but have her checked by a new medical man in the community—someone who dealt with psychoses as well as physical problems. It would be expensive but necessary, in his book, to put their minds at ease.

Her mother agreed somewhat reluctantly. She had to do it. What would it look like to refuse the best care for your own child? The new doctor would visit the next afternoon.

That night Mattie slept on a cot in the hall outside Evy's door and was awakened sometime after midnight by a strange dialogue coming from Evy's room. Cracking the door Mattie watched as the sightless child felt her way around the walls, her small chin pointed in the air.

"Do you know where Emma is?"

"No. She didn't come this way."

"Could you check?"

"We'd know if she were here."

"But where is she?"

"I think she went away."

"I think Edward killed her."

"Edward killed a puppy."

"Yes, yes. A puppy, not Emma."

"The wasps killed Emma."

"And I'll kill the wasps. All the wasps in the world."

The door creaked open. "Evy? You needs to be in bed. It's late, honey."

"Mattie?"

"I'm right here. Let's walk down to the bathroom and then you let me tuck you in."

* * *

Da came back three weeks after the funeral. Transportation was difficult and messages often took days to reach him out in the villages. But he came as soon as he could. Evy didn't think it was fast enough. She wanted her father. Aside from Mattie, there was no one else she could stand—not her mother, not the priggish Ella, and never Edward.

The new doctor had been nice and talked to her for a long time. He understood about Emma. How much she missed her, how she felt responsible. Evy had suggested the game. If she hadn't told Emma the story of the moving picture, she'd be alive. But he said it was an accident. Not anyone's fault.

She'd asked him if he believed in God, and was Emma

with God right now? He had paused, said that it wasn't his belief exactly that counted but what would make her feel better. She guessed he didn't and was mystified that a grown man didn't have to believe in God. And nothing would happen to him.

A few days after this meeting, she was propped up in bed staring at her walls but seeing nothing, when light pushed into a corner of her left eye and then the right and then shadows loomed up at the foot of the bed. She blinked and hollered for Mattie. Suddenly, the color of the wallpaper appeared its crisp yellow and her people looked fine, waved even from their walk around the room.

Not waiting for Mattie, she hopped from bed and ran to the top of the stairs.

"I can see!" She sang it out at the top of her lungs, then skipped two steps at a time and ran into the kitchen.

"Will miracles never cease," Her mother said and turned back to washing Edward's hair. He leaned over a bucket set on the floor beside the sink and her mother poured tepid water through his thick curls. "Hand me that towel on the chair back."

"When's Da coming?"

"He'll be here tomorrow afternoon."

"Da will take me to visit Emma."

"Yes. I'm sure he will." A wail from Edward, as water and soap reached his eye, stopped any further conversation, but Evy skipped outdoors to sit on the porch swing and dream about her father's return.

Evy had never seen her father cry, but that first night home he sat in the parlor with tears streaming down his face, his great chest constricting.

"I wouldn't let the children see you like this."

"Mourning is not a weakness, Connie."

"Well, it was God's will. We can't undo what's been done. That's that. We'll go forward."

"Emma never had a chance at life."

"Emma was called in Edward's place."

"What? What are you saying?"

"God needed to take one of my children. I prayed that it wouldn't be Edward, so he chose one of the girls."

"Connie, I do not worship a punitive God. You're not making sense."

"Think what you'd like. She was such a plain thing and really slow-witted. Why, I still don't think she knew all her letters after two years' schooling. Don't you think I haven't wondered that it was a blessing, her being taken young. Now, don't look at me that way. This life wouldn't have had much to offer our Emma."

Her father turned away. "Your callousness astounds me."

"Practicality is not callousness. Can you look at me and tell me I'm wrong?"

"There is more to life than having a son."

"That one child safeguards all our futures. Do not ever forget that."

"Have it your way. I'm returning to Africa in a week."

"So soon?"

"I'm needed there."

"Will you be gone long?"

"Possibly. I need to stay through one planting season, see my efforts through to harvest. I'll be taking machinery with me this time. It'll take time to teach them how to operate it all."

"Take Evy with you."

"Evy? Why? Whatever would she do in the wilds of Africa?"

"You've always talked about the plantation, the test station, the community of researchers and their families. There's a church. I've seen pictures. I'd hardly call that the *wilds*. It would do her good. She's struggled so much with Emma's death. And she's so attached to you."

"Let me think about it."

Crouched in the hall, Evy couldn't believe her good luck. Da said he'd think about it. He'd do it. She just knew he would.

* * *

But by the end of the week, Evy knew something was wrong, very wrong. For the first time that she could remember, her mother left Edward in the care of nurses and spent her days in town.

"She's at the bank," Mattie whispered like it was some terrible secret. "They's been big moneys lost," she'd say and roll her eyes. "All my little ones goin' be poor. Your Mattie goin' to be turned out to go home to Africa."

"What's poor?" Evy asked.

"When you don't has enough to eat or clothes to wear."

Months later, when her mother found the gunny sack of moldy bread hidden in her closet, Evy couldn't make her understand that she was trying to save the family from being poor. But they weren't poor, her mother reprimanded, less affluent at the moment, but not poor. But the way her mother said the word with a mixture of disgust and fear, Evy knew it was something to guard against.

In fact, her mother explained that she was working

hard at economizing and asked both girls to help. She dismissed four of the six house servants and the same number of farmhands. Evy helped Ella with the laundry and making beds. Her mother cooked, and Mattie did a little of everything. Evy's father worked from dawn until dusk, exhausting himself preparing the fields. He and Clemetts had the help of only one extra man. The harvest that year was only so-so. There had been very little snow, and the usual spring rains were non-existent.

Her father looked grim-faced in the evenings when he came up from the fields.

"It's as bad as I've ever seen it."

"What's bad, Da?" Evy asked as she handed a plate of bread to him. Bread and potatoes dominated their meals now. Fresh vegetables gave way to canned ones, starting fall. Helpings were small and doled out by her mother who filled plates from the head of the table and handed them around. Extra portions for Da because he worked so hard and extra for Edward because he was poorly. But Edward's extras were mostly sweets, a second sliver of pie, jam on his bread at dinner, two slices of streusel for breakfast. Still, he stayed thin.

"The land, Evy. It's begging for moisture. We had a dry summer and a worse fall."

"What happens if it doesn't rain?"

"Any wind will take our topsoil."

"What's topsoil?"

"Evy, for heaven's sake, let your father eat. His dinner is getting cold."

"Let her be, Connie. She's old enough to understand what it means to be tied to the earth, to pray it will produce for you."

He turned to Evy. "The first six inches of dirt is the richest. It contains the minerals, the nutrients that make everything grow. Lose any portion of that and your crops are spindly, more apt to die and not mature."

"Is that what made the Weber's corn fall over?" Evy remembered the tall stalks in a neighbor's field suddenly lean and collapse against each other.

"Yes. That's exactly right. The plants didn't have the strength to stand upright."

"And the same thing could happen to our wheat?"

"More or less. We'll plow under the winter wheat and not replant until next year. A rest is good for the land."

"There won't be a harvest next summer?"

"No."

Evy watched her father begin to eat. She couldn't think of anything else to say. It was shocking to think there wouldn't be a harvest. But she had her Da. He'd stayed almost two whole years after Emma's death. And she was thankful for that.

Then one morning, Evy got up to find a note on her pillow. He was gone. Da had crept away in the middle of the night. He wrote that he was sorry that he couldn't take her with him. Maybe some other time. But it sounded false. Evy doubted there would be another time, and she was heartbroken.

There was only one thing to do. She ran away, sneaked into the back of a wagon going to Hillsboro, and hid in the town's library. She hadn't meant to get locked in overnight, but she'd given everyone such a fright by the time they'd found her, her punishment was light——stay in her room for three whole days, leaving only to go to the bathroom.

But this didn't last long. By the second day her mother

ignored her. She slept in Edward's room and had retired
that evening by nine. Evy was also in bed early and was
startled by the noise of her bedroom door opening.

"Shush now. Don't go waking your mama. Mattie's
found you a big ol' surprise but you gots to come with
her. An' you put on some shoes, you hear?"

Evy took little prodding. Escape. She was out of
prison. Pulling on her robe, she bent to fasten the buckles
of her good black leather dress shoes and followed Mattie
downstairs. The kitchen was dark, and Mattie told her to
leave the lights off.

"I'd be in a heap a trouble if your mama finds us. We
gots to be quiet now. You follow close."

Quietly, Mattie opened the back door and shut it by
letting the handle turn slowly in her hand. Even after the
click, she motioned Evy to stay still, and the two of them
waited and watched to see if a light came on upstairs.

"Looks like we's off." With this, Mattie gathered up her
skirts, grabbed Evy's hand and took off across the lawn
heading toward the barn.

The lone bulb in a socket that dropped from a black
electrical cord beneath the hay loft glowed a soft yellow.

"Remember, you be quiet now. I's got to find some more
light." Mattie disappeared into the tack room and came
back with an oil lantern. "This here's gonna help." Turning
up the wick, Mattie struck a kitchen match on the side of
a stall and ignited the filament. Replacing the glass globe,
she held the lantern in front of her, and beckoned Evy
to follow. They were almost at the last stall before Mattie
pulled opened the wooden half-door and stepped inside
after hanging the lantern on a nail.

"What's you think?"

At first, Evy didn't see anything, then a rustle of straw in the corner caught her attention.

"What is it?"

"You drop down to your hands and knees and crawl over there real slow."

When Evy was two feet from the corner, she saw the bundle of fur, not one but four bundles. Hissing and jumping sideways, the kittens postured and tumbled over one another getting braver when they saw their mother rub against Mattie's leg.

"They're so cute. I'm going to name them right away." Evy plopped down cross-legged and picked up the first kitten. "You look just like buttermilk, so that's what I'm going to call you. And you, you'll be Fudge. That's Licorice and—"

"Well, ain't this cozy."

Mattie screamed and reached for Evy.

The man was dirty and smelled, and he hung over the stall door gaping at them, a long-necked bottle, half full of some yellowish liquid, swung loosely in his right hand. Evy hugged Mattie, the kittens forgotten.

"You gets on out of here. Nothing be said if you just keep on going. This ain't no place to stop for the night."

"You the missus here? 'Cause if you're not, you're real high and mighty to be telling me anything. Nobody ever teach you your place?"

"Watch your mouth and do as I say."

"Go away. This is not your house," Evy added.

"Well, well, even the young one don't have no manners. Looks like the two of you need a lesson in hospitality."

He pulled the stall door open and lunged for Mattie. She

screamed and sidestepped but his weight bore her backwards and she stumbled, striking her head on the feed trough.

"Mattie. Mattie!" Evy was frantic. Mattie wasn't moving and the man was straddling her and pulling at her skirt.

"Stop that." Evy threw her weight against the man but caught a blow to the shoulder as he batted her away. "Now. Go away now!" Evy again jumped on the man's back and pulled his hair. His blow this time bore her backwards into the open door and knocked the wind out of her. Gulping to catch her breath, she struggled to her feet and hung onto the door for balance.

"People's brats that don't know no manners needs a lesson or two. You stay back, and you won't get hurt. I'm gonna have some fun with your mammy-friend here, and then maybe I'll show you a thing or two. Pretty as you are, you could stand a little fun."

"No!" Evy screamed the word, then continued to scream until a slap across the mouth snapped her head sharply against the door's wooden edge. Why wasn't anyone coming to help? Where was Clemetts? Or the stable hand? Then she remembered, the young man who used to exercise the horses was gone, had been "let go" her mother called it. The farm needed mechanics now, not those who knew nothing but stock. And weren't all the stalls empty, save one? The carriage house held three shiny new automobiles.

The man in front of her lurched to grab her hair and pull her head backward, brushing his mouth across hers.

"You're a real beauty. Anyone ever tell you that? Jus' look at these little buds pushing up outta your nightie here." One hand pinched the front of her. She screamed and kicked, arms flailing but not connecting with flesh. The man only laughed.

"You'll get your turn, my pretty. But's now I gotta give your mammy something she won't forget."

Suddenly releasing Evy, the man fell on top of Mattie, pulling at her clothes, but the process of undressing her was hampered by voluminous petticoats, a long wraparound apron and not a little by her attacker's inebriated state.

A whimper escaped, but Evy quickly clamped her lips together. What could she do? Putting her hand out, she inched along the rough plank wall and the answer almost fell on top of her. The long handle was smooth and cool to the touch. She half-turned to close both fists around it before leaning back squarely against the wall, the pitchfork held tines-out like a shield.

"Leave Mattie alone."

"So, you can't wait your turn? Is that it? You want ol' Buster to be a foolin' with you now?"

"If you touch me, I'll poke your eyes out."

The man glanced over his shoulder then laughed when he saw the pitchfork braced against Evy who was backed up against the door.

"Now what's this?" He staggered to his feet, then leaned down and found the bottle in the straw. He paused to take a swallow. "Is this a threat? Little bit of a nothing like you goin' to poke my eyes out?" His laugh rocked his body and he took a couple steps backward before he leaned against the opposite wall to steady himself. But his merriment seemed short lived and in a burst of anger he threw the bottle in the corner and stepped toward Evy.

She saw him lurch forward, catch a toe on Mattie's skirt

and lunge, catapulted full length toward her. She screamed and held on.

The shuddering impact reverberated along the handle of the pitchfork and shivered through her body. The force had wedged her against the wall, but she hadn't let go. She'd kept the pitchfork extended in front of her, and he'd been caught in mid-leap, the tines puncturing his neck. For a long second, pitchfork and body formed an inverted V before both collapsed to the floor of the stall. The weight of the body forced two of the tines to protrude from the back of his neck.

She couldn't look. His eyes were open and any minute he would grab her. Dropping to her knees, Evy frantically shook Mattie.

"Mattie, please get up. Hurry." She glanced over her shoulder.

The man hadn't moved, nor had he closed his eyes. He looked just like Emma when they had laid her on the bed. Only there was blood coming out of his mouth that spilled over his chin and dribbled down his neck.

Mattie moaned and opened her eyes.

"Mattie, there's been an accident. Get up. We've got to leave."

Mattie struggled to a sitting position, glanced to her right and sank back in the straw, a hand clutching her forehead. "Bring your mama. Now, child, run."

"No. You come too."

"Child, you listen to me. Mattie's hurt. An' it don't look like he's gonna do any more damage. You go on now. Mattie will be waiting right here."

Evy flew to the house, threw open the back door, and screamed for her mother. As soon as she saw lights come on, she ran back to the barn to be with Mattie.

The rest of the night was a frenzy of police. She was questioned and applauded for being so brave. She didn't feel brave. She felt scared and couldn't close her eyes without seeing the face of the man she'd killed. At last the body was released to the coroner.

Her mother was calm but abhorred the commotion. "Don't give people things to talk about, and they won't talk."

Well, Evy guessed they'd talk now. But the nice sheriff said that the man was a vagrant, someone who was out of work, traveling from one area to the next working odd jobs.

"Down on his luck. Simple as that. Lack of jobs hit a number of folks hard and not just here. This country's got some answering to do. Things can't go on like this. Just last week we found a body over by Marion Lake. The man was so malnourished, he likely starved to death. Now you tell me what's happened to the land of plenty. It's a sin to think a fellow could go hungry."

The sheriff droned on, mostly for her mother's benefit, Evy thought. But it dawned on her that no one was blaming her. She'd held the pitchfork, but no one actually said that she'd killed him. It seemed to be more a problem caused by circumstances, a child forced to defend herself.

"I don't want you to worry, ma'am. No way your young'un could have done different. You should be real pleased that she stood up to him that way. Could have saved her from exactly what he was planning to do to your cook." The man cleared his throat and made eye contact with her mother before looking at the ground.

"God help us. I don't know what I would have done

then," her mother said.

"Man like that ain't much better than an animal. With the liquor and all, he don't know what he's doing. But like I said, that little girl of yours was lucky, real lucky."

Evy had never seen her mother so upset. She kept running her hands through her hair, recently cut into a short bob that made her long face seem overly narrow and pinched. "No woman ever lives through rape. Survives, that is."

"I agree. See it every once in awhile. The poor girl is plain ruined for life." He'd lowered his voice. "How old is your daughter?"

"Coming thirteen."

"Oh, a bad age for something like this—a lasting impression, if you know what I mean. A man with his pants down to his knees, ready to do his business. You don't think she saw—"

Constance looked startled, then cleared her throat. "Well, Mr. Weens, I need to get my daughter to bed, if there are no other questions. I'd like to think this could all be forgotten. I wouldn't want people to know what almost happened here, what she might have seen. My daughter's reputation and all. Do you understand?"

"Surely do. But townsfolks gonna get word of it one way or the other. Can't stop a healthy curiosity."

"I'd ask that you not add to the story in any way. Bad enough there was a murder. My daughter is highly emotional, the strain of this will be damaging enough … I ask that you try to understand."

"I'll do my best, ma'am."

"Sheriff?"

"Ma'am?"

"I'll be sending my daughter to live with her father for awhile. He's on mission in Africa. The Congo, actually. You don't see any problem with that, do you? You, yourself, said that there wasn't any reason to detain her—that what she did was brave and called for."

"Yes, ma'am. Right brave and quick thinking. You have a lot to be thankful for—and proud of—in that girl of yours."

"Good. Then I'd like to have her gone by the end of the week. What I can't get packed in that time, I can ship. I just think we need to move quickly. Wouldn't you agree?"

"Absolutely. Probably a good idea what with the townsfolk and all, talking, that is. No, that's a right fine idea."

* * *

Evy slept in the next morning. When she finally came downstairs for breakfast, her mother had already had trunks pulled from the attic. The plan had been set in motion. Her mother's mind was made up.

And Evy was ready. This wasn't like having to push a reluctant child to do something she didn't want to do. To escape the farm and see Da? And live in some strange and wonderful land? That was heaven to Evy. The answer to her wildest, most fervent prayers.

Of course, Reverend Schmidt was consulted. More out of courtesy, Evy thought. She didn't understand everything Reverend Schmidt said about Da's mission, but it was apparent that he had been successful in supplementing the production of rubber on the large plantation by introducing crops and teaching local workers how to plant and harvest.

Successful harvests that would feed themselves and the surrounding villages.

The mission now had a school—more of Da's doing—taught by a Jesuit, an itinerant Catholic priest who traveled the countryside, establishing centers of learning. The fact that the founder was Catholic made the good reverend wrinkle his nose. But as he told her mother, "Everyone under God must work together in His name."

The school seemed to be a coup of sorts. A breakthrough for the Congolese living in the area. On the whole, natives were not offered educational opportunities beyond primary schooling. Da's emphasis on advancement—making some secondary classes mandatory in order to work on the mission grounds—was novel and met with local support.

Evy listened as Reverend Schmidt extolled her father's virtues, simply beaming with pride—as though he had discovered her father and was somehow responsible for his success. He repeated how Da was an exemplary example of the church and its mission—its dedication to the less fortunate.

CHAPTER SEVEN

Her father hadn't had a lot of warning. Maybe, not any. Evy was certain of that as she slipped off the bus, a great gray, rambling, stinking thing filled with crates of chickens—apparently with the same destination—as she watched them being unloaded and stacked high to the right of the road. Most were panting in the heat, their heads and unblinking eyes lolling through round holes in the crate's sides. She was certain that a great number of the birds were dead. The smell was overpowering. She pinched her nostrils shut and took in short bursts of air through her mouth.

"This is where you go. Somebody come soon to get you." The bus driver leaned out the window.

Evy nodded. Was he asking a question? His lilting English rode up at the ends of sentences, and she couldn't tell. She hoped "somebody come soon" because she was hot and tired and a little out of sorts. Her last clean dress had literally come un-pleated, mussed as it was from the train ride across half the continent. It had taken six weeks to get where she was and instead of being elated, she felt like crying. She was almost thirteen, which was mostly grown, Mattie had said, old enough for an *adventure*. But it didn't feel very grownup at the moment.

The driver helped two other men unload the chickens and stack the crates. Sweat glistened on his dark arms and beaded across his forehead. After the last crate was wedged up against the others, the three flopped on their backs under the only shade and jabbered in a language that Evy had never heard. Then, after sharing a canteen of water, they got back on the bus. Still, no one came to the gates to greet her, so the driver honked his horn. One short blast, two, three. Then he continued in rapid succession to squeeze the bulbous rubber ball to the right of the steering wheel. Incensed at the disturbance, a raucous flock of parrots lifted in a blast of color from a nearby tree.

"You be all right now. We go."

"No. You can't leave me." It hadn't dawned on Evy that he'd drive away. She'd be alone.

But the driver just waved, letting the bus roll down a slight incline before shifting gears. His wave was friendly enough. But Evy was thoroughly put out. Why hadn't her father met her at the station? What could he be thinking? Granted, she'd had an escort until she reached Nairobi. One of the missionaries, a friend of Reverend Schmidt, had been with her during the long trip by ship, then rail.

The good woman had sent another telegram just two days ago. Since her father expected her, she had then put Evy on the train early this morning and sent her off with a native girl for company. The two had rolled out of the dirty, fly-ridden city into the cooler country at six a.m. Evy's companion spoke little English but smiled a lot. When they got to the rail station, the nearest stop to the mission, Evy found her bus with the help of the station master, and the girl waited for a train to take her back.

But what if her mother's telegram hadn't reached Da in the first place? It was easy to see how the second one might not have been delivered yet. What if he didn't know? Her mother hadn't waited for an answer in her haste to *spare* Evy the talk of the town. Was she even in the right place? She'd had to trust the bus driver for that. He'd nodded when the station master had summoned him, assuring both that he did indeed know the missionary, Papa Ev and the plantation, New Hope.

What a strange thing to call her father, but didn't it fit this strange country? It wasn't at all like what Evy thought. She hadn't seen one animal that wasn't domestic. And those were pretty scrawny. An emaciated dog had followed her from the station to the bus, but the driver warned her not to pet him because he was sick. The minute she landed— walked off the ship to dry land—transportation to the next hub had been waiting.

What a journey. First the ship, then a bus trip to a boat to take her down a river to another dock where she waited for a train and then the last jaunt by yet another bus and now at mid-day, she was standing alone but for fifty-some crates of half-dead chickens on a rutty dirt road out in nowhere. A place that even God would forsake.

The first tear left a track down her cheek. She dabbed at the wetness and grime with the only clean hanky she had left and sat on her trunk, now filled to bursting with dirty clothes. Other than the dress on her back and a hat, she had nothing else presentable.

She moved to a patch of shade provided by a sprawling, frondy tree to the left of the big iron gate and sat down. The chickens made funny garbling noises and continued to poke their heads out, eyeing her. Or were they envious of the shade? Evy carefully tucked her hanky under her belt and walked to the stack of crates.

"I imagine you'd feel better in the shade." Was it her imagination or did the rooster closest to her wink? It took her most of an hour, but one by one, Evy carried and dragged the two-foot square wooden crates across the road to rest under the tree.

"There. Try to rest now and you'll feel better."

But it was apparent that the chickens didn't want a nap. Their scratching seemed even more frantic. Evy eyed the heavy iron gate with an "N" and an "H" welded in the middle of black twisted metal. Beyond, a dirt road disappeared into the distance, miles, Evy guessed from where she was standing. But if her Da didn't come to meet her, why couldn't she just go meet him?

It wasn't like the gate was locked. It didn't have to be because it wasn't attached to anything. There was no fencing on either side, just a big black iron gate across the road between two tall trees with roots that humped up out of the ground in a twisted mass. Beyond the gate the ground looked better cared for, and Evy guessed that the gate marked a boundary, that passing through would put her on the mission grounds. But what to do with the chickens? She couldn't leave them and she couldn't drag all the crates that distance. She'd let them go and hope they followed.

One by one, using a thick stick, she pried the tops off of the crates. The mess inside was worse than she imagined. Every crate had held six chickens—in a space that would have cramped three. Most had lost their feathers and had large pus-filled sores from being pecked. There wasn't one crate that contained more than two live chickens. Some were too weak to even hop out of their squalor, but the lively ones fairly burst from their confines and flew and flopped onto the road stirring up quite a dust cloud.

She counted as best she could and came up with one hundred and one more or less live birds. Some staggered and fell and couldn't seem to get up. Those she carried and placed inside the gate, the others she rounded up and herded to the other side. No easy feat since the healthiest had scattered like buckshot from Clemetts' shotgun.

"If I leave you out here a wild animal will eat you." She yelled trying to get their attention. And then immediately wished she hadn't used that phrasing to scare the chickens because she'd done a good job of scaring herself. And wasn't the sun getting lower all the time? It was fast becoming evening.

"All right. Anyone who wants to come with me better do so right now." She stamped her foot for emphasis but this was lost on the flock as they fanned out through the foot-high grass along the road, clucking, and scratching up a late lunch.

There was really nothing to be done but go on by herself. She left her trunk where the bus driver set it. Even if someone stole it, they'd get nothing but dirty clothes, so if they opened it first before dragging it off, she was pretty certain that it would be left.

Darkness crept around her, and she struggled with

the rocks and dips and holes in the road, her shoes long discarded. This was certainly different from the wide, bricked front drive at home. Then she topped a rise and saw the house.

Lanterns swung from posts planted at three-foot intervals around the wide porch. Some twenty-five of them bobbed and swayed in the light breeze. Amazingly, the house's vast roof was made of grass, domed across the center, falling well past the eaves, and supported by poles as thick as her waist.

To the right was a series of barns, but on the left was a building that must be a school or a church. It was low and flat to the ground but with windows that ran the length of the side nearest her, all with heavy shutters on hinges, propped open with two-by-fours. And again, the roof was thatch, long green-brown strips matted solidly to curve over the edges of the building.

The place was eerie in the golden light from the lanterns. The porch had been white-washed, but the planks were rough and uneven. All the windows, and there were many across the front, were shuttered. Evy couldn't see one speck of glass. But it was the lawn that sparkled in the late light. An emerald carpet spread around the house, broken only by fenced circles containing a sapling or flowering bush.

Altogether, the place was pretty, Evy thought. She clasped her hands in excitement. This is where Da lived. And he needed her. Out here by himself with only natives. He'd be so glad to see her. And they would spend time reading together and riding.

It didn't seem like home, it could never be that. What was it her mother always said? "Beggars can't be choosers." Suddenly, she was so happy and so relieved that her long trip was over that she broke into a run covering the last bit of dirt road and cutting across the thick green grass.

She took the porch steps two at a time, landing in front of a double door of carved wood. An elephant trumpeted in *bas relief* and long-necked birds strutted through tall grasses. The door was partly open but screened on the inside. From somewhere in the interior, someone was playing a piano. Not well. Not like Ella. But the tune was fast and lighthearted.

There was a bell-pull to her right. Evy tugged once and heard a tinkle of bells coming from the center of the house, then voices. The piano music had abruptly stopped.

Evy didn't hear anyone approach the door and was startled when the wooden door was pushed back and the screen squeaked open a few inches.

"Yes?"

The woman was a creamy tan, a skin color that glowed with life. The screen blurred but couldn't hide the flawless amber of bare arms and legs. Her black, full hair was caught at her neck with a yellow ribbon but ballooned over her shoulders while several tendrils fell forward around her face. She was wearing a yellow sundress caught in a bow below the waist, and she wasn't wearing shoes. A foot with five scarlet toes rested on the threshold. She would be considered beautiful, Evy knew that. A beauty that could turn heads.

But it was her eyes that Evy stared at—large, dark with long lashes that could actually touch her cheeks when she blinked. Evy would have assumed that she was a servant but for a certain air of ownership. The woman slouched ever so slightly against the door jamb, her arms crossed over ample breasts.

"I'm Evy." It was all she thought to say.

"And who is this Evy?" The woman's voice was melodious. An accent gave the words a musical sound.

"Evy Everett. I've come to take care of my father." Evy couldn't have told why she chose those words, "take care of" instead of "visit" or just plain "live with". They just tumbled out.

"And this Mr. Everett needs looking after? He's not doing so well? And he's sent for his little nurse?"

Evy couldn't tell if she was making fun. She thought she was. But what was aggravating, Evy wasn't being invited in. She was Harold Everett's daughter, this was his house, and she was kept standing on the porch after coming thousands and thousands of miles.

"I think you better let me in. This is my house now." And then Evy jerked the screened door and literally pushed past the woman. "I'll thank you to tell my father that I'm here. And then I would like a sandwich and a glass of milk." If the woman was going to act like an insolent servant, then Evy could treat her like one.

"I see. I don't like pushy little girls without manners."

"I don't care what you like. I want to see my father."

"Your father isn't here."

Evy felt like she'd been slapped. "Not here?" She'd just assumed her father would be waiting. "Where is he?"

"At the agricultural station. He was expecting a shipment of chickens today, not one little messy chick by itself."

Evy ignored the reference to her clothes. What was she expected to look like after traveling all day? "When will he get back?"

"Maybe in a week. Maybe two."

"But didn't he know that I was coming?"

"No. A telegram came two weeks ago, but he was gone." The woman moved to a sideboard just inside the door and picked up a folded yellow paper, a set of six bangle bracelets jangled as she shook the paper out. "So, you are this Evy that is supposed to arrive? The telegram is from your mother?"

"Yes." Now, Evy was exasperated. If this woman knew she was coming why all the questions? "Are you a friend of my father's? Do you live here?"

The woman seemed about to say something but simply shrugged.

"You can call me May." Then she turned and started toward the center of the house. Evy simply watched her go. What was she to do?

"Come on, come on. That milk isn't going to come out here and hop into your hand. I'll send someone to get your luggage. Where did you leave it?"

"Back on the road. By the gate."

"*Outside*? Outside the gates?"

Evy nodded.

"Ninny. By now all your things will be gone."

"It's only a trunk with dirty clothes."

"Dirty, clean? What is the difference if you have none to start with?"

Evy wasn't sure she understood, and she was too tired to wonder about not having any clothes. Da would fix everything. He'd buy her new dresses.

"They left the chickens by the gate, too."

"Chickens?"

"Crates of them. Most were dead. I tried to bring some with me, but they ran away."

May threw up her hands and continued through an arched doorway. "I can't believe it. Your father is waiting for the chickens at the station, and they leave them here."

She said something sharply and a young girl struggled to her feet from a pallet in the corner. Evy guessed that the big, airy room was the kitchen. A large wood cookstove took up one full wall, what with counters and cupboards that stretched out on either side. There was a sink and drainboard with a pump attached. And a huge table, rough hewn with plank seating along both sides. There was no ice box. A loaf of bread sat on a sideboard alongside a crockery pitcher covered by a doily.

May sank down on a plank seat and waved Evy to the opposite side. She studied Evy with a frankness that was unsettling, then reached into her pocket and brought out a packet of cigarettes. Evy had only seen people smoke in moving pictures and tried hard not to stare. The girl who had been so rudely awakened scurried around preparing food.

"You look like him, you know? Do people always tell you that?"

"Like Da?" No one had ever said that. But, yes, Evy guessed she favored Da more than her mother. Her dark hair waved in layers down her back when it wasn't caught in two fat braids like now, and she was petite, somewhat robust, not lanky like Ella or her mother.

May struck a match on the table. The first fizzled and in a poof, blinked out.

"Damn." May struck a second that flared to life and leaning forward she touched the cigarette's tip to the flame and sucked quickly on the end in her mouth.

Evy didn't know what was so amazing—the use of a

curse word or her agility in lighting the cigarette.

"Yes, you are very like him. In a crowd I would pick you out as being his. And pretty. Do you know that you are very, very pretty? The boys have discovered this, no?"

Evy was saved from answering this embarrassing question by the arrival of her meal. The milk that the girl put in front of Evy frothed above the rim and a mass of bubbles slid down the side of the cup. It was warm, sickeningly so, and smelled of fetid earth.

"The milk is warm." Evy carefully put the cup down and willed her stomach not to churn.

"So?" May eyed her suspiciously. "The little princess only drinks milk that is cold?" She turned and barked something at the girl who was cutting the loaf of bread. The girl shook her head and excitedly babbled an answer.

"She says it is fresh. The goat was milked at sundown."

"Goat?" Evy didn't even know that you could get milk from a goat. No one in Hillsboro would keep goats. A respectable household kept cows, big brown Guernsey with friendly eyes.

"I never drank goat's milk before."

"There are always new things to learn, my little Evy. I suggest you get used to it." May pointed at the milk. "Drink up now."

The servant girl placed a plate of sliced, dry bread in front of her with a small flat dish containing a square of something white.

"Goat's cheese." May pointed with the cigarette. Her nails, long and tapered, were perfectly manicured and painted to match her toes. Evy tried not to stare.

"Do you have any cows?" Evy ventured the question as she stared at the colorless food in front of her. She wondered if she could pinch her nose closed and still swallow.

"Cows out here? You have much to learn. Eat. It is well past the bedtime of everyone at the mission." With that, May stubbed the cigarette out in a saucer, pushed away from the table and left the room.

Evy tried to smile at the thin, dark-skinned girl who had served her, but she'd already gone back to her bed in the corner. Evy managed to drink half the goat's milk by imagining a cold glass of cow's milk being served by Mattie. And then she ate a slice of bread and had to admit that the cheese was good, a little bland, but perfectly edible.

"What an appetite. You had nothing on your trip?" May stood in the doorway and didn't wait for an answer but simply motioned her to follow. "Leave your dishes. I will show you to your room."

At last Evy could get a look at the house. Every time she looked up, she was startled to see grass. The outside was thatch and the inside, too. No painted embossed tin here for ceilings, but the walls were plastered. White and smooth and cool to the touch, they gave off a comforting feeling of familiarity. At least something seemed normal.

May walked ahead of her, leading the way through a large open room that held a smattering of overstuffed chairs, a divan and end tables, a magazine rack and pictures—photographs of a hodge-podge of events. What looked to be a safari, a group of men standing around a dead elephant and then many of buildings clustered in groups, probably other missions judging from crosses perched on rooftops. The piano was in the corner, a spinet of polished black wood with a lamp on top. A stack of sheet music was on the bench.

"The sleeping rooms are this way." May walked easily over the stone floor and never stubbed her toe. Unlike Evy who had tripped repeatedly trying to look down as well as around her. "You may wash in here." May indicated a dark room on her right. "And here is where you sleep."

The room was small in comparison to the others. But maybe small because the bed was so huge, draped in white netting.

"Here is a gown. Never mind it is too big. Leave the rest of your clothing outside your door. Someone will wash your dress and bring it back before morning."

May handed her a folded silky pink bundle that smelled of flowers and lemon. A scent of lemon so strong that it brought tears to her eyes. That was the scent that made her think of her father. It was what he wore all the time. His citrusy fresh smell would wash over her as he bent to push her hair off her cheek or kiss her.

Suddenly, overpoweringly, she wanted her father. The tears welled up and she turned away.

"Is something the matter?" May leaned against the door.

"I'm tired."

"So? You go to bed now, and the rest of the house can sleep, too." The scent of gardenia lingered after May left. One time Mattie had shown Evy a bottle of the same scent in the five and dime in Hillsboro. "De flowers are big as dinner plates and pure white," Mattie had said. "An' smells so sweet."

Evy had to agree. She hugged the gown to her and closed her eyes.

"Missy don't want clean dress?"

Evy's eyes flew open. Sunlight burst into the room as

the young native girl pushed the wooden shutter outward and propped a stick underneath its edge. Bright, blinding light now illumined every corner. The girl who stood by the window was the same one who had prepared her dinner. Evy didn't even remember falling asleep. She had apparently just leaned back on the bed, in mussed dress and dirty feet, hair still haphazardly braided.

"I forgot." What would she do now? She had no other clothes.

"You wait." The girl disappeared and returned with a white shirt.

Obviously her father's and not exactly white but more of a rough cotton, and someone had torn the sleeves out. Recently, too, judging from the threads that tickled over her arms as she slipped it on and buttoned it up. The collarless straight tunic hit her just below the knees, but a rainbow-hued cord belt cinched the fabric at her waist. The girl gathered up Evy's dress and underthings and left the room. Now what? Was breakfast being served? Evy had no idea of the time. She pulled the ribbons off the ends of her braids, unwound her hair and tried to comb the thick mass with her fingers, then gave up and decided to find breakfast.

"Sleeping beauty decides to join us, does she?" May was seated on the piano bench and got up as Evy entered the room.

"Is it to be luncheon or breakfast?"

May could be so daunting. Evy thought it was on purpose.

"Have you eaten?"

"Hours ago. Here we get up early and do our chores. There is much to be done before the sun is overhead."

Evy didn't say anything. She couldn't believe that May in lacquered nails did any manual labor. What would her mother call May—a hothouse flower? Being beautiful was what May seemed to do best. Evy tried not to stare at her sheer, lavender dress with matching slip.

"Go to the kitchen. There will be something to eat. Ask Catha. And I will leave a comb on the dresser top in your room. Put it to good use." And then she turned back to the stack of sheet music.

There was something on the sideboard for breakfast— wonderfully tasty berry turnovers hot from the oven. Evy ate five with another glass of goat's milk. It was beginning to taste better. And Catha was friendly, probably close to her age, and seemed willing to talk. Evy saw the chance to make a friend.

"I'd like to go get my clothes. I left my trunk on the road. Would you like to go, too?"

"No clothes there." Catha seemed to have her information on good authority, but Evy thought she might be kidding.

"Do you know where my clothes are, the ones from my trunk?"

Catha shrugged, "Maybe, they go walk-away."

"They can't do that without help."

Another shrug.

"Missy want to go with Catha to pick more berries?"

"Okay." Anything to get away from the snotty May. And it didn't seem like she'd be getting her clothes anytime soon. What a puzzle.

* * *

The berries were sticky and a little sour and at the end of two hours, Evy was ready to go back. She was tired of overgrown foliage and bugs that dropped off the trees and slithered down her neck. Most seemed to be the biting kind that raised welts on both exposed arms.

She longed for a bath and thought she'd ask Catha how she could get one. But loud angry voices drifted out across the porch when they approached the house. No one needed to tell her one was Da's. Catha went on to the kitchen, but Evy hung back and waited outside one of the large shuttered windows, reluctant to go in, dreading that the argument had something to do with her.

"Just when were you going to tell me about this other family? Your dear little Evy and her mother."

"May, they're nothing to us. They can never take away what I feel for you. My life is here."

"And I remind you, mister, now your little Evy is here, too."

"She's a child."

"She has breasts."

"What?"

"She is more than a child. She is nearing an age that is dangerous. And what do you tell her about me?"

"Nothing. Why do I have to tell her anything? We met last month in Nairobi, you have been staying at the mission while I was gone."

"So, I am just a house-sitter who also sleeps with her father."

"Maybe she won't notice."

"Like I say, she has breasts."

"For God's sake, May, stop saying that. She's eleven, maybe twelve."

"That is not so young for a girl-child."

"How can I send my daughter away? I love Evy. I don't want to hurt her. Something terrible must have happened at home or she wouldn't be here."

"So, you jus' toss me out?"

"Of course not."

"There is room for only one woman in your life, I think."

"And that *woman* is you."

"Men do not understand. That is not a little girl who showed up on my doorstep last night. But what I think you need to know is that I don't share. You are my lover. I will not be a mother to someone over half my age."

"May, I'm not asking you to be her mother."

"No? So it is you who will tell her about the ways of the world?"

"If she's old enough to know that, she's old enough to understand about us."

"Ha! Men are so crazy. Say that you will send the little meddler back where she came from."

"I'm not sure I can send her back."

"If you care for me then do this. I will not stand for having her live with us. When she comes back from picking berries, she can just keep on going."

The conversation abruptly halted, and Evy knew without looking that May had left the room. She ventured a peek and saw her father sit heavily in one of the overstuffed chairs. Eyes closed, he leaned back and pressed fingertips to his forehead as if he had a headache. He was so handsome. Even now in distress, she longed to hug him and tell him everything would be all right. She was here to take care of him. But did he want her anymore?

A bird sat in the top of the sapling closest to the edge of the porch. Evy tried to concentrate on his song. Better that than letting her mind dwell on what she'd just heard—sickening evidence of her father's sins. And betrayal. How could he care so little for his family? And what could she do? She couldn't get rid of the horrid May. That's what she wanted to do—make May go away. Wasn't Evy more important to her father than this intruder? Evy's mother was her father's wife.

Tears threatened to pop over her lower lids and streak down her cheeks, but she snuffled, rubbed her eyes and kept them in check. Tears would be excused, but she didn't want her father to see her that way. Not until she had a plan and not until she'd mastered her anger. How dare her father play house in Africa when Edward and Ella and her mother needed him at home?

Evy was acutely aware of how she looked—dirty summed it up. She couldn't face Da this way. Who could want some urchin to live with them? No, she must make herself pretty. She'd sneak into her room, brush her hair, wash, and hope her dress had been cleaned. And she'd be nice—sweet and obedient—as much as she could, to throw May off. She had always been her father's favorite, and now she'd put that to the test.

She crept around the long side of the veranda and ducked below windows until she came to May's room. And her father's, she supposed. She looked in. All was quiet. The draped bed loomed large but was almost dwarfed by the size of the room itself. A desk in one corner fronted four tall shelves bursting with books and papers. This must be where her father worked. On the wall opposite was a vanity, ornate, side drawers draped with wine-red cloth, an oval mirror hanging directly overhead. A white stool edged with gilded flowers perched in front.

But it was the glitter of bottles that mesmerized her. Tiny crystal decanters sparkled in the sunlight. Perfumes? They must be. And then before she could reason that what she was about to do might not be a good idea, she'd slipped over the low sill and stepped into the room.

Standing before the vanity she tugged a cut-glass stopper from the nearest bottle. Gardenias. She'd been right. And three more bottles held the same scent. Would May miss one? No, she couldn't think that way—that was stealing, still ... There were lipsticks, pots of rouge, powder with puffs that sat in separate china dishes and a wad of hair ribbons fluttering from a nail on the wall. The array was dazzling.

Could May honestly know all that was there? Quickly, Evy picked a bottle of fragrance, a lipstick, a tin of rouge, a small box of powder and a bright yellow ribbon and tucked them all in the pocket of her made-over shift. This was terrible. But she would bring everything back. She was only borrowing. And that thought made her feel better as she opened the door to the hall and tiptoed to her room.

A fresh basin of water was on a stand by her door. Not the tub she longed for, but it would do. She'd just take one of her mother's "canary flutters." As long as her feet were clean, she'd feel better all over. And her one and only dress, pressed and almost perfectly clean, rested on the bed. If May thought she was "very, very pretty," then she would be. Pretty for Da.

She dampened her hair and willed it to behave, then brushed a hundred strokes. There was a small round mirror on the wall by her bed and she squinted into it, pleased with the burnished highlights that capped the crown of her head. The yellow ribbon against her naturally dark long waves was a good contrast. As an afterthought, she pulled several tendrils of hair to frame her face. If May could do it, so could she. The effect was quite striking, if she did say so herself.

The makeup was a different story. Evy had never seen these things before, outside magazines. First, she scrubbed her face and grimaced at the dark smudges on the piece of muslin meant for a towel. Then a light dusting of powder blotted with the towel left her face smooth, evenly tan and healthy looking.

The rouge was more of a challenge. At first she dabbed her lips, but the stuff was gooey and thick. She carefully rubbed it off and when she looked in the mirror saw that the color left looked great—not too red, more like a hint of rose. So far, so good. This was fun. A tiny bit of color on her fingertips and a gentle rub along her cheekbone and presto—a pale blush that looked natural.

She was certain that May penciled in her brows, filled in at the corners and gave them a straighter line. But Evy's were naturally full and arched. Her lashes weren't as long as May's but they were thicker. Evy propped the mirror against the edge of the basin and leaned over to peer at her reflection. And for the first time ever, she could see what May saw. She was pretty.

Da sat with his head back and his eyes closed. Dozing? It would seem so because she was able to walk up behind him and cover his eyes with her hands—hands that smelled of gardenias.

"May?" Startled, he sat upright.

"No, Da." Evy stepped to the side of the chair, quickly

leaned to kiss him on the cheek and then sat on the ottoman at his feet. "I feel terrible that Mama's telegram didn't reach you. I must be quite a surprise."

"Yes ... Evy, let me look at you. You've grown since I last saw you. I can't believe it's my little girl in front of me. But what happened? Why did your mother send you without making certain that I knew you were coming?"

Making it sound like the rape had been directed at her and not Mattie, Evy told the story and enjoyed her father's anger displayed by a clenched jaw.

"Dead was he?"

"Yes. Mama was worried about my reputation. She and the sheriff agreed that I should go away. People talk and all, ask questions. Mama really couldn't bear it. So, I'm here until things are forgotten. Maybe a year or two."

Now her father got up and walked to one of the windows, keeping his back to her. He was quiet. Evy bit her lip but didn't say more. The year or two had been her idea. No one had ever said how long she'd be away. Ultimately, it would be Da's decision. Would he keep his mistress and send his daughter packing? Evy really didn't know. Ever so cautiously she crossed her fingers and added, "May seems nice, but I don't think Mama would approve of her living here."

There she said it. Why not let him know that she'd tell. And instinctively, she knew that not only would her mother not approve, she'd very likely do something awful. It was important that things went as her mother wanted. There was little room for surprise. Still her father didn't turn around. He leaned a forearm against the window casing and continued to gaze at the lawn that spread out away from the house.

"I suppose we could engage May as your governess. That way, she'd have to live with us. Your mother couldn't find fault with that."

"True." A compromise—so like her father.

Did that mean that she was to stay? Evy waited.

"So that settles it. I'll tell May." He was beaming.

He hugged her and danced a few steps, swinging her lightly off the stone tile floor, and said how glad he was that she'd come, how she could go to school with the mission children but take private lessons here at home with May, maybe piano and art, sketching. Wouldn't she enjoy drawing some of the hundreds of birds that visited the orchards and fields?

Yes, she said, that would be wonderful but intuitively, Evy knew she'd both won and lost. Somehow, she'd just provided her father with an iron-clad excuse for having his mistress under the same roof.

* * *

Three oxen carts piled high with boxes and trunks pulled up to the front door on Monday morning. May fluttered from the front steps to the big bedroom, jabbering excitedly and ordering five young men to pick up this, leave that, move more quickly.

Evy watched from a safe distance. She'd ventured closer only to be barked at. May even had furniture. A spindly black lacquered chaise and embroidered settee with matching footstool were hoisted on the shoulders of the movers and gingerly carried into the house. It was a two-hour production and Evy soon lost interest. At least, May was being nice to her.

Supper that evening was strained. May was beginning to take her governess duties seriously and ordered Evy's elbows off the table, then admonished her to use a knife and fork as she'd been taught in a French boarding school. Evy thought of informing May about how Americans eat but caught her father's frown before she'd said anything.

All in all the meal was a trial. But they had meat. A chicken had been roasted in a pit outside and the skin puffed up from juices caught next to the flesh. The juices dribbled across her plate from a large chunk of thigh. Evy couldn't remember eating anything so tasty.

And she knew her father was happy. She'd never heard him laugh so much. It dawned on her that he was *really* handsome—not just because he was her father. She was beginning to notice the men of the world and her father leaning across the table in the candlelight, shirtsleeves rolled to the elbow had a movie star quality about him. His thickly lashed eyes sparkled as he looked from May to Evy. At one point he caught each of their hands and kissed the backs, first one then the other, each with a resounding smack.

Later, when she crossed the great living room on her way to bed, she looked the other way when she caught them kissing. It was so disgusting. Never in all her life had she seen her mother and father display their affection openly. Her mother always said that touching was unclean and a sign of weakness on a man's part.

But there was Da hugging May, openly pressing his mouth to hers. She had seen this in the movies, men and women sighing, holding each other tight. She felt a prickly, warm feeling that spread throughout her body. And it slowly dawned on her that she was jealous. But more than anything she wanted someone to hold her in that way.

CHAPTER EIGHT

Nigerian Dwarf goats—lots of them—met her at the gate to the wire enclosure next to the house before the sun even topped the trees. Catha became her outdoor tutor because to the best of her knowledge, May never went outside unless it was to ride in the car.

Evy set her two buckets of warm water down, careful not to slosh them over into her shoes. Catha opened the gate and coaxed the hungry animals away from the entrance until Evy could enter and lock the gate behind her. Morning after morning the antics of the frolicking kids never failed to make her laugh. Always some little one would chase another up a milking stand only to throw itself in a twisting motion off the top, hitting the ground and pronging sideways to come bouncing back and do it again.

Milking them was an entirely different matter. Even with heads locked in the milking stand stall, the does would bleat and fuss and stomp until Evy was in tears. At first Catha laughed but after days of futile attempts she lost patience, finally enlisting a younger brother to help with milking and making Evy muck the stalls.

Evy didn't mind. The sweet smell of heather that she spread after raking was a perfume all its own and, to Evy, rivaled anything May kept in a bottle on her dressing table. Evy loved the goats. She named every one of the thirty-one and at kidding time helped bring more small creatures into being. Life was a dream and Kansas was a world away.

The days flew by in a blur. Chores that really weren't a burden included tending to chickens and geese and tilling, planting, and harvesting the garden. Predators were more of a problem than anything else, but the fuzzy bundle that Da brought home after a trip to the south turned into her best friend. He was a mix, a mutt, Da said but came from guard stock. Evy didn't care, he was the puppy she'd never had—the replacement for the one lost many years ago at the hand of her brother.

Da mentioned that Skippy might not be the name a hundred-pound watchdog merited but after that one comment, Skippy it became. Skippy slept beside her bed until Da pointed out that predators were more of a threat at night and Skippy was assigned to the goat pen and a pallet of soft rags that had to be taken up every morning so as not to be eaten.

There were school days in the one-room schoolhouse at the back of the property. Lessons for her taught by the aging Catholic priest who traveled over a hundred-mile area, lessons given to all the children on her father's farm. Da was very avant-garde in this, as it was not a popular concept.

She was curious about this man's religion and would often stay after class on the days he was invited to supper, to question him. Catholicism was foreign to her. It was just something her mother disapproved of. Da and the priest would often good-naturedly argue far into the night—long after Evy's eyes had drifted shut and Da had helped her to bed. She knew her mother would be appalled. A "cat-likker" in their home? And a priest at that. Unthinkable.

There were fun times, picnics beside waterfalls, swimming in holes made by backed-up springs. Da brought her a camera which became her prized possession—an awkward fold-out model that was big and cumbersome for smaller hands but never far from her side. Film could only be developed sporadically—when a trip into a large city was planned—so she labeled the spools and kept them safe. It was as if her memory was in a box, never to fail her when recalling her years growing up. But growing up would have its boundaries. It would not, and could not, last forever.

May stayed for exactly three years from the time Evy arrived. In the end when she left, Evy missed her. There had been piano lessons and singing lessons in addition to the ever-present reminders of etiquette and broken sticks of charcoal waiting to be smudged against white poster board in the likenesses of animals and flowers—real or imagined. Surprisingly, May had a good voice and coached Evy to develop her own somewhat dubious musical talent.

Her father had visited the States twice in that time. But

Evy declined to go. Her life was in Africa with Da and the woman who slept with him. Plus, she was scared to death that if she went back, somehow her mother would find a way to keep her there. She couldn't even think of never seeing Catha again, or Skippy.

There were letters from Ella and her mother with a postscript now and then from Edward. Their life seemed dull, but the farm was flourishing. It just was not Evy's kind of life. The confines of a Hillsboro, Kansas would never measure up to the freedom and beauty of the farm in Africa.

Her father had purchased a touring car and taught her how to drive. She would never be willowy tall like her mother, but she had gained enough height to reach the pedals. By fifteen, almost sixteen, she was aware of how people stared at her. Men, especially. She had "blossomed" to borrow one of May's favorite words. A trip into the city made her father nervous. Finally, he simply left her home. "Great beauty is a greater burden," he used to say.

Her life could have gone on forever at the mission. She had Skippy and the goats and chickens; she loved her studies and the books Da brought her from his travels. She was now old enough to teach younger children from a nearby village and found she loved it.

Every morning during the rainy season, she taught the ABC's to twenty-one natives aged seven to ten. Her father became moody and spent longer and longer times in the city. He missed May. For the life of her, Evy couldn't figure out why May had left. Things had seemed normal enough, and then one morning she was gone.

It was a Sunday morning. They had celebrated Evy's sixteenth birthday on Saturday with a picnic early in the day and a trip into town for dinner and shopping. May bought her a silk scarf and a bottle of gardenia perfume. Her father bought her a charm bracelet complete with ten small gold animals and a thatched house with *school* etched on it—her favorite was a whimsical goat and three chickens—a mama and her two babies. Dinner had been roast goat and new potatoes with vegetables and a chocolate cake for dessert. Evy couldn't remember being so happy or feeling so grown up.

And then May was gone. Her father had vaguely referred to family obligations—May's father, a diplomat, now aging and ill—and May, the only daughter, called home to attend.

Evy didn't think much about it. But the months stretched on—six to date since May had left. It was difficult for her father. May didn't come back to visit and it was difficult for him to go to her. When he did, he stayed weeks at a time, leaving the mission to Evy and some help from the village. He was always out of sorts when he came home—acted like the mission was a burden. She hated to see him so morose. But then her life changed forever.

The Saturday morning gave no clue of the devastation that was to follow. It was simply another day. She fixed coffee for her father, letting the water boil then pouring it through an elaborate double filter in a tall French china pot. Balancing a tray with cups she carried everything out to the veranda. The cups with hand-painted poppies looked bright against a dark green linen cloth.

May had taught her how to "arrange" things, set a table, use flowers as an accent. As the daughter of a widowed ambassador, May had often acted as her father's hostess. And it seemed important with May gone to continue these little niceties. She didn't want Da to think she couldn't make a home for him.

He had already pulled two chairs up to the white wicker table and sat reading a week-old newspaper. Fresh news for those who lived outside a city. She poured his coffee and offered sugar.

"I'll be taking the car into the city this afternoon."

As always, he took two lumps. She poured herself a cup and waited. Perhaps, he wanted her to drive him. The seventy-five miles was the extent of her long-distance experience but she'd done it before.

"I may be gone for some time."

"But you just got home." She hadn't meant it to sound like a wail. She stopped herself and caught her breath. Now she was on alert. There was something different going on—something her father was reluctant to talk about.

"I haven't said anything before … I just didn't know what your reaction would be—"

"Da, tell me."

"May is about to have a baby." Slowly he looked up from the ground to meet her gaze with the beginnings of a lop-sided grin. "The pregnancy has been difficult. We thought it better if she were closer to a doctor's care."

She was stunned. Baby? And there was her father looking all goofy and happy and maybe a little ashamed.

"Does Mama know?" She clapped a hand over her mouth. What a stupid thing to ask.

"Not unless you tell her." His smile faded and he fixed her with a stare.

"No, no, I won't. But what will happen to it?"

"The baby? May and I will raise it. Evy, listen to me. I don't want to hurt you. I love you. You know I do but I need to be with May. I'll write and tell your mother when the time is right. And ask her for a divorce."

"Divorce?" People didn't get divorced. They were married forever until death. This Evy knew.

"Evy, you must know that I've not had much of a marriage with your mother. You might say we were never happy together. Our marriage was an … an arrangement. May is everything to me. A new beginning." His voice trailed off and Evy sat there waiting for him to continue. "I'll be sending you back at the first of the month. No, it's not like you think. May offered for you to stay but this is no place for a young woman. You need to finish high school. Meet people your own age."

Or your own color? Wasn't that what he meant? "You're sending me away?" Her voice sounded far away as though in a tunnel.

"Don't say it like that. It's for your own good."

In three weeks she'd be gone. Suddenly, everything around her seemed unreal. She was just sixteen and being replaced in her father's affection. No, if she were truthful that had happened a long time ago. She saw the need for May written across his face— raw in its wanting.

"I can't go. You'll need me here. May will need help with the baby."

"Evy, look at me. May and I love you very much, but we need to get on with our lives. We won't be staying here. We'll live in Europe after the baby is born." He paused, searching her face. "I won't see your mother again."

You won't see me again, she thought but didn't say it out loud. Tears were already sliding across her cheeks.

"Evy, don't." He reached for her hand. "Be happy for us. Never in my life have I wanted anything as much. Don't begrudge me this happiness."

Her father held open his arms and she realized that he was crying, too. He drew her onto his lap and when it seemed he could trust his voice continued. "I've given your mother eighteen years of my life. I'm not young Evy. I'll be forty years old next year. Old to start over, but so very lucky to even have the chance—the chance to start a family and be together with the one I love. This has not been an easy decision. It's been an agonizing one. But I can't be who you want me to be if I love someone else. I need to be with May and our baby."

Evy pulled away to stand. She looked down at him. "You already have a family. A wife and four babies." Her voice sounded dead, devoid of inflection.

She slipped off his lap and walked away. She couldn't control her tears, being so close. She leaned over the whitewashed railing of the porch that curved around the house and counted the azalea bushes. They were newly planted, just twigs that had arrived bunched in damp gunnysacks and now struggled to survive. The whole lot was pitiful but she had been the one to insist, had seen pictures in magazines of crimson beauty—

She turned toward him, but still he didn't speak.

"Oh, Da, how can you? How can you send me home? I hate Edward, I hate Ella, I hate—"

"Evy, don't."

"Well, it's true. My life will be hell."

"Don't use that language."

"It's the truth. Hell." And she noted that he didn't correct her a second time.

"I had hoped that you would be the one to understand. I always thought you were like me—liked an adventure, could take things on the chin and stay standing."

She didn't say anything.

"I'm having a few household things moved this afternoon."

"Today?" She hadn't meant to raise her voice, but today? So soon?

"Just the piano and my bedroom furniture. May has missed having a piano. Her father's house is very grand but he always thought musical instruments were frivolous. And now he's quite old and complains about any noise."

Evy nodded. She wasn't certain what comment was expected of her. "So, you won't be staying with him?"

"We have an apartment."

Evy waited but there didn't seem to be an address forthcoming. Her father didn't even want her to know where he would be. She turned back to stare at the sickly azaleas.

"I'll never see you again after today." She said it matter-of-factly. She didn't mean it in a melodramatic way—it was the truth. She simply knew it. Felt it in a way that she didn't understand, but she trusted her intuition.

"Don't say that." There was pain in her father's voice that made her know he believed she spoke the truth.

"Don't lie." Where had she gotten the courage to say that? "Will you write?" She added after a moment. "You have my address." She tried to make it sound light, a joke.

"I'll always know where you are, Evy."

She turned back to gaze at the azaleas and waited for more, but only heard the scraping of a chair and knew he'd gone into the house.

Well, she'd just treat this day like any other. She stood and patted her dress smooth. She'd go down to the school house and put the storeroom in order. If she were to be gone so soon, she'd need to leave notes. They were dangerously low on chalk and primers and hymnals.

Surely, there would be a new family, someone from the States, to take her father's place. And she couldn't cry. She was through with tears. She couldn't give into that enormous fist of sorrow choking the very breath from her body. If she did, she might not ever recover.

She ran from the porch but hadn't crossed the first field before the sobs caused her to stumble and then collapse until she could get her breath. *How could he?* How could her father pick his mistress over his daughter? What made men leave their families, desert wives, abandon children?

That would never happen to her. She'd learn how to keep a husband—whatever it took—she could learn how.

She compared her mother to May. Her mother took no joy in her life. Only Edward. He was her mother's reason for being. And that was wrong. Why had her father stayed as long as he had? Her strange skinny mother with the thinning hair had driven her father to this—another woman and a new family. It was all her mother's fault.

Dusk had pushed into the classroom when one of the servants found her washing chalkboards.

"Missy, you come."

"Moses? What is it?" The elderly man stood in the doorway. He'd helped out around the mission for years and was proud of his biblical name, but tonight he seemed agitated. "No can say. They jus' ask for you."

"Someone on the phone?"

Moses shook his head. "At da door."

Visitors? She wasn't expecting anyone. How strange. She hadn't wanted to go back to the house until Da was long gone. She simply could not face him again. The gathering darkness assured her she wouldn't. But company?

She wiped her hands and carefully shook out the apron she'd been wearing and folded it. It was likely that the visitors were from a neighboring mission, some new preacher come to pay respects to her father. Well, no problem, she could handle this. Instinctively, she reached in her pocket and pulled out a hair ribbon. She didn't want to appear a banshee and then smiled at her father's term for the bushel basket of long curly dark hair that sprang from her head in a thick feathery halo. She neatly tied it back from her face.

"Will our guests be staying for supper?"

"Dunno, Missy." Moses impatiently swung a lantern out ahead of him and waited for her to follow.

When they reached the house, she recognized the car in the drive as belonging to the state's police regiment. Three black men stood tall on the front porch in khaki uniforms liberally sprinkled with brass buttons.

"Miss Everett?"

His English was flawless, British accent and all. It always struck her as unusual and she'd try to imagine Clemetts talking that way.

"Won't you come in? Could I get you something to drink?"

"No, Miss, excuse us please, but here is fine."

"Is there some problem?" Her thoughts raced to permits. The mission was expecting delivery of two new tractors and there were always bribes, extra fees to cover safe transport.

"I am the unhappy one to inform you of the passing of your dear father." The man almost clicked his heels as he bowed slightly.

"Passing?" Evy wasn't following.

"We have determined that the accident was unavoidable."

"Accident?" Something had happened to Da?

"We must ask that you come with us back to the city. There are forms."

"What happened to my father?" Evy screamed it, then rushed to grab the wooden man by the arms. "Tell me. *Where is my father?*"

"Now, miss, you must control yourself. This is not easy. I am sure your father is a very good driver but after the rain, him swerving to miss the bus with everything so slick—"

She pulled back. "Is he dead?" She forced the words out.

"Yes, miss. And the woman, his wife, is still in the hospital."

CHAPTER NINE

Evy walked up the front steps of the hospital. She nodded to two orderlies but couldn't have said what they looked like. All her senses were deadened. She was simply going through the motions—ride back to town, try not to think, maybe there was a mistake, don't waste energy on sorrow—not until the truth is known. She'd meet with the doctor who'd attended her father, then, see May. Make arrangements ... that is, if May wanted her to.

But arrangements? What if there was some mistake? Well, wasn't that why she was here?

"May I help you?" The woman had the starched presence of cardboard. Could she even bend in the middle? "Are you ill?" The woman walked around the corner of a great wooden desk.

"No." Evy focused. The woman was a nun, stiff apron, wax-like complexion, a trifold bonnet and flowing veil, three black hairs protruded from a mole on her upper lip. "I'm here about my father."

"Ah, Miss Everett, is it? Father Albert is waiting in the chapel. Come with me."

Evy almost had to half-run to keep up as the nun glided along the marble-smooth corridors. The building hadn't looked large from the outside but here under the ceiling fans, hurrying ever deeper into the recesses of whitewashed walls turned cream in the evening light, Evy felt dwarfed by the tomb-silence and hallowed emptiness.

Wheeled carts rested next to wheeled chairs but occupants were nowhere to be seen. The nun skated past some half-dozen closed doors. But it was the silence. The whoosh and crackle of the nun's stiff habit seemed overly loud in the almost total quiet.

Then she stopped, rapped her knuckles sharply against a dark wooden partition, a half-door like the ones in the barn at home and, folding her hands under her surpliced smock, waited. A round-faced man appeared almost instantly.

"Father Albert, please. Tell him Miss Everett is here."

The face at the door disappeared. The two of them continued to wait. Evy wasn't tempted by conversation. Certainly, the nun didn't think it necessary. Maybe she'd taken a vow of silence and only said a bare minimum of words. Evy had read about that once and was intrigued enough to try it, betting herself she'd last a whole day. But she'd lost. In the first half hour to be exact. She decided then and there that she'd never make a nun.

"Miss Everett." The man in white collar and black robes nodded at the nun who almost curtseyed before disappearing back the way they'd come. "I want to help you in any way that I can."

He held the bottom half of the door open and motioned her to follow. He sounded kind, yet there was something. Did he know she wasn't Catholic? Or that Da and May weren't married? Her mother thought Catholics were heretics. Did it show on Evy's face—this history of hatred for his church?

"I am very grateful for your help." Her voice sounded small, a whisper.

"I know how difficult this is. We must ask God for his support."

Only then did she realize that they had entered a chapel. An ornate dais filled the far end of the room where, up from its center, loomed a twelve foot ebony cross with life-like carving of Christ. To her left, twelve stained glass windows showed the same bearded Christ moving through the tableau to his crucifixion. A four-foot Virgin Mary dressed in a flowing egg-shell blue gown appeared to oversee a bank of small red glass jars most with flickering candles. It was all very grand and more than a little overpowering. And strange.

"It's a beautiful place, isn't it? Inspiring, actually. I often come here." The priest followed her gaze to the windows. "But I think we might be more comfortable in the arbor."

Evy nodded. The room was stuffy and smelled of paraffin and stale flowers. She wished her dress wasn't so mussed from the two-hour ride in the officers' open car. She'd chosen the pale ivory whose tucks rounded nicely over her newly matured figure and nipped in at her tiny waist. Her father loved that dress. Maybe because May had chosen it? Perhaps, but wearing it was the least she could do to cheer him—she must believe that he was still alive. Mutely, she followed the priest through a rear door catching her breath as the scent of jasmine settled around them.

"Here. We won't be disturbed." The priest was pointing to a wooden bench nestled against a wall. He sat opposite her on an identical bench. Then he folded his hands in his lap letting his thumb and forefinger run absently back and forth over a pleat in his cassock. He didn't speak at first, simply studied her. "You're very young for this burden."

Evy forced herself to breathe evenly. There was a frankness in his stare. She experienced this all the time now. Men would stare, ever so slightly lower their eyes to her breasts, then back up to meet her eyes. Yet, with the priest there was admiration, not something to be acted upon but more of an appraisal. And she sensed that she'd passed.

"You look very like him." The priest rose abruptly and walked to straighten a tilted trellis. "Did you know that I worked with your father?"

"No, he never mentioned."

"We pooled resources some years back to provide a clinic in the bush that would serve several villages. The project was highly successful. We had hoped this spring to add—Ah, even I have to remind myself that God has his reasons, yet your father's death is so premature."

He didn't notice Evy's sharp intake of breath or chose not to comment. Yet, his eyes flicked across her face before he continued. "You must be eighteen or nineteen now?"

Evy nodded. There was no way that she would ever correct him. Sixteen would sound too babyish.

"I was sorry to hear of the death of your mother last

year. Ah, the death of both parents so close together. So young to be cast out into the world alone." He shook his head in mild disbelief.

This time Evy almost gasped but stifled the sound before it pushed between her lips. Wouldn't her very-much-alive mother love to know that she'd been dead almost a year? This was Da's doing, but why?

"I can understand your reluctance to celebrate your father's wedding—it must have seemed so soon. Did you know they were married here? In this chapel?"

Evy shook her head. Wedding? Here in a *Catholic* chapel? There was no way that she would trust her voice. She pressed her lips together.

"He'd said that you'd chosen not to come, indicated that there were some feelings of jealousy concerning May." The priest stood before her now.

"It wasn't like that." Her voice sounded small but she had to say something. She didn't look up—didn't trust eye contact.

"Of course, your father could have misread the situation. Yet, May was so close to you in age. I would expect there to be some difficulties. Two beautiful women under one roof vying for the same man's attention." The priest chuckled. "It would be human nature for you to feel slighted when your father decided to remarry and start a new family. I simply don't want you to feel guilty. Children can sometimes get the fanciful notion that if only they'd been more supportive, perhaps more attentive, things would have turned out differently."

"When can I see May?" Evy needed to change the subject. She simply could not listen to more duplicity. "Is she all right? And the baby?"

Her father had lied. Lied about already being married, lied about her feelings. The mounting anger was helping her remain dry-eyed.

"Oh, my dear Eve, no one's told you? Both were lost. Your father and then May. We had a choice in May's situation. But her father supported the church. The mother's well-being is secondary when there's a question of the child's life. The choice was clear. It was not easy but her father understood that." The priest knelt and took her hands. "To become an orphan and lose one's status as an only child in one night must be quite shocking. What can I do to help you?"

Only child? Would the lies never stop? She pulled her hands back. More because the trembling embarrassed her, and it wasn't from grief but an overriding flood of anger.

"I would like to see the baby." She didn't, really. The child had nothing to do with her. It was just some mistake by her father, the liar. But it seemed to be the only thing to do. She should at least pretend interest. And she wanted to get out of the confined space, away from the chapel and the garden, the scene of her father's debacle. And this man who obviously believed all the lies.

"Of course. That's wise. I know the Sisters are expecting us."

The child was a boy, a tiny cherub that looked just like her father with May's creamy coloring. The nuns had placed him in a separate room making excuses for not having a nursery. But someone had found a cradle; rough hewn and makeshift and he slept, making soft sucking noises and fluttering his eyelids.

Suddenly the enormity of the evening washed over her. She sank beside the cradle and couldn't keep the tears back. He was so innocent. But wasn't she? And now their lives were changed forever. And joined forever. That was the momentous thing—this was her brother.

"If I can get you something …" The priest touched her shoulder.

"No, thank you."

"I'll leave you alone for now. We can talk later."

She didn't turn around when she heard the door close but nearly flew upright a moment later when it crashed open.

"Here's all you'll be a needing for the night. I'd be waking him up before too long for this bottle, if I was you. I believe the little ones should be on a schedule. I hope you're not going to be too lenient now. Those mothers just ask for trouble later. Let's see, he had a meal about 5 and it's 9 now—"

"I'm not his mother." Evy faced a large woman in a blue pinstripe dress and white apron. A nurse? The sliver of a cap hiding in a tangle of auburn curls said she wasn't a nun.

"Not his real one but the only one he's got, the poor little bugger." The ruddy-cheeked woman pushed a bottle toward her.

"Why are you giving this to me?"

"Well, just who do you think is going to come in here and take care of him? We're short-handed. Not that I'd spare someone anyway. He's not our responsibility now—not as long as he has family."

"His family—"

"Well, that be you, correct?"

"I guess until someone claims him. His mother's family needs to be informed."

"That's been done. There's only the mother's father and he's too old—frankly, I'm not sure he even understands what has happened."

Evy took the bottle and looked from it to the baby.

"Don't just stand there. The little one needs a meal. He's had a tough afternoon, too." She laughed. "Get going girl. Ones younger than you have their own and they figure out how to do things. I'll be back to check on you later." And with that she was gone.

Evy was transfixed. Only the baby's fussing brought her back to the present. Her brother. Her father's child. But what was going to happen to him? Tentatively, she leaned over and unfurled a tiny fist. He was so small. Suddenly he began to wail. Nothing was wrong with his lungs. Hastily, she scooped him up and held him close. Where had she set the bottle?

He didn't take to the heavy rubber nipple at once but with some coaxing, four ounces of whatever was in the bottle disappeared. Then it was time for burping. She'd watched Mattie pat Edward on the back with him almost upright on her shoulder and she tried that. The baby gurgled, spit up but finally settled. She put him back into the cradle.

She was tired and needed to change her dress or at least rinse the sour baby smell from her shoulder. Should she talk with the priest about her father's body? Her mother would expect to have it shipped home.

Her mother. Evy sank into a chair by the crib. What was she to do about her mother?

She couldn't mention her very-much-alive-mother to the priest. If Da had still been married when he remarried, wouldn't that make the baby a bastard in the eyes of the church? She couldn't have that. This tiny thing was innocent. He hadn't asked to be brought into this mess.

She still couldn't stand to dwell long on her father. He lied. Not just a little white lie but this all-encompassing lie that threatened to ruin those he'd left behind. Especially a child with no parents, married or not. She must think. There had to be a solution.

"I want you to call him Daniel."

The door was only open part way but Evy could see the tall man as he bent to enter the room leaning heavily on a fat, gnarled ebony stick decorated with shells. He looked like he could have been a hundred years old, he was so frail. And his skin parchment-dry and paper-thin with large purple circles scattered down his arms seemed an unlikely covering, not quite up to keeping his life from oozing out.

"I don't believe we've met." He bowed slightly; the brimless cap of brightly colored ribbons bobbed forward. Grizzled gray hair hugged his scalp but his eyes were sharp, small and almost black.

Of course, the man must be May's father. Even now his stately bearing spoke of a life of service to his country. She got up and pulled the only chair in the room away from the crib.

"Please come in and sit. I'm Evy."

"Thank you." Lowering his weight, even into a chair, was tortuous. He did not grimace but simply paused as he eased his body downward, all the time staring at the baby.

"Daniel is a good name, don't you think?"

"Yes."

"Do you find it odd that this late in my life, God has given me this miracle, a namesake? A grandson to continue after I leave. I must say that I'm not surprised. God giveth and taketh away. But he provides for all of us who believe."

Evy sat on the edge of the cot in the corner. He must have servants with him to take the baby. At any minute someone would come to take the two of them back to their house, wherever that was.

"You'll be good to him won't you?"

"Me?" It came out as a startled squeak.

"You're his mother now."

"No. I couldn't ... but surely you have servants, a household—relatives of May who—"

He raised a hand to stop her saying more. "I want him to go to America. He is an American like his father. I understand that you have money. After your mother's death, you are well off. There is a farm somewhere for my grandson, for the two of you. He will prosper and never want. Isn't this true?"

What could she say? How could she make her father out a liar? And it was true. The baby was an American. And there was a farm, albeit a little crowded. Suddenly, the old man pounded on the floor with his cane.

"What are you thinking, you selfish girl? You would leave this child? This brother you've never had? You would take all your father's money for yourself? What kind of daughter are you? Your father is dead not one day and already you are shirking your responsibilities, thinking only of yourself." The old man's voice rose and spittle collected at the corner of his mouth.

"No. The baby will go back with me as you wish. I will raise him as my own."

What was she saying? But if she didn't, wouldn't there be lawyers and legal issues? Daniel disowned, cast aside, put in a home. Her father's reputation would be ruined—

the mission, all his good work and dedication … all for this one selfish, foolhardy act.

And they would all suffer—her mother, Ella, Edward—no, this was the best way, the only way. Her mother would never accept her father's child. She'd have him disinherited, banished from their lives as if he had never existed. Her father's deceit would kill her mother, give way to an anger that would consume them all. Of that she was certain.

So, she would say the baby was hers. It wasn't impossible. Lots of girls her age started families. The nurse had said as much. It would take a lie of this magnitude to get Daniel past her mother. She'd accept him only if she thought he was a grandchild, no threat to Edward. A cousin, not a half-sibling. It was the right thing. But could she do it? Lie to cover a lie?

"When will you leave?"

Evy had no idea. "I need to know how soon Daniel can travel. And, of course, I'll be taking my father's body back—"

She was interrupted by the pounding of the cane on the floor. "No. I am adamant. My daughter must rest next to her husband. And that is here on the soil where she was raised. Where she was happiest."

Evy didn't contradict. She didn't have the energy to face that issue now. It was enough that she had bound herself to an infant, a catastrophe in the making if the truth were known. She felt tears somewhere just behind her eyelids but willed them to go away. There was too much to do, to think about, to plan. She couldn't have made conversation if she'd had to, but the old man seemed not to expect it. He rocked for awhile, told her of his life, dozed only to wake with a start and continue where he'd left off.

There was a father, this baby's great grandfather, a powerful landowner, mixed in ancestry who purchased a life of government service and handed this position to his son. A mother from India, lovely but in ill health, who died young leaving an only son. Then his own wife, the daughter of a British missionary, disowned when she chose to stay, to marry a man of color some twenty-five years her senior, then dying when she gave birth to May.

Evy picked up Daniel when he fussed, changed his diaper, folding a fresh cloth from the stack left by the nurse, pinning the corners securely. She never interrupted nor wakened the old man when he slept. Finally, he asked to hold Daniel, not trying to hide his tears. He gently crooned to the baby, and it wasn't her imagination—Daniel relaxed, little arms and legs waved less frantically. Then he nodded for her to take him, rose and held out his hand.

"My thoughts are with you. You are strong like your father. You will do what is right."

The door clicked shut behind him and Evy sat, gently rocking. She didn't even protest. What was there to do? The only way out was to tell the truth and ruin the lives of everyone she loved. The decision seemed so black and white. But she had never felt so alone and abandoned.

Daniel slept until midnight when his cries brought the same freckled nurse running with another bottle, huffing and complaining about the noise and the inconsiderate demands of infants.

"When do you think he'll be able to travel?"

"Why in the morning, I'd imagine. He's a strong lad. With a few precautions, he'll do just fine until you can get him back to the mission."

That wasn't exactly what Evy had meant. But then

wouldn't she have to stay until the church had found a replacement for Da? Or had he taken care of that already seeing as how he was leaving anyway?

"But his formula?"

"Goat's milk, honey and a trace of cod liver oil. I know you have goats on the grounds."

"Yes. I didn't realize it was so simple."

"Keep 'em fed and dry and warm for the first six months. That's about all there is to it."

Evy wanted to ask her if she had children of her own but the nurse was bustling out the door. Or what happened after six months, but she guessed she'd find out. And to think she had to leave in the morning. She looked at Daniel, blissfully unaware that his caretaker was only sixteen and had not a thought about how she was going to handle everything.

She'd talk to the priest first and wait until she got to the mission before calling her mother. Yes, Moses could bring the truck and have them back before mid-afternoon. She put Daniel in the crib and fell back across the cot.

Like a gramophone needle stuck in a groove, her mind played over and over—Da was a liar. A terrible, hurtful liar. He didn't care about her mother or her, and she could not grieve for such a man. She had loved him so much but he was selfish and deceitful. Then she forced that thought from her head and drifted into fitful sleep.

* * *

"I cannot leave him here. I want to honor his grave, have him near me on the farm." A young nun had stayed with Daniel when the priest had summoned her early the next morning. His office smelled of cigarette smoke and furniture oil. But Evy was too aware of how she must smell. A blouse stiff from repeated rinsing, yet reeking of rancid milk.

"Eve, I understand. I'm only presenting the wishes of a bereaved father. I confess I believe that Harold would want to be buried in his home land."

Beside his one and only true wife and Emma, his true daughter, and all the rest of us who came first, Evy added to herself. She dreaded the call to her mother. How could she keep her from coming here herself? Only Edward's health—it was a terrible thing to ask of God but Evy prayed Edward would keep her mother home.

"I guess that leaves taking May—burying the two of them together. I think I could present that option to May's father and have it accepted."

"My mother—" Oh God, she'd almost referred to her mother as living. Evy swallowed. "Before my mother died, she had chosen plots for her and my father. I don't think it would be fitting to squeeze May in somewhere."

The priest was silent. "I'm telling myself this is not some immature, prideful remark by a child who resents her stepmother even in death. That would not do, not do at all. A man has a duty to remarry after losing his mate. He must carry on. The obligations of a Catholic can be quite different—"

"My father was Mennonite."

"But converted shortly before his marriage. My, my Eve, I'm certain he told you. Wasn't it your decision not to join us? I had thought that it would make a more cohesive family, each of you in the same faith. But he honored your wishes."

The priest paused to light a cigarette, all the while peering at her with a quizzical wrinkling of his brow. "He attended instruction here in my office. I must say I'll miss our discussions. He was quite well read when it came to the Bible." Then, as he scooted an ashtray closer, "Daniel, of course, will be raised in the church."

It wasn't a question. Evy simply gaped. She couldn't say a thing. One more word and an anger like she had never felt before would spew out into the room and she'd tell all and blaspheme her father, but wasn't he already damned and in Hell?

The priest seemed not to notice her agitation. "I cannot condone casting May aside. These were two people very much in love, anxious to start life together. They were inseparable—let them be so in death."

"Of course they should rest together. Have them cremated and mingle their ashes. I will see to the building of a mausoleum." Where had that idea come from? But it was a good one. Evy looked at the priest squarely, willing herself not to blink, to be strong.

There had been so much lying, did it hurt to add another? It was only a teeny lie and this way May's father would be happy and Constance would never need to know. Shouldn't Daniel at least have the ashes of his parents?

"Good grief, I think you've found the solution. How astute." The priest rubbed his hands together, clasping and unclasping. "Yes, a more than tolerable solution for all concerned. There would have been considerable expense to transport two bodies—as I'm sure you imagined. But this way ... I bet the old man could even provide a suitable urn."

"You'll make the arrangements? Have the cremation completed and then ship the ashes?" Evy rose. She needed to pick up Daniel and get back to the mission.

"Yes. I'll take care of everything." He followed her to the door. "There's also the matter of your father's apartment. I'm sure you'll want his effects. Here's a ring of keys, and a packet of papers, Daniel's birth certificate, your father's conversion, a copy of their marriage certificate."

"Thank you." Evy slipped the envelope into her skirt pocket along with the keys. Would these be things that Daniel would want someday or should she destroy them? They had such lethal potential.

"I wish you well. The burden is great but God will be at your side."

Evy smiled. *No, he wouldn't be. He didn't support liars and now she was one, too.*

CHAPTER TEN

Evy poured a tumbler half full of whiskey. Wasn't this the way to courage in the movies? She took a sip, then another. Nothing happened. The liquid was warm, hot actually, and roughed her throat up on the way down, stinging well past the end of her esophagus. She pushed the glass aside. She had to make the phone call, whiskey or not.

It took a full fifteen minutes before her call went through but Mattie sounded like she was standing beside her. A good connection. At least she wouldn't have to repeat herself a dozen times.

"Missy, Missy I jus' knowed you'd call. I had a feeling. I misses you so much. I bets yous just growed up without me. Your Daddy says you're beautiful. When you coming home? I ain't seen my little girl for three years now."

"Soon, Mattie. I'll be home soon. But get Mama. I need to talk to her. I'll write to you."

As much as Mattie might have wanted to stay on the phone, Constance would be livid at the cost of a transatlantic call being used for chitchat. Well, Evy's news wasn't in that category.

"Eve what a surprise. Is anything wrong? Why isn't your father calling?"

"There's been an accident …" Evy told her mother about the rain, how the touring car went out of control, striking a bus before tumbling end over end into a ravine. Yes, her father was alone, in town on business— had driven in that morning.

Her mother never made a comment at the end. A beat or two after Evy had finished, the line went dead. It wasn't some malfunction. Her mother had hung up. Somehow, of all the things that could have happened, Evy didn't expect this.

An hour later her mother's solicitor called to assure her that he was wiring money. Her father's body must be brought back for burial. Her mother wouldn't be able to come but they had total confidence in Evy. Once her plans were solidified, would she wire them of her arrival? And, yes, of course, he sent his condolences. Such a tragedy.

Her poor, dear mother was quite distraught, but he had called her mother's personal physician. If Evy had questions, she should direct them to his legal office until her mother could better cope. He gave her the number but she didn't write it down.

Evy sat by the phone in the hallway a long time, pressing her cheek against the cool plaster of the wall. A beetle worked its way through the ceiling thatch and fell to the floor in front of her, stunned and disoriented. She watched as it finally gathered itself and marched off toward the kitchen.

A survivor. That's what she had to be—along with Daniel. Thousands of miles away her mother was struggling to cope, supported by her children and servants. Across all those miles, Evy could feel her mother distancing herself, mourning Da as if no one else could feel pain, as if he were hers only to lament the loss.

But the truth? What if her mother knew the truth? Evy shuddered. The truth would always be hers to guard. And someday when the anger had receded, she'd be able to mourn Da. But not now, not for awhile, not until she could forgive him. She roused when she heard Daniel's wail from the back of the house. A servant stayed with him night and day and he seemed to be flourishing. His skin was less flaky and wrinkled and he spit up less.

She'd received a telegram from a Dr. Elton Alridge—a doctor of divinity who would be arriving on the twenty-seventh with his family of five to assume management of the mission. But she'd be gone by then.

She'd made lists of the things she had to do—she'd put off going through her father's belongings at the apartment in town as long as she could. Yet, it had to be done. There would be things her mother would expect her to bring home. For the life of her she couldn't imagine what those things would be, perhaps some of his clothing. Maybe she would recognize what they were when she saw them.

The less she had to do with her father, the better. When she looked at the baby, she willed herself not to see her father, only the helplessness of an infant who would never know his parents. Would she ever tell Daniel the truth? She didn't know. Maybe when he was a grown man himself.

* * *

The days seemed to be flying by. Because she dreaded going home? Evy thought so.

She now had only four days before all her trunks would be picked up at the front gate and carried into the city to travel by rail to the coast. She'd follow her baggage the next day—first, a bus ride, then train, then steamer—short or long they would all be tedious journeys with a baby, now a mere one month old. It would have been so much quicker to fly to the coast, but she'd chosen not to or rather her mother had instructed her not to. Still not to be trusted, to paraphrase her mother, these tin-cans in the sky.

She agreed to everything her mother's lawyer said. She was instructed to send him her father's papers—anything she could find that would indicate bank accounts or investments. He would, of course, take care of transferring any monies to her mother's accounts. The lawyer seemed reluctant to discuss these issues with her. He had expected there to be a secretary at the mission and then insisted that she put him in touch with her father's banker. Clearly, discussing business with her was not acceptable.

She had no idea if there was money, a personal account, perhaps, something her father had put aside for his life with May. As far as she knew, the mission provided for her care. But where did that money come from? She knew her mother had made sizeable donations. She had to find out. It wouldn't do to have the lawyer make inquiries and come up with accounts in May's name.

She'd put off going to Da's apartment, but couldn't any longer. She left instructions for Daniel. Only one bottle and only then if he fussed and, fussing or not, he must nap. A crying, overly tired baby was the last thing she needed on a long trip. Almost as an afterthought she picked up a large tote from an open-air shop near the taxi stand. Ready to face the apartment ... ready at last.

* * *

The squat, white, two-story building stood out from its taller neighbors. Less than five years old, according to the cab driver, it was squeezed onto a corner in a nice neighborhood, not luxurious, but safe. There was a doorman who helped her from the cab and escorted her to the door of her father's second floor apartment. He offered to stay but she insisted that she preferred to be alone. And that was the truth. She was walking into her father's other life, and it was difficult to sort her feelings.

The monotony of creamy ivory walls and slipcovers was broken by peach flowers that trailed up and down drapery and accented silk throw pillows. An oriental rug spread across polished oak flooring—ivory with woven flowers in lightest orange. The room was sparsely furnished. Mission-style furniture was dominant along with stained glass lampshades on floor lamps and table lamps alike. Windows were covered in billowing sheers that silently rippled in any hint of a breeze.

The piano sat in the corner with sheet music piled on the bench in front, two selections open above the keyboard. For all the world, it looked as if May had just gotten up to get a cup of tea or glass of water. The picture in the gilt frame above the keyboard was of a beautiful woman in white, veil thrown back to reveal her smiling at the man on her arm—his dark hair trimmed close, beardless, elegant in tails, boyishly handsome and smiling back. A wedding photo. A wedding lie.

Evy picked up the photo and imagined what they must be thinking on such a happy occasion. Caught up in such a lie. She put the photo down and turned in a half circle. The room screamed cozy, everyday, a haven for two people very much in love surrounded by the things that meant most to them in life. There wasn't one picture of her or Edward or Ella or—

Evy quickly squelched that way of thinking, walked to a window, and opened it. The sheers were sucked outward immediately. Evy leaned forward, gathered the filmy material and knotted it, a blob of pink hanging askew against the casement. She breathed in deeply and exhaled. She knew this would not be easy.

Everything, everywhere she looked were echoes of this woman—her father's wife. Her father's bigamist transgression. Did May know of her father's lie? No, she couldn't have and now she'd never know. She took another deep breath. Where to start?

So far, there was nothing in the living area that would be worth shipping home—nothing her mother couldn't live without. Nothing Daniel would want to inherit someday. She had to consider that as she looked at his parent's belongings. Maybe the picture on the piano but she'd have to give that some thought.

She started down the hallway; somewhere Da had to have had an office. But it was the nursery that took her breath away. She stood in the doorway and simply gaped.

Animals from the countryside marched around the room while others were grouped together at a watering hole. Brightly feathered birds crisscrossed the sky—reds and greens and yellows against the palest blue. Some taking off from the branches of gnarled trees to continue their flight across the ceiling.

It wasn't a room, it was an adventure, though neutral—no pinks or blues, but, of course, they didn't know that their baby was a Daniel. The crib was also Mission-style with embroidered linens tailored to size. This time, colorful birds crowded around the edges of the sheets in cross-stitch perfection pulled tight across a four-inch mattress. A bassinette with holders for glass bottles of lotions, and folded diapers stacked to one side.

She sat down in the rocker by the window that flooded the room with sparkling light. She then took note of the photos. They seemed to be everywhere—on table tops, bookcases, hanging above the crib. May and Da hugging, the two of them riding in an open car, then both standing beside May's father, then with the priest. May wearing a long white gown and holding a bouquet of lilies and orchids ... she squeezed her eyes shut. She couldn't bear to look at this happy couple—so young and vibrant—with a life ahead of them. And then she reminded herself—he'd planned never to see them again. Edward, Ella, Emma's grave, her mother ... herself. He didn't care.

Everything would have been perfect—his beautiful wife, his baby boy—but now he was dead. They were dead.

Without looking back, she stood and went into the hall. She only glanced into the room that must have been their bedroom. If there was time, maybe she'd see if there was some piece of jewelry that she could keep for Daniel.

And pictures … ones of May, of course. She needed to take some for him. That would be important. She couldn't let her anger, her feelings, get in the way of what would be best for Daniel.

She presumed the last door on the left at the end of the hall was his office—why ever else would it be locked? She dragged the ring of keys from her pocket and found the perfect fit in four tries. She pushed the door inward and stepped across the threshold. The suffocatingly still air danced with dust motes in the light streaming through half-closed shutters. The first thing she did was tie back the heavy drapes and open all of the shuttered windows. Better, but her first deep breath brought on a fit of sneezing.

The room reminded her of her father's study in Kansas. An overstuffed couch with matching arm chair flanked the overly large, ornately carved wooden desk. A monstrosity to say the least.

Evy wondered where her father had gotten it. But it was a place to start. She pushed the chair to one side and pulled out the center drawer. An ink bottle, several pen points, lavender paper with a peppery scent. She was about to close the drawer when she noticed the key. She compared it to the ones on the ring but this one was different. She slipped it into her skirt pocket. She quickly pulled out the desk's side drawers and examined the contents—bills, one for a hundred English pounds for an ivory satin wedding dress and veil—a dress encrusted with over five hundred seed pearls and Austrian crystals. Evy closed the drawer.

She hadn't noticed before but the entire back wall was floor-to-ceiling books. And books on many topics—predominantly religious, there were also ones on history, geography, African tribes and general anthology, a series on Italian operas, a collection of plays by Shakespeare, most in gold-embossed leather bindings... would Daniel want something that was dear to her father? His father?

Certainly cartons of books would be a safe thing to ship home. Something her mother would understand and accept. She began pulling volumes from the shelves that she could reach. She wouldn't take all of them but a representative few that would give Daniel an understanding of their father's interests.

She had instructed the cab driver to wait for her and now she went downstairs and asked him to bring back cartons—several wooden crates used for shipping or storage. Of course, this cost more money but her travel allowance had arrived and would be put to good use. At his insistence upon helping, she excused him to wait in the car by insisting she needed the time to go over the belongings of her dear dead father by herself.

The truth was she needed to be alone—alone with the duplicity of it all, the fact that she hadn't been loved—not by a mother and now, if the facts were known, not by a father.

It was the emptying of the third shelf up from the floor that first revealed it. Small, its green enameled door snugly shut with only the key hole raised to indicate that behind that innocent looking façade could reside even more surprises. Evy wasn't certain she could handle any more unknowns. But she took out her circle of keys and knew instantly that the key from the desk fit this lock.

The entire interior of the safe was about the size of a picnic basket. But it was what was inside that took her breath away.

Quickly, she walked to the door of the office and

locked it. It wouldn't do to have anyone else see what she was looking at—gold ingots crudely formed in varying sized molds stacked irregular row after irregular row front to back until the space was entirely filled. She dragged a chair to the bookcase, hopped up and gingerly took out one of the small shiny bars. How much money was she looking at? Thousands upon thousands, she thought. But what now?

It struck her that she would not give this money to her mother. It belonged to Daniel. To be held for him until he could maturely handle it. So where would it be until then? A bank, she thought, but a bank in the States, and that posed the question of how to get it there.

She wasn't certain what had prompted her to decide to sew the ingots into the hems of the baby quilts and pillows that would be easy to keep with her on the trip. But it would work. Heavy, a little cumbersome, but workable. In addition, she would be shipping the crib and bassinette— ample storage for these treasures. It would be possible to take every single ingot home. Or at least to somewhere where she could put it safely in a bank.

But wasn't she lying ... stealing even? Whose money was this? Could she convince herself that it had come from astute investments made by her father from his personal income? Or was it, as she suspected, monies from crops and from her mother? Money meant to do good, further the church's good deeds?

She felt sick but knew there would be no one to safeguard Daniel's future and, perhaps, her own. There was every likelihood that her mother might disinherit her ... but a grandson? That was a bargaining chip. Mattie had told her long ago the high stakes her grandfather had invoked—the reason Edward was so precious in his mother's eye.

No, the gold would mean the difference between bondage and freedom. She would treat it as her own. And then she had a brilliant idea—possibly even the truth—she would convince herself that it had come from May. A dowry. Surely May's parents had been wealthy—the old ambassador would have had something set aside for his only child. Instantly, she felt better—one less lie to pin on Da, and didn't it excuse her taking it?

In the end it wasn't so sad to leave. An ornate, hand-pounded brass urn of mingled ashes would be her reminder of all that was here. Of promise that never came to fruition.

The land where she left childhood and innocence to be catapulted into adulthood without ever having been taken into anyone's confidence—only left to inherit deceit. A deceit that would change her life forever.

She walked the land that last evening, remembering the picnics by the water. She held her favorite goats close until they squirmed in defiance. Skippy sensed something was different and dogged her every step. The new pastor coming to the mission had children. Skippy would love that. She had to believe that he would be fine.

No, there was a feeling of finality. And deep down she knew she would never return. At the first drops of water she sought shelter on the porch and sat, swinging long after the rain had passed. Collecting her thoughts; sorting her thoughts. A wet nurse had been found in the village and Daniel was content and growing by the day. A trip by steamer would be challenging but a crate of tinned milk—evaporated milk—had been sent by train to be loaded onto the ship and would be waiting for them. She would be traveling alone without Catha or other help. At least her mother hadn't chosen to come. A certain disaster averted.

Now she was just eager to get the next phase of her life underway—a sixteen-year-old widow with a baby to raise.

CHAPTER ELEVEN

The transatlantic crossing took less than a month and ended none too soon. There had been two other stops and a put-in for repairs. The trip had been tortuous. Evy kept to her cabin with Daniel most of the time, venturing out for meals in the evening and only after he was sleeping. She had trays delivered at all other times.

Daniel hated the canned milk and only settled a bit when one of the kitchen help added a generous dollop of honey to each bottle. Even then it seemed he spit up more than he took in. And he couldn't abide the tablespoon of cod liver oil that the doctor had recommended. Evy would try to talk her mother into having a goat—a nanny who was fresh. But that was assuming her mother would let them stay at the farm.

The telegram from her mother arrived just as the ship docked in New York. It was simple and straightforward (after all, didn't each word cost money?): She was to go directly to the hotel listed. A room had been set aside in her mother's name. Money for a train ticket had been wired via Western Union to a bank near the hotel. Constance expected her to board the train home no later than the third day after arrival.

Evy had kept the pram with her—complete with its sparkling cargo hidden from sight. Most of the ingots were there and the others in the crib now crated and sitting on the dock. She had spoken with the steward about renting a truck and one was waiting.

It took almost all her ready cash to pay for it plus the five porters and two dock workers to load the trunks and other crated goods onto the truck's bed. Three young men rode with them to the hotel and the unloading meant enlisting three more strong bodies from the hotel.

Evy was exhausted and Daniel was at his fussy best. She'd totally forgotten to have a bottle made up ahead of time not realizing how long the loading and unloading would take but finally she was in her room, stripped to her bloomers and watching Daniel suck down his breakfast.

Dusk had fallen and she ordered a tray of fruit—fresh strawberries and pineapple with whipped cream—and the biggest piece of chocolate cake that the hotel's kitchen help could find. All served with a huge tumbler of cow's milk. Cold, in a frosty glass. Wasn't this heaven? She didn't think she'd ever been so full. She got her best night's sleep in two months.

* * *

But the morning brought new adventure and new concerns. It was fortuitous that she had to go to a bank to claim her travel money, but how could she deposit the ingots without arousing suspicion or, worse, have bank personnel inform her mother?

No, she needed a plan. And a plan entailed opening an account under another name. That negated drawing out her travel money under her right name at the same bank. She was going to have to go to two different banks. A full morning's running around, she guessed.

She was doubly thankful that her mother hadn't sent an escort. Things were challenging enough as it was. And she could only imagine what would have happened if someone like the pastor's wife saw her holding a mixed-race baby that looked exactly like her. She was putting off even imagining what her mother was going to do.

In the end she had saved Da and May's personal papers—passports, Daniel's birth certificate, travelling papers that luckily matched his last name with hers, Da and May's wedding license, May's birth certificate ...

She had the paper work to look legitimate but Evy's plan would only work if she could look six years older. And pass for someone named May Smythe-Nelson Nutanda Everett.

Evy dressed in one of May's mid-calf length, silk shirt-waists in the palest ivory with an attached delicate pink cape that just touched her elbows. She parted her hair down the middle and rolled each side, pinning the great lustrous loops together and tucking the ends beneath a narrow-brimmed hat of dark coral.

Brown, almost black, wisps of hair escaped to frame

her face in curls that stood out prominently against her perfectly smooth, creamy tan skin. Her complexion was flawless and she was getting quite good with May's makeup kit. She accentuated her brows with a touch of pencil and lightly smudged her upper lids. Her long thick lashes required no embellishment. The lightest touch of rouge across her cheekbones and lips and she was ready.

Shoes were a different matter. The shoes that best matched the outfit and instantly made her look older and three inches taller required two linen hankies balled up and stuffed into the toes in order for them to fit. She wouldn't be able to walk a long distance but in and out of a cab she could handle. And she knew without looking in a mirror that she not only would pass for twenty-two but that heads would turn.

She paid for a young woman who worked in the hotel kitchen to watch Daniel and marveled at what a natural the girl was—Daniel bubbled and cooed and kicked his round little legs and didn't fuss when offered a bottle. Evy promised herself that she'd try harder to be a good mother. It didn't look to be all that difficult.

* * *

She put every ingot in a large satchel. A bag of leather that her father had carried in his business before he met her mother. It was large and roomy and double-sided, offering protection or, even better yet, defied detection of its contents. The only drawback was its weight. She allowed the cab driver to carry it to the door of the bank for her and then hand it to a guard who escorted her to a room separate from the bustle on the floor.

She had chosen the bank because it was the biggest on the block. Big, ornate, and grand. It struck her that it would be in business for a while having survived the economic downturn of the last several years. It was stalwart and robust. Those were her words for it. She congratulated herself for choosing well.

The transaction went surprisingly quick. May Smythe-Nelson Nutanda Everett opened an account and deposited in a safe deposit box—after an initial weigh-in and test for purity—two hundred and fifty thousand dollars worth of gold. She was given two keys and written proof of the box's contents. She listed the second name on the account as Daniel Nutanda Everett. She wasn't even surprised when the bank vice-president proposed lunch but she deferred, citing impending travel and various errands in order to get ready.

She boarded the train for Kansas the next morning. This time she remembered an extra bottle and handed it off to a porter to be placed in the train's ice box in the dining car. This time she had a compartment big enough for the fold-down bed and a crib. Luckily the train's rolling motion lulled Daniel to sleep and she could relax. It was good to have time to herself. It wouldn't last for very long.

CHAPTER TWELVE

Mattie and Clemetts met the train. Mattie didn't bat an eye but took Daniel and began cooing and snuggling him stopping only to ask, "Where's this baby's father?"

"Dead."

"Oh my poor little thing. And my Evy … You loses your husband?"

"Yes." Evy had had six days across country to decide on a story. "He was the tutor at the mission. He was in the car that night with Da."

If Mattie thought Daniel's creamy-brown skin would be a problem, she didn't let on. All she said was, "Your momma gonna be real surprised."

And she was. Evy stood in the large circular foyer of the house and waited for her mother to appear at the top of the stairs. When she did a frail and very thin ten-year-old Edward was hanging onto her skirt.

"I'd like you to meet Daniel—your grandson."

Her mother didn't miss a beat, but continued down the stairs to stand squarely before Evy. She surveyed a robust baby boy with lightly tanned skin, a head full of black curly hair, long-lashed eyes, and overall chubby good health. A perfect baby in every way. Evy sometimes called him her angelic cherub. Perfection was a gift that only God could bestow.

"Is that my brother?" Edward stood on tiptoe to look at Daniel.

"Of course not. This is a mistake. Something your sister did to ruin her life. I knew I could never trust your father to look after you. And just look at you. Is that rouge?" Her mother spat on her finger, then reached out and swiped Evy's cheek. "Why I believe it is. You've turned into a rather proper tart, haven't you? And now I suppose you expect to move in here and bring your shame with you."

"Your grandchild, Mother. He had a proper father. Daniel is not a bastard."

"What's a bastard?" Edward stepped forward to take another look at Daniel, but Constance jerked him back.

"That's a bastard." She pointed at Daniel who was now starting to cry. "And don't think I'm going to fall for this 'proper father' tale. You expect me to believe that the heathens in that country marry properly? I'd be shocked if the father were even Christian. To think you let a man of color touch you. It makes me sick. I'll thank you not to parade this abomination around town."

"Abomination? I'd rather call him *insurance*." Evy almost imperceptibly nodded toward Edward. "I believe you'd be the first to admit you could use a little of that."

Two could play the blame game and Evy wasn't backing down. She could see the truth of her words sink in and watched as her mother put a protective arm around Edward but still didn't utter a word.

"He's a mix, a mutt of the worst kind—a negro and a white one."

"He's a child of God. A gift from God." Evy had almost said God saved his life but luckily caught herself.

"I have to live in this town. I can't even imagine how Reverend Schmidt will react."

"Just buy him another college." Yes, Evy knew how her mother kept her place in the community. Hadn't her father shared that with her? "I don't think you have to worry. That's always worked before."

A tic below her mother's left eye was the only indication that Evy had struck a nerve. That and a hardened gaze that took in both her and Daniel. "I know these people. He won't be accepted."

"It's 1936. Times are changing. We need to lead the way."

"Time will tell. But I'm not holding my breath." Her mother seemed about to say more but turned instead to go back up the stairs. "And will you tell Clemetts to bring the coffin inside. My husband doesn't need to be left on the porch. The viewing will be here in the parlor on Thursday and I have the memorial plot almost ready. The granite headstone was chipped and is being replaced."

"Coffin?" Evy bit her bottom lip. Oh no. Of course, her mother would have expected the body to have been shipped with her. Why hadn't she told her mother sooner? "There isn't a body. It's the custom of the country—I'm sure it's for health reasons—that the dead are cremated."

"What are you saying? You've brought back *ashes*?" Constance turned back to face her daughter.

"Yes."

"Did you see the body? Were you the one to identify it?"

Evy nodded.

"And you didn't tell them my wishes? That I expected a body? That I will be laid to rest next to my husband when that time comes? I can't imagine that they wouldn't have honored the wishes of his wife."

"I thought you had been told—the lawyer from the mission didn't consult with you?"

Her mother shook her head.

"I'm sorry there's been this misunderstanding."

"I shared my views with your father. I know he must have had it written down somewhere. Your father and I might not have seen eye to eye on everything but we honored our vows—respected each other's wishes as husband and wife. I shared the plans for the memorial with him. He knew he was to lie beside me."

"No one knew that he wished this. I believe there are laws—if not for the country certainly within various provinces."

"I was moving there at the end of the summer."

Evy was stunned. "You didn't tell Da?"

"It was to be a surprise. Edward has had a good year and I'd discussed traveling with his doctors. I was meant to be by your father's side to help with the mission. We were a team whether it was bringing in the harvest or doing God's bidding. And this ..." she waved a hand in Daniel's direction, "I would have kept this from happening."

Evy noted that it didn't seem to dawn on her that Daniel would have already been born—a little late for intervention—but what a fiasco if she had come.

"Do I dare ask what the community thinks of your ... indiscretion?"

"My marriage and my family were well thought of."

"And you expect me to believe that? I'm sure there were people of breeding in the community ... not everyone was a heathen, surely."

Evy shrugged. "It would have been good for you to have seen the community."

"I'll thank you not to go into town until Reverend Schmidt has been consulted."

"Consulted? On what?"

"On how this is to be presented to the church."

"There's nothing to *present*."

"Well, I'm sure you had to get married—a fifteen-year-old girl ... a child, no less."

"If I remember, Christ's mother was thirteen." Constance stepped toward her so quickly and the slap was so sudden, Evy rocked backward almost dropping Daniel.

"I will not have someone who spreads her legs for a heathen defame our Lord in my house."

"Whatever you say, Mother, but this heathen is a direct descendant of your father and heir, along with Edward, to all that is here. That you cannot deny—you cannot undo."

"I'll pray on it." With that Constance turned and, half-dragging Edward, briskly climbed back up the stairs to the second floor.

Victory? Evy didn't know. Maybe. But she marveled at how little her mother's words hurt. God was making her strong enough to withstand this verbal punishment of which she knew there would be more. But she sensed a victory. Daniel was the answer to what would happen if Edward did not reach maturity. She knew her mother was, above everything else, practical.

Not a day went by growing up that she and Ella weren't made to realize that their worth was nothing in comparison to their brother's. The terms of their grandfather's will was openly discussed. Flaunted, even, because Evy knew her mother had to win—to best an old man long in his grave who'd thought to control her, dictate her mother's life. Demean her mother's abilities. Relegate her to non-existence because she was a woman.

No, Daniel was another card in a winning hand. Her mother wouldn't fold.

"Well, it doesn't look like I'll be having any competition for beaus."

Evy turned. She hadn't heard Ella walk up behind her. Rail-thin, no bust, slightly prominent upper teeth, and wispy limp, dish-water blond hair, at seventeen and a half, she was a younger replica of their mother.

"Ella, how wonderful to see you. This is Daniel."

"A bastard, I'm presuming."

"No, there was a marriage but his father was killed." All true, Evy just wasn't giving the players' names.

"I'll be leaving for college in the fall."

"Ella, that's wonderful. Have you picked a course of study?"

"Medicine. Mama thinks that is best. What a shame that you can't go to school, too. But I imagine your little bastard keeps you busy."

Evy didn't correct her again, but simply shrugged and walked to the kitchen.

"You don't pay them no mind. Mattie's your friend. They just mean. No difference between those two—your mama and your sister. They never took no happiness from anything unless it was hurting someone else. You be so beautiful, they ain't never gonna be nice. Here, now. Give me our little man." Mattie held Daniel while Evy fixed a bottle of fresh cow's milk with honey. "He's just a miniature of your daddy." Evy held her breath. "But then, so are you. I was sorry to hear about his accident. He should be here to love this child. You was his favorite—that's no secret. He'd a just loved this little boy to death. Poor thing ain't going to get any love from the missus."

"That's all right. We'll survive." And they would, Evy was convinced of that.

Her mother never said one more word about Daniel being in the will. But Constance put all her energy into building a mausoleum—an above ground, white marble edifice to hold Da's ashes. And May's. It was six months in the planning and building. Stone from Italy, carvers from an Amish community in Pennsylvania.

There were carefully crafted angels at the corners and the ceiling was in *bas relief*—characters from the Bible. Acting out a flood. There were four crypts in addition to the glassed-in case for the urn. One for herself and each of her children? Evy didn't ask.

The brass container that had come over from Africa with her disappeared. The new urn was a last-century baroque monstrosity of hand painted china and carved jade. Ornate might be the nicest word for the whole thing. Ostentatious and cheap in its fake grandeur might come closer. Could her mother really have spent more than one hundred thousand dollars on it?

When the memorial was finished, there was a service. The back field was filled with cars. Mostly the curious, Evy thought. But Reverend Schmidt did a bang-up job of making her father sound like a saint—extolling his virtues, his accomplishments, how he was truly God's chosen. Evy felt like throwing up.

Africa already seemed light years away and it had only been eight months. Daniel was flourishing; Constance relented and bought a milking goat—a pretty Nubian with large brown eyes that had just come fresh. She was kept in a pen behind the carriage house but Clemetts tethered her once a day to a fence post and let her forage on weeds that grew along the edges of the garden. Sunshine would let anyone milk her and stood quietly without a milking stall. All was well until Edward tried to ride her and fell off, breaking his collar bone. Sunshine was gone the next morning.

It was the first normal, boyish thing Edward had ever done that Evy was aware of, and she was proud of him. But the bone didn't heal cleanly and required two operations, and the whiney, sickly child was back getting his way, ordering his mother around, and in general, being demanding, conniving, and mean—unless it had something to do with the baby. Daniel seemed a focus for Edward. The friend and sibling he never had.

As Evy looked back on that afternoon, she would never understand why she hadn't seen Edward's preoccupation with Daniel as something unnatural.

Now almost nine months, crawling and sitting up on his own, Daniel was becoming more of a little person, which seemed to fascinate Edward. Yet, most of Edward's attention seemed more like a game than anything sinister.

He'd sit on the floor, making faces and playing peek-a-boo with a paper sack and the baby would shriek with delight. Sometimes Edward would roll a big stuffed ball across the floor crawling after it himself encouraging Daniel to follow.

The games seemed so good-natured and genuinely kind that Evy let her guard down. Then, on a hot humid Friday in August just before Daniel's first birthday, once again Evy's life was changed forever.

She'd spent the morning in town. Driving the big Buick Roadmaster was a treat and not unlike driving her father's touring car. More and more she ran the family errands— shopped for groceries, did the family banking—there was talk of unrest in Europe. The Germans again.

The Mennonites in the community, many of German descent, were Conscientious Objectors. They would not go to war and would refuse the draft if it came to that. And, then what? Would they be incarcerated, as rumor had it? There seemed to be far more weighty matters to worry about than a sixteen-year-old girl and a mixed-race baby.

Yet, her father's memory seemed very much alive in the church. She was taken off guard when Reverend Schmidt had extolled her father's virtues during his sermon on Sunday. Evy tried not to think about it but there was simply no way that her father wasn't in hell. And no way that she could tell the man about Da's duplicity damning him forever and taking his soul out of reach of saving.

To save herself from hating him, she simply stopped thinking about him. "Out of sight, out of mind" as Constance liked to say. She never even went near the mausoleum. She could see the shiny white angels from her bedroom window, sentinels kept spotless from bird droppings and mold—by Clemetts? She thought so.

Errands took longer than usual that day. She was late for Daniel's mid-afternoon feeding but knew that Mattie would take care of it. So when she finally unloaded the groceries and had carried two of her mother's best dresses upstairs—both recently shortened to meet with current fashion—she stopped in the nursery but the crib was empty.

Probably still in the kitchen. Sometimes Mattie would keep Daniel with her until he became tired. The baby loved playing with measuring spoons and pots and pans.

"Where's Daniel?" Evy quickly looked at the empty high chair.

"I's put him down for his nap maybe thirty minutes past."

"Where?"

"Why Miss Evy, where would I put him? In his crib." Mattie took two rounds of cornbread from the oven, tapped the pans' bottoms, ran a knife around the inside edge and plopped both onto cooling racks.

"I was just there. He's not in his crib."

"He gots to be." Mattie's voice rose in alarm. "He's crawled off then and fallen asleep. Check the cupboards, under the beds—those empty rooms on the south side. Don't be too loud, now, your mother's taking a nap."

But a ransacking of the house did not turn up the baby. Evy was fighting panic.

She needed a clear head and they had no indication that there had been foul play. Foul play? How could there have been? There had been no visitors, no strangers—this was not the Lindbergh baby—they were not famous.

It wasn't until the officer from the Hillsboro precinct asked the question, "Is there anyone else in the household who might be able to help us? Someone who might have seen the baby?"

And at that moment she knew. She had no proof, just the bone-chilling realization that Edward was also gone. He had taken Daniel. Still, she admonished herself, there was no need to panic. Edward was so good with the puppy ... no, baby ... he was so good with the baby.

Why had her mind fed her the word puppy? Edward had killed the puppy from so long ago. He wouldn't kill a little human. Not now. He was eleven. He knew right from wrong.

She swallowed hard. There was a terrible taste in the back of her mouth.

"Get Clemetts. Maybe he's seen Edward. I'll wake mother." If she stayed busy, she would find the answers.

But with everyone convened on the front porch, no one seemed closer to an explanation. Constance pooh-poohed their concerns. Couldn't Edward have just taken Daniel for a walk? Was the pram still in the carriage house?

Constance might raise her hem to abide with the times, but she thought the term, garage, to be vulgar. The common man could have a garage; she would have a carriage house. Still, no one had thought to check.

Clemetts volunteered and ran to the two-story structure behind the house, throwing open the big double doors and disappearing inside. The rest of the little group followed to the corner of the house but stood back waiting for him to reappear. Evy wasn't sure she'd even taken a breath until nodding and pointing behind him, Clemetts was walking back toward them. It was still there.

"The pram be there, but Mister Edward's wagon be gone." Clemetts was out of breath from rushing up and back the driveway. "It was there this morning."

"Where would he have gone?" It was a rhetorical question and would seem Constance didn't expect an answer because not one adult standing on the porch could even venture a guess.

"I'm gonna get some help out here. Some of the boys from the station, if I can use your phone." Constance led the way back into the house showing him the phone in the kitchen.

The "boys" turned out to be two young men with bloodhounds. Bloodhounds? Wasn't that over the top? But then, maybe not. A combing of the fields closest to the house had turned up nothing—not one trace of a red Flyer wagon, a pale, slightly built eleven-year-old boy, and a baby.

And then the hounds caught a scent. A diaper and one of Edward's T-shirts had been used to bait the dogs. But it didn't take dogs to see the small figure in the distance trudging back across the stubbled field pulling a wagon. Evy broke from the group and ran to Edward.

"Do you have Daniel with you?" She was screaming, running, then stumbling, she fell to her knees on the uneven ground and grasped Edward by the forearms. She thought her heart was beating loudly enough for everyone to hear. "Answer me. Is Daniel with you?"

"No." He squirmed away, pulling out of her grasp.

But Edward wouldn't look her in the eye. He kept his gaze averted and then ran to his mother when she got close. Suddenly Evy realized that the sounds of gasping, the snorts and racking coughs were from Edward—Edward trying to gulp in air. He was having an asthma attack. Quickly she stood and again grabbed his arm.

"Have you *seen* Daniel?"

"He went swimming." This between wheezing and gasps, mouth open, head thrown back.

"Swimming? How could he have gone swimming?" Evy was screaming now and jerked Edward to face her.

"Leave him alone. He's sick." Her mother pulled Edward's arm back and held him to her.

"And Daniel could be dead." There she'd said it but wasn't everyone thinking it?

"How melodramatic. Leave us alone. Go find your pickaninny baby. You'll get what a slut deserves. God doesn't forget or forgive those who cavort with the devil."

"Daniel wanted to be Moses. I was the Pharaoh." Edward was wheezing so badly he was difficult to understand.

"What? What are you saying? Wait." Evy tried to run alongside as the policeman who had picked Edward up was hurrying toward the house, but her mother pushed her back and sent her sprawling.

"Leave us alone. Sometimes I don't even believe you are my own flesh and blood." Her mother turned and hurried after Edward.

What had Edward said? Swimming? Moses? Had it been some kind of game? But if she remembered her Bible stories, the Pharaoh wanted all Hebrew babies to be drowned ... Moses was saved by being set adrift on the Nile in a basket. Oh my God, could Edward have wanted Daniel dead? Could he have been so cruel or demented to have taken the life of a baby? His own brother, if only the truth could be known.

The creek was less than a mile away. She pushed herself upright and instead of dusting off her clothing, she turned and started to run. The thick green belt of trees that lined the water's edge was maybe a half-mile to the right. Cottonwoods and elm. The creek snaked its way along the entire southern edge of the Warkentine farm, offering up its water to irrigation during the summer months. It was now running full after the harvest and before planting, not needing to be tapped for the sustenance of crops.

In late summer it was always swift and dangerous.

Edward had been coming from the creek. But just where had he been playing? The boundary was over a mile in length. Where should she start? How would she know where they had been? Please, please dear God let her find Daniel alive.

"Missy? Follow me. I'm bringing one of the dogs otherwise this will just be huntin' a needle in a haystack."

God heard prayers. Evy was sure of it. Here was help. She nodded and fell in step with the man being pulled along by an overly fat hound with flapping ears, its bulbous, twitching nose snuffling along the ground.

Once they got close to the water, the dog didn't hesitate but turned to the north and continued its lumbering gait, seemingly purposeful like it knew exactly where it was going. And when it stopped by a toppled tree, half submerged in water and started baying, Evy rushed ahead and struggled to reach the creek's edge.

The mud boundary was like quicksand pulling at her feet sucking off first one sandal and then the other as she tried to pull each foot free in order to move forward. She fell, flailing wildly, catching at a branch above her head to keep from sliding forward. But she wasn't the first one here; she could see the imprints of one set of smallish oxfords. The size a young boy might wear. Those prints skirted the mud but also ended at the water's edge.

At first she didn't hear it. Muffled, weak, the mewling of an injured animal … or a baby. She shouted for her companion to help her look.

The overgrown tangle of weeds and branches and young sapling cottonwoods that lined the bank made any movement almost impossible. But the man had a pocketknife and could cut the smaller brush and push back the larger in order to continue.

"Stay close. Watch for branches that'll spring back and whip you good right across the face."

"I hear it. It's coming from over there." She pointed toward a thicket of dense underbrush and trees. "Hurry." She didn't want to stand around talking about branches, they needed to move, find Daniel.

"Easy now. We need to carve out a path to get down there so's we can get back up."

He was right. But the sound had stopped. She strained to hear but there was only the lapping of the water. She hadn't realized she was barefoot until she stubbed her toe on the jagged, pointed tip of a rock sticking up in the muck and fell, slipping onto her side in two feet of still water that formed a four-by-four foot pool.

And had she not fallen, putting her at surface level, she might not have seen the basket, masked as it was by foliage. She struggled to her feet, toes buried in a slippery layer of silt, her wet skirt wrapped around her legs. She could barely reach the rattan wastebasket from her father's office now wedged firmly in the exposed roots of a giant cottonwood.

The basket's sides were too steep for the baby to tumble out, and there was Daniel in the bottom. Naked, soiled, streaked with mud with no energy left to even cry;

he could only put two arms in the air to be picked up when he saw her peering down at him.

"Baby, baby …" She snuggled him close and didn't try to stop the tears.

She realized she couldn't even imagine life without him. All the anger toward her father had nothing to do with this little life. He was innocent. And she loved him. And she'd never ever put him in danger again.

"Here let me take him. I'll put him out of harm's way and come back an' help you."

"No, I can make it back up the bank. Just take Daniel."

Slipping and sliding up the bank, the minute she was on sound footing, she scooped Daniel up and sank down in the tall grass to check him for cuts or bruises.

The officer leaned in, "I think to be on the safe side we should have a doctor look at him. Looks like he's got some black and blue marks there on his side. We don't want there to be anything broken that goes unattended. I'll go put the dog up and get my automobile. Meet you on the County Road." He pointed to a bridge not far from where they were—a one-lane crossing over the creek. "Give me fifteen minutes."

* * *

Bethel Deaconess Hospital—a block square filled with a clinic, hospital, adjoining home for Mennonite sisters, a dormitory for the school of nursing, and on the opposite end of the block, a home for the elderly. Farms and homes could be deeded to the church for lifelong care.

The church was a force within the community. And money had always given her mother power within that force—leaving her father an afterthought. Evy knew this. Deep down she believed that Africa and missionary work was Harold's way of being his own person, having something that wasn't owned or dictated by someone else, such as an unmoving, unforgiving woman who grew more shrill with age. Could she really be angry with someone who was just trying to escape an oppressive life? Someone who had found happiness in someone else in a land half a world away?

But wasn't the question really how much would Evy share with Daniel about his father? Would she ever be able to give up the charade of being his mother?

She asked the officer to stop first at the house and she grabbed a diaper and a blanket; then, changed her own clothes, rinsed and tied her hair back. She needed to look halfway decent.

The exam was thorough and later the doctor requested that she meet with him in his office. Daniel napped in her lap, having proved to be none the worse for wear.

"There is bruising along his side. I would imagine from being buffeted about in the basket. I'm more concerned about the swelling and bruising in the scrotal area. Again, this certainly could be the result of his little adventure but I'd like you to be aware … know who is taking care of him." Evy's intake of breath made the doctor pause. "No, I don't think it's anything to be alarmed about—just keep an eye out."

Edward. Evy's thoughts were racing. Sexual perversion? What had he done? How could she take Daniel back into that house?

"And now I'd like to see how you're doing."

"How I'm doing?" Evy jerked back to the present but

wasn't following.

"Let's see, your baby is almost nine months. Have you had your follow-up exams? You've certainly lost any excess baby-weight—I hope not at the expense of any nutrition for the little fellow. Are you still lactating? Nursing for a full twelve months following delivery is recommended."

Evy froze. Why had she not anticipated this?

"I … I … was unable to nurse him. The doctors thought it was due to the shock of losing my husband and my father at the same time. I went into labor early; then my milk never came in." Was that a term only for cows not coming fresh? Or could she use it for humans, too?

"I see. Let me call a nurse to look after your son and I'll give you a quick examination. Sometimes when the flow of milk is thwarted like that, there are complications. You've not had any discharge?"

"Discharge?"

"From your nipples?"

Evy shook her head. She looked away and adjusted the blanket more tightly around Daniel. But now she realized that Daniel was too warm. Her own hands were damp and ice cold. But she pulled the blanket back allowing air to reach his arms and upper torso. Anything to kill time. Think. She had to come up with something. She couldn't allow an examination.

"I'll make an appointment but today has been emotionally draining. My younger brother became ill, and I know my mother needs my help at the house." With this, Evy stood and, shifting Daniel to her shoulder, held out her hand. "Thank you."

She moved to the door, then into the hallway. She didn't look back. She didn't stop at reception. She continued out the front door, down the steps, and slipped into the front seat of the officer's car, finally taking a deep breath.

"Should I have someone from the farm come get me? If you're on duty."

"This accounts for being on duty. I'll see you home, Miss. Did the little guy check out all right?"

Evy took another steady breath and shared that he had, in fact, passed with flying colors. As if to prove her point, Daniel slept contentedly in her arms. The rest of her evening didn't go as smoothly.

Her mother met her at the front door. "Put the baby down and meet me in your father's study."

"Edward?"

"Asleep. Thank you for asking. I'm sure you're wondering how he is." This said with derision. "I know how much you care."

"Mother—" Evy stopped, then added, "I'm sure you're concerned about Daniel, too. Aren't you interested in how he's doing? I know how much you care."

She had never challenged her mother before but it felt good, right—but she was afraid once she started, stood up to her mother, it would be like opening the flood gates. And she couldn't risk it—she knew too much. There was danger in standing up. She lowered her eyes and looked to the side.

Her mother paused, lips pressed together in a thin line, the ever-present tic under her left eye when she was trying to control her anger. She opened her mouth, then closed it again. "Just do as I say."

The study was dark when Evy came back downstairs. Daniel didn't wake when she changed his diaper and put him in his crib. The afternoon had been exhausting—and not just for Daniel. She wasn't up to some haranguing by her mother but also knew she couldn't escape a confrontation either.

Evy stepped inside the study door and switched on an overhead light.

"I'm not wasting electricity. Turn the desk lamp on if you want light."

Evy did as she was told and sat opposite her mother.

"I'm going to come right to the point. I don't see how the two of you can live here any longer. I've spoken with a psychiatrist—someone suggested by Edward's pediatrician. He thinks, as do I, that the addition of a male child in the household is causing Edward to act out."

"When did you consult someone? Today?"

"Of course not. If you'd had your eyes open, you would have realized that Edward was feeling pressure."

"Pressure?"

"He was thrown into the role of older ... for lack of a better word, sibling. He was expected to share—to go from only male child to number two, or so it seemed in his eyes. Yet he was expected to show concern, give time to this new addition, show affection and appropriately play with an infant. In his delicate state these were all stressors for him. He just isn't capable of adapting as quickly as you or I might."

"Where are we supposed to go?" Spare her the *poor Edward* litany. Hadn't she heard it all her life? They were getting thrown out. She hadn't expected it, but it wasn't a surprise and she was simply too tired to fight back.

"I want you to know this wasn't a sudden decision. I've consulted Reverend Schmidt." What was going on? Her mother was licking her lips and twisting a frayed edge of her apron. And not looking her in the eye. "A number of people have prayed on it."

"And?"

"The church has sponsored a young man from the Congo—his home is not far from the mission where you lived. He has just completed studies for the ministry. He is in need of help with schools and a clinic to be built in his village. You have experience in these matters. And I can think of no better role model for Daniel than an African man—a church leader, a leader among his people. Daniel must have a life and a country he can identify with. He's certainly not a fit for rural Kansas—here he's an abnormality—you must see that? I would think that Daniel would be your first concern. Our missionary will be going back to his country within the month. I will help you prepare for travel to your new home."

"How much is it going to cost you, Mother, to get rid of an embarrassment and what you perceive as a threat to your son?"

"I've always been generous with the church. And if there is a romantic connection between you and the minister, then I want you to know I fully support it. You will have my blessing."

"Romantic connection? Between me and a man of the bush?"

"Well, it certainly wouldn't be your first time to show interest in such a man."

Careful. Evy paused; she had to be careful but she would not return to Africa. Especially to the region where she had lived. There would be questions—and possible knowledge of Daniel's true parentage. And maybe none of her fears would be realized, but living with the possibility of being discovered—always wondering if this person or that would remember Da and May's wedding, the accident ... the baby. And worst of all would share this knowledge.

"We won't be going to Africa."

"You'll go where I say you'll go."

"No. This is our home. Daniel or not, I'm still under age. I know my rights by law."

If Evy had expected outrage, there was none. Her mother stood staring at her. Was the look one of hatred? She had been bested. She had lost—something Evy knew her mother found intolerable.

She waited but her mother only turned on her heel and walked past her out the door of the study and up the stairs. Was she accepting defeat? There was no way of knowing. Had Evy won? But at what cost? Evy knew, could sense, that this was a hollow victory.

CHAPTER THIRTEEN

1940

They never spoke of it again. Ella went away to school and Evy, Edward and Daniel lived on the farm. Evy finished high school and Daniel flourished. At three he knew his colors, the alphabet, numbers past one hundred and could recite short poems from memory.

He was his father's son—in dark swarthy, chubby good looks and intelligence. He followed Clemetts everywhere, and other than a remark by her mother that Daniel certainly recognized his roots, they all lived in harmony.

Ella dropped out of medical school. No one talked about it. Was it too difficult? Evy thought so. Ella finished her schooling with a degree in education and moved to Halstead for a job in an elementary school. At twenty-one she was unmarried and without prospects in sight. She took her mother to church every Sunday and joined the rest of the family for dinner at the farm.

The talk of war was still impassioned and divided families. What would Roosevelt do? Would he drag the United States into a bloody global argument that wasn't of their making? Germany had invaded Poland that fall but that seemed to not even cause a ripple other than some *tsks* between "pass the corn" and "I'll take a second helping of those potatoes."

The harvest that year was one of the best. Plentiful rain but dry fields by the end of June meant machinery and men could work quickly. Evy helped her mother feed the crew that summer—young men from neighboring farms as well as out-of-state. Evy still didn't date but it wasn't because young men didn't try to interest her. She was just coming twenty with all the time in the world. And who could she ever trust with her secret? Then that changed.

Walter Wayne Schuler was twenty-three with a shock of dark brown hair that fell over one eye and muscles that strained the seams of his work shirt. He was tall—a good four inches taller than her mother—and had that easy way about him that drew people to him. His eyelashes were probably the envy of every girl he met, long and dark, framing laughing blue eyes. Even Mattie called him Mr. Handsome.

Home was Texas, the panhandle, and he worked his way across the Midwest early every summer, signing onto one crew or another. He was the youngest of seven boys so there wasn't much left in the way of an inheritance once he was grown. He had to make his own way. So, every year it was corn in Oklahoma and Nebraska and wheat in Kansas. Winters found him driving cattle to market—

finding the nearest railroad yard and loading his herd for shipment to Chicago's stockyards. The money was good, but it was never quite clear whether he was an owner or just a hired hand. It didn't really matter. What was clear was how talented he was. Good at whatever he touched.

On this particular Thursday afternoon, he'd come driving up in an old pickup the day before harvest was to start. He'd seen the flyer in the post office about the farm hiring, and he met with her mother for over an hour. When the combines wheeled out into the fields the next morning, he was boss—Clemetts' right hand man.

If anyone thought it odd that a "johnny come lately" got the top job, he soon proved he was worth it. He was good with the men—firm, yet fair. And it wasn't Evy's imagination—he got more work out of them than Da ever had.

He wasted no time singling her out. He was attentive and generous. Movies didn't change that often in the theater downtown, but he took her to *Rebecca, The Philadelphia Story,* and *My Girl Friday,* sometimes going as far as Wichita just to catch one they hadn't seen. There were countless lemonades and malted shakes, hand-dipped chocolates, bouquets of flowers and a dinner in a real restaurant. Ella was so jealous she stopped coming to Sunday dinner.

If there was one thing disquieting, it was kissing him. She'd never kissed a boy, a man, before. Once, years ago, she'd asked Mattie how she'd know what to do. "You'll jus' know. Ain't gonna need no lessons." And that was true.

Evy amazed even herself. That first evening in the front seat of his truck, her arms came up and around his neck and her lips parted. Even when his tongue sought out hers and she felt her heart stutter, she knew what to do. It was only when his hand clasped a breast or crept under her skirt along her inner thigh that she pulled back.

"I can't."

"Hey, it's okay, baby. I'm not going to do anything you don't want to do." He tipped her head back. "You can trust me."

Walt never pushed it but smartly left her wanting more. Wanting *him*. And he was good with Daniel. A pony ride around the yard after a long day in the fields seemed to not faze him one bit. He taught Daniel to swim under Evy's watchful eye and took the three of them to town in her mother's Buick for ice cream every chance he got. And every night before they went to bed, before he went to the barn and the bunk bed assigned to him, and she went upstairs to Daniel, he held her under the stars and stroked her hair and made promises to always take care of her.

By the twenty-fifth of July, the last day the harvest crew would be in the fields, Walt told her that he loved her. And then he proposed. One month to the day since they met. Too sudden. Too soon. Too everything, but Evy said, yes. Her happiness was only marred by something that had taken place the week before.

She had promised to spend the night with Ella in order to help her hang wallpaper in her new apartment. But an upset stomach—maybe a touch of food poisoning—had sent her home early. Arriving at the farm around two a.m., she walked barefoot up the stairs so as not to wake anyone and went straight to Daniel's nursery. He had slept in his own room since the first of the year and was quite proud of himself for being grown-up. They had cut out "choo-choos" and pictures of tractors and cars from magazines and pasted them all around on the walls after Clemetts applied a bright new coat of yellow paint. Daniel loved his room and his grown-up bed without safety railings.

She quietly turned the knob but the door didn't budge. It was locked but not by a key—by a slide-bolt on the inside. She fought down the first blip of panic when she realized that a three-year-old, even one almost four, could not have reached the bolt. Daniel was too short to even reach the door's lock, let alone reach above it to maneuver the sliding piece of brass with his short, stubby fingers and press it forward through the bracket.

Without a second thought she began pounding on the door. Mattie came flying up the stairs only to come racing to the end of the hall two steps behind Constance.

"Evy, what is the meaning of this?" Her mother looked disheveled, hair in curlers, tucked under a scarf.

Evy didn't have to answer because at that moment the bolt rattled back and the door opened. Edward stood there blinking into the light. He was naked but so was the small boy standing beside him.

"Is there a fire?" He was rubbing his eyes and looked confused.

"Why are you in Daniel's room behind a locked door?" Evy kept her voice low and steady but her hand was shaking.

"I'm sure he was just comforting him. I thought I heard Daniel cry out earlier."

"And that explains nakedness and a locked door. To my way of thinking, you lock a door when you don't want to be disturbed—don't want anyone to see what's going on."

"Oh Evy, what an imagination. It's a warm night. Why wouldn't a child strip down to nothing just to be comfortable? After all, it's just boys."

"A fourteen-year-old sleeping naked with a toddler …? And you don't see anything wrong with that? You say 'it's just boys'?"

Her mother grabbed her arms and jerked Evy to face her. Even in the dim light of the hallway, Evy could see the red splotches of color dotting her mother's neck and cheeks. Her voice shook. "Why don't you take your filthy mind somewhere else? I don't know what you are insinuating but I won't stand for it."

"As always, your head is firmly in the sand. You see only what you want to see. I suggest you consult his psychiatrist." Evy pulled away, scooped up Daniel who was whimpering, and walked to her room.

But it was Edward, smirking as he lounged against the doorjamb, who would haunt her. Knowing nothing would happen—no matter what he'd done, there would be no consequences. In the morning Evy had a daybed moved to Daniel's room. She wouldn't be comfortable, but Daniel would be safe. In hindsight, the incident was to play out in a way she couldn't have imagined.

* * *

The wedding was simple. A Justice of the Peace in the living room at the farm. Evy wore a dress of May's—palest green satin, ruched halter-top with matching jacket, long flowing skirt that circled her feet, barely letting her gold wedge sandals show. Something else from May. Her hair was piled on top of her head and long, dangling earrings of Venetian crystals swung from her ears. She wore two jeweled combs that matched the earrings. She looked breathtaking. Even her mother offered a simple, "The color suits you," before disappearing downstairs.

Ella was her maid of honor and Daniel was ring-bearer. She was adamant about Edward having no part in the nuptials. A few of her mother's friends from church were there, a family from a neighboring farm, Clemetts and Mattie. Walt's family declined to make the trip. Later, Evy was to wonder if he'd even told them … or worse yet, did they even exist?

In the middle of a supper of cold roast beef, potato salad and hot crescent rolls, her mother rose to announce that she was giving the lucky couple a house. It had been kept as a surprise but now she could tell everyone the wonderful news. And the only thing that Evy thought was, I'll never have to live on the farm again.

It was in town, a whole five miles away. That, at least, was a separation of a sort. No matter that her mother had chosen everything without consulting either Evy or Walt. They would discover later that the furnishings were dated and second-hand, the house was a charming Victorian but sadly in need of repair and there was no talk of a remodel.

That night she and Walt both thanked her profusely. The honeymoon was a trip to Kansas City for a long weekend and then Walt was taking a harvest crew north, and she would return to Hillsboro to deal with their new living arrangements.

There was talk of Walt managing the local hardware store when he returned in August. That and helping local farmers put in winter wheat would give him plenty to do. And enough for a young family to live on. No one knew about the gold in a New York bank safe deposit box. And no one would.

As the long afternoon wore on, Evy became more

nervous. She was a virgin masquerading as a young mother with a child—and not just any child. A child who, if the truth were known, was bound to arouse hatred and shock—maybe excommunication, certainly shunning for his father. The congregation would not take Da's indiscretions lightly. Her father's name was on more than one church memorial, thanks to her mother. Could they excommunicate the dead?

The night promised to be traumatic—she would have to share her secret. This was not something that could be hidden. There was no way she could have been honest before they were married. And could she be honest now? Did she trust even Walt not to tell someone and the news somehow getting back to her mother? Would he be understanding? Of course. That was silly of her to even think he wouldn't. He loved her. He promised to protect her forever and now she was his wife—bound by law.

Constance had loaned them the Buick for the ride to Kansas City. They had reservations at The Elms in Excelsior Springs, Missouri, and Mattie and Daniel were going with them. If Walt found it odd that Evy wouldn't leave the boy behind, he didn't say. But there was no way that Evy would leave Daniel in the same house as Edward.

The trip took hours. The highway was two lane and treacherous at night. It was late evening when they arrived. Evy found herself dreading being alone with her new husband more and more as the evening wore on. She even feigned hunger but the dining room at the hotel was closed. Maybe a drink? The bar looked open.

Walt shushed her and said he had other things on his mind and winked. Her heart sank. Other things. Walt declined help with the bags and squashed all four of them into the elevator off the main lobby already crowded with their luggage. Daniel was too sleepy to even push the button that would get them to the third floor. He and Mattie had a room across the hall and Evy helped Mattie unpack and tuck the dozing Daniel into a trundle bed.

"Now yous scuttle back across this hall and tend to that young husband of yours. I can take care of things here."

Walt was sitting on the side of the bed waiting for her when she opened the door to their room.

"Come here, beautiful."

Reluctantly she sat down beside him. He wound her thick hair around his hand and gently pulled her head back. The kiss was soft, tentative even, and Evy felt her body respond. He kept her tethered by the handful of hair while he undid the buttons on the front of her blouse.

"I think we need to talk." She tried to wiggle away.

"Hey, now's not a good time exactly for conversation."

"I have to go to the bathroom."

He stared at her but released her hair. "You got anything else you can put on?"

She nodded, slipped off the bed, and bent over her suitcase. She quickly hunted through her clothes until she found what she was looking for, grabbed it and shut the bathroom door behind her.

May had a peignoir of ecru colored silk trimmed in matching lace. The gown was cut low with a solid V-shaped lace panel covering most of her breasts. The gown's skirt brushed her ankles but draped over her body like another skin. Every curve was accentuated. Was this the gown that May had worn on her wedding night? The day she became the bride of a bigamist?

Evy quickly shut down that train of thought. She was in the mess she was in because of her father—she didn't need to dwell on it.

And she was torn. How could she want this man in front of her so much? Want him to think she was beautiful? Want him to make her world right—it had never been right. It had always listed to one side. There had never been a time when everyone in her family had been truthful, had openly and without doubt loved each other. Told each other that they cared. That's all she wanted now. To be loved, understood, cherished for who she was—for what she'd tried to do—save her father and her family from shame.

She opened the bathroom door and walked back into the room. His eyes roamed her body and his breathing quickened. He had taken off his clothes and it was difficult to tear her eyes away from his erection. Of course, she was familiar with the male anatomy—just not a grown man's. There was something both exciting and frightening.

"Come here."

She walked over to stand in front of him. She slipped the outer matching robe to the floor and willed herself to stand immobile. He put both hands around her waist and drew her closer. Then, with maddening slowness, he stood and slipped one narrow strap from her left shoulder, then the right. With a tug the gown slithered over her hips and fell in a heap at her feet. She willed her arms to stay at her sides and let his eyes take in all of her.

"You're the most beautiful woman I've ever seen." His voice was husky; the words whispered in her ear as a hand found a nipple and caressed it. Then he swiped his thumb across his tongue and the slickness intensified the pleasure—his thumb now gliding easily in a tight circle. The rush of feeling almost buckled her knees.

He put both of her arms around his neck and lifted her, bracing her back with one hand and lowering her slowly onto the bed. She sank underneath him stretched full length, legs parted. He didn't wait. He barely touched the outer edge of her vagina before positioning the head of his penis and thrusting full forward with a force that threatened to cleave her in two.

She had told herself she wouldn't scream, that it wouldn't hurt—she was a grown woman, not a girl—wouldn't that make a difference? She read in a book she'd found in May's room that the vagina could accommodate all sizes of male sexual organs. But they lied, she did scream, at the sheer enormity of his member and the lunge that drove it deep within her. She pushed against him, struggling out from beneath him and rolled to a standing position. She clutched at her abdomen, doubled in pain and saw the blood dripping onto the floor.

"What the fuck?" He was furious. "You're a virgin." He got up from the bed and just stood there staring, trying to comprehend.

It wasn't even a question. And she didn't even acknowledge it. She was terrified and couldn't stand up straight. The pain was low and throbbing and didn't go away. He walked to the bathroom and came back with a towel. He wiped himself first, then threw it at her feet.

"Clean yourself up."

She did as she was told but still couldn't stand. The room tilted; Walt's face had fuzzy edges and seemed to be retreating. She held out her hand, "Help me." Her head lolled backwards and she slipped to the floor, unconscious.

* * *

The doctor motioned for Walt to follow him back through the waiting room to the admitting desk. "I need your consent to operate—to check for any internal perforations. This will be done under general anesthetic. I expect we'll be in OR for a couple hours—I'll come get you when I'm done."

After lighting a cigarette and offering one to Walt, he turned on his heel and briskly walked back through the swinging double doors that separated the hospital's interior from the emergency room.

Walt quickly signed the form and took a seat. This wasn't exactly how he'd expected to spend his honeymoon. And what exactly had happened? A virgin? With a four-year-old? Brought to mind a bad joke about immaculate conception.

The wait was three hours instead of two, but finally a nurse took him down the hall to the doctor's office. A name plaque on the door said Harvey Nettles, MD. It wasn't much of an office—a dark, stale, hole-in-the-wall with an overflowing ashtray and a carved oak desk that was way too big. The room was made even smaller by floor to ceiling bookshelves loaded with thick, heavy volumes that looked well-used.

The doctor bustled in after a brief wait and scooted sideways around the corner of the desk to reach the chair in back. He sat for a moment, drumming his fingers on a stack of papers.

"I'll get right to the point. Your wife has *Primary Vaginismus*. Not sure when I've seen a case quite so constricting. Let me explain." He turned to the bookcase in back of the desk and after consulting two different books, chose one, opened it and turned it for Walt to see. "This is a diagram of the vaginal area. Vaginismus is the physical condition that involuntarily constricts the pubococcygeus muscle" ... he paused to point with a pen ... "but we don't rule out the involvement of other muscles—the levator ani, bulbocavernosus circumvafinal and even the perivaginal muscles. All are suspect or even a combination of these muscles. We just don't know all we should about the condition. It's rare—maybe I've seen five cases in twenty years."

"And you're sure she can't help it? I mean if this is a muscle thing, why can't she just relax?"

"That's a good question. But trust me, she can't." Without warning the doctor reared up and thrust a pen toward his left eye.

"What?" Walt pulled back.

"There. Could you have stopped your eye from blinking shut as a reaction to perceived danger? Of course not. Well, this is much like what happens to the pubococcygeus."

"So, there's no possible way that my wife could have given birth at some time in the past?"

"Mr. Schuler, your wife was a virgin. Whether childbirth can correct the situation from this point forward, there first needs to be a reversal of her present condition."

"It can be fixed? Or changed?"

"It's going to take a lot of patience. The only thing prescribed at this time is dilation—the vagina has to be stretched to accommodate a penis. There can be no entry until this is done. I'll send you home with a vaginal dilator set. There's a set of five, graduated in size, true to life forms—medical-grade synthetic polymer—that she'll need to insert at night to allow the stretching action to gradually open the canal. She needs to keep them inserted for a minimum of eight hours and move up in size as quickly as she's able to tolerate a bigger form."

"A little box of fake dicks."

"Well, uh … um, … yes, that's one way of describing them. Might I remind you that out of consideration for your wife, you should pleasure yourself and not attempt to rush the treatment. It might be some time before she's receptive … able to be, that is. I'll be keeping her here for a few days—observation. There were stitches … just need to make certain everything is healing properly."

* * *

They kept her for four more days. She had an allergic reaction to ether and couldn't keep any food down for seventy-two hours. Which gave credence to the lie to Mattie that she had acute food poisoning.

By the morning of the second day, Walt was tired of being cooped up, still seething at being lied to, and bound and determined that he wasn't going to be saddled with someone else's mixed-race child to raise. But why would Evy ruin her life to lie about the child? None of it made sense but there was one way to get to the truth. Evy's mother.

The woman had paid him fifty thousand dollars to marry her daughter—to take on the support of her daughter's son. Only Daniel wasn't Evy's child. What the hell was going on?

Walt called the hotel and had a message taken to Mattie. They would be leaving in thirty minutes. Going back to the farm. Evy would stay in the hospital and he would drive back and pick her up at the end of the week, barring any setbacks. Daniel and Mattie were already packed and waiting on the hotel's front steps when he got there.

"Mama, Mama." Daniel ran to the car but burst into tears when he didn't see his mother.

Or, as Walt reminded himself, the one he thought was his mother.

Walt just shook his head. Why would anyone lie to a kid? If Evy had adopted a child—he knew she'd lived in Africa—why would she present it as her own? Suffer the shaming and gossip of a small town full of people who would surely point fingers and ostracize her. And the crazy thing? Daniel looked just like her.

Constance met them on the front porch having watched the big touring car lumber up the long drive-way.

"Where's Evy?"

"In the hospital. We need to talk."

Mattie carried a sleeping Daniel up the steps and Walt followed Constance into her office.

"I need answers." He remained standing.

Constance balanced on the edge of the desk. "What's the meaning of this?"

"That's what you're going to tell me." He reiterated what had happened, not leaving out one graphic detail, slowing only when he saw Constance's two hands grab the edge of the desk to stay upright.

"Virgin? Could never have had intercourse? Is that what you're saying?" Her voice was shaking. "But Daniel? Why the lie?"

Walt watched as a look of realization washed over her features—a dawning of maybe something she'd already known at some level. Or could she be as shocked as he was? He watched as her face turned a pasty-white—healthy color simply draining away.

On unsteady legs she walked to the back of the desk and slumped down in the big swivel chair. "Leave me. I need to think. Give me an hour and then let's meet back here." She made a motion toward the door, dismissing him. The meeting had ended.

Constance closed her eyes, squeezed them shut. *Think. Be logical.* No, it wasn't true. The baby wasn't his. He wouldn't have done that to her. He was a man of the church. He had been her husband. She trusted him. She gave him money, children, a home, made him respectable, made him successful—he owed everything to her. He would have never thrown all that away. And for what was probably a cheap whore? No, not her husband. He had integrity. He'd learned his lesson long ago.

There might be one way to find out for certain. Evy had brought back a trunk of keepsakes—things she'd wanted to keep for Daniel—native paintings, beads, things that made up his heritage. It was all in a trunk in the attic. She'd directed Clemetts to put it there. But could there also be a birth certificate? Maybe other proof of the baby's parentage?

Constance walked up the stairs and took the long hallway that ended in a door to the attic. The trunk was in a far corner. She couldn't stop her hands from shaking. But she told herself what she feared just was not possible. Her fear was groundless. She was overreacting, letting her imagination get in the way.

She sank to her knees beside the trunk. She fumbled with the hasp pulling the tight-fitting wooden peg from the metal loop. Then paused before heaving the trunk's heavy lid up and back. The first layer was filled with brightly colored costumes and carved bone and wooden jewelry. A crude giraffe and stuffed lion—stiff hopsacking cutouts with bright beading and frayed yarn for eyes and manes— obviously baby toys, possibly made by some relative. She carefully laid all these things to the side until she found the large manila envelope at the bottom.

It was thick and double bound by a string that wound around two circular clasps. It was difficult to get her fingers to work—to stop shaking long enough to unwind the twine. But finally she was able to upend the contents onto the floor.

It was the picture that first caught her attention. An 8x10 black and white in a silver frame. How young he looked, how handsome … and how happy. He was dressed in a dark suit, very formal and the young woman on his arm was wearing white—a long white dress and a veil that trailed the ground behind her. A bouquet of white calla lilies and orchids resting on a white, probably leather-bound, Bible.

He must have been asked to give the bride away— probably someone's daughter, someone he worked with. She was breathtakingly beautiful and not much older than Evy. Even in black and white it was evident that she was of color—not dark but, perhaps, a rich toffee with flowing black hair and luminescent eyes. A beaming priest was standing in the background. Odd that Harold would have attended a ceremony in a Catholic church, let alone taken part in one.

She slipped the photo out of its frame. Ah, this might explain it. There were papers behind the photo—a rather official looking document that Constance separated from the others and held toward the light—the one window in the room. It was a certificate of marriage issued by the church, the Catholic Church, signed by a priest for a Harold Everett and May Smythe-Nelson Nutanda.

Her hands were shaking uncontrollably. She felt a terrible tightening in her chest and it was difficult to breathe evenly. These were lies. Whatever she was looking at was simply wrong—the certificate said they were both of the Catholic faith. And marriage? Of course not. He was married. Already married. Already a member of the Mennonite church.

She tossed the photo aside and quickly picked up a newspaper clipping. *The death of Harold Everett and his wife, May Smythe-Nelson Nutanda Everett occurred on ...* With the taste of bile rising in her throat, she picked up another document. The death certificate for Harold Everett clipped to the death certificate for his wife who died in childbirth. May Smythe-Nelson Nutanda Everett.

One last bit of paper ... Constance picked up the birth certificate of Daniel Nutanda Everett, son of Harold Everett and May ... her vision blurred; she couldn't even see the words printed on the page in front of her. A marriage, a baby named Daniel ... she leaned against the trunk's cool surface, pressing her cheek against the metal stays and waited until the throbbing in her head subsided.

An hour later she handed the birth certificate to Walter Schuler. "It would appear that Evy was trying to make amends for her father. Daniel is her half-brother." She didn't say more. Let him think what he wanted. It suited her if he thought the child's real mother was a whore.

"You can have your house back but not the money. I've enlisted. I leave for camp next week. I'll be stationed in California and will take Evy and Daniel with me." He turned and walked out of the office.

* * *

He picked up Evy at the hospital on Friday. He'd brought pillows and a quilt so that she could stretch out and wouldn't have to sit up—still something that was difficult for her to do.

"I know Daniel is your half-brother. Your mother showed me his birth certificate." He watched her in the rear-view mirror. Her eyes got big and she blinked rapidly, opened her mouth as if to say something, then closed it. "I think she was as shocked as I was." Still nothing from the back seat. "Your mother had paid me fifty thousand dollars to marry you. Make you 'legitimate'—not so much of an outcast—whatever that meant. I'm giving the house back but not the money. I'll share it with you. She's not going to want to give Daniel his father's share of the farm—not under the circumstances—and you'll need money. I guess I should tell you I've enlisted. I leave one week from today."

"So, there's no harvest crew or managing a hardware store?"

"No, Evy. There never was going to be. I told your mother I'd take you and Daniel with me. I'll stay long enough to see that you have a place, a job if you need it before I ship out."

"Do you love me?" The voice sounded small and afraid.

"I don't know, Evy. That's God's truth, I just don't know. It's been six weeks since we met—that's not very long. I don't think we know each other. This country is going to have to go to war. Everything points in that direction. I know I want to do my part. I know when I took your mother's money, my conscience wouldn't leave me alone. I guess I'd just as soon get the marriage annulled. You don't need a marriage now—you're free, out from under the stigma. You don't need me to be 'legitimate.' You could go to school, travel—anything you wanted." He glanced in the rearview. "Maybe we could try again after the war?"

She nodded but looked out the window. It broke his heart when he saw the tears. But he wasn't going to lie anymore. She was beautiful but young, naïve—only now a woman who could tell the truth about her young charge—her half-brother, his mother and father dead. She had a right to experience life. And fall in love with someone who was worth it. Someone who wouldn't take money to perpetuate a lie.

He drove the rest of the way in silence.

* * *

Mattie saw Constance go to the barn but went back to mopping the kitchen floor. It was only when she was wringing the mop out in the bucket on the porch that she realized what Constance was going to do. The first alabaster angel wing flew off as a head rolled. Mattie watched all four sentinel angels dissolve into dust and chunks of marble. Constance swung the sledge hammer again and again. The heavy tool almost carrying her over backward with the effort. The pedestals, the door to the crypt, the stained-glass windows—their crimson red and cobalt blue chips glittered in the sunlight before scattering on the ground—all in ruins. The mausoleum was no more.

Finally, Constance dragged the jewel encrusted china urn from the rubble and carried it to the privy behind the barn. There was still outdoor plumbing for the hired hands. Mattie turned to go back inside. An hour passed, she was preparing supper when Constance came up onto the porch and sat in the swing. Nothing was said. And the urn was never seen again. The last trace of the caddis man was gone.

* * *

It was eight that night when Evy and Walt returned. Daniel was beside himself and wouldn't let go of Evy's skirt the entire evening but trailed her everywhere. Constance stayed in her room and didn't join them for a late meal. Evy made up the cot in Daniel's room and went to bed early but had to read five nursery rhymes before Daniel nodded off.

"Missy, Missy Evy. Wake-up. You gotta come. It's your mother."

It took Evy a minute to get oriented. The sky was barely streaked with color. A pale peach stripe stretched across the horizon. It wasn't fully dawn yet. She was home on a cot next to Daniel. Then the fear in Mattie's voice registered.

"What is it?"

"You jus come—somethin awful happened."

Evy knew the minute she crossed the threshold of her mother's bedroom that Constance had had a stroke. The left side of her face was pulled sharply downward, her right arm was flailing in the air, a claw-like hand grasping at nothing. The garbled sounds had no meaning and didn't even mimic language. And she had soiled herself. Her urine-soaked gown stuck to her legs—her left leg grotesquely twisted beneath her.

"Call Dr. Schroeder."

The morning was taken up with an ambulance ride to Bethel hospital. Tests, consults with doctors and then home again. Evy was exhausted. And the prognosis wasn't promising. Her mother suffered with high blood pressure—yesterday's shock was the trigger. At fifty-two, she was old before her time and now infirm—possibly to spend the rest of her life tied upright in a wheelchair. Speech might not come back nor the ability to feed herself. In all likelihood, for however long the rest of her life proved to be, Constance would be an invalid.

The doctors suggested a home. Evy promised to consider it. At the moment a lengthy hospital stay was predicted—at least until she stabilized. Evy divided her time between Constance and Daniel—driving the ten miles round-trip to the hospital three times a day. After the first visit Edward refused to visit his mother again. He didn't like the smells of the hospital. Evy thought he couldn't stand to see his life's champion incapacitated.

On the third day Walt met her in the hallway. "You're not packed." He had stayed on the periphery and out of the way—usually only coming up to the house to eat. He helped Clemetts with readying the planting—fixing machinery, even putting a new clutch in a combine.

"I'm not going." Evy couldn't look at him. She knew he'd disapprove, think she was throwing her life away—and, well, she was ... sort of. She just knew what she had to do and didn't feel like arguing over it.

"You can't stay. This is no life for you, or Daniel."

"Edward is fourteen. Mother can't take care of herself,

let alone a child."

"Put your mother in a home; send Edward to boarding school—"

"And the farm?"

"Sell it."

"It's our life, our *way* of life—I want Daniel and Edward to have their heritage, live their heritage."

"Ella could run the farm."

"And leave her job? She's never liked it here. It would be disastrous."

"Evy, listen to reason. Don't sentence yourself to this prison, taking care of a woman who has never been kind to you, raising a child by yourself."

"And what am I supposed to do? Go to California where I have no relatives or friends, and raise Daniel by myself out there?"

"You don't owe these people—not a father who would have abandoned you, chose to start a new family and not honor the old—not a mother who never showed you love."

"Please … stop. I know what you're saying is true. Yet, I cannot in good conscience abandon them. I didn't choose them, but they are my family."

He stood and looked at her as if he wanted to say more then walked away, slamming the front door a little too hard. He was angry, and not willing to honor his wedding vows. Under the circumstances she understood and if truth be known, she was unsure of her feelings for him—unsure enough that she couldn't promise to spend the rest of her life with him.

Their chance had come and gone; maybe, her own chance ever at marriage—her mother had seen to that. But one thing she was sure of. If a husband came her way now, he wouldn't need to be purchased.

And Daniel's secret was safe. No one needed to know. Someday she'd share the truth with him but he'd have to be older, mature enough to understand why she had to perpetuate a lie. But for now she was still his mother, the only one he'd ever known.

CHAPTER FOURTEEN

The war came closer. More than a year after Walt had left for California. He was in the Navy and stationed in Hawaii. There had been letters—business-like at first—had she gotten a copy of the annulment? Had she remembered to check the terms of the bank loan for the seed—winter planting was fast approaching. Again, an apology, then finally letters written by the man who had become a friend and who counted her as his. He had strep throat and missed a night in town with the boys; he rescued a kitten and found it a home; he gave his hat to a kid who looked just like Daniel and used to hang on the fence outside the barracks.

As pen pals they found a bond. A comfortable commonness.

At first she was surprised but saw his reaching out as yet something else to assuage his conscience. But then she looked forward to his letters. He was showing her a world different from hers—he was helpful, thoughtful, whether it was preparing her to run the farm or comments on raising Daniel. It wasn't too early to introduce the boy to sports. Maybe he'd like baseball? Or get him a pair of skates, let him skate on the pond next winter—then introduce a hockey stick and puck. Evy wasn't certain what a five-year-old would like but she bought him a glove and played catch.

She answered all of Walt's letters—sometimes eagerly waiting for mail delivery, out on the road by the box on a fence post. She mostly shared small talk, the farm, the community, Daniel, her mother … she was careful not to let her eagerness show on paper. She never referenced how she missed him, longed for help with the farm or Daniel … how she was lonely, tired of making decisions all on her own … how she thought of him every day. And he never professed love but she read between the lines and gained comfort.

She followed the war news in the paper and listened to Roosevelt's fireside chats. How could the United States not get involved? Wasn't it inevitable? Walt never mentioned the war. Maybe he wasn't allowed to. He kept his stories confined to the base—had she ever seen the ocean? The water was blue. And he shared what he was doing—he was learning to fly. She felt his pride as he described feelings of being "on top of the world." He even sent a picture of himself standing on the wing of his plane.

Then after December seventh there was silence, and she assumed he had been killed. No one saw her tears and no one could fill that hole that widened to encompass her very being. He was bigger than life. How could he be gone?

And if she could have been a wife—a *real* wife—would he have left her?

She said a prayer for his soul to a God she was more than a little uncertain of. But it was all she could think of to do. She had no idea how to find out for certain if he was dead. She could recall no family that he'd mentioned other than a lot of brothers. Wouldn't they be in the war, too?

And it wasn't just her life—the world seemed to be in utter chaos. A madness that was all consuming. Stories of an entire people being annihilated. A madman wanting to "cleanse" his country, purify his race. It made no sense. But somewhere there was a God that just seemed to be standing by, hands off, watching His people annihilate each other.

She stood in line at the post office for the family's ration books. There was one for each of them. Edward, at almost sixteen, bragged about going into the service as soon as he turned eighteen, but Evy doubted he could pass the physical. Asthma was never far behind him.

And his food had to be specially prepared or he could be laid up for days with an irritated colon. What was it her mother used to call it? Having a "nervous constitution"? It certainly seemed like it took little or nothing to throw him into a full-blown spasming, wheezing fit or doubled over with stomach cramps. With his mother no longer able to take his side, he'd turned into a morose teen, bullying Daniel whenever he got the chance. But, to the best of her knowledge, otherwise leaving Daniel alone.

She'd had to hire a nursing staff for her mother. Round-the-clock care could not be provided by someone also running the farm and raising two boys.

Ella stayed away, coming home only for holidays. She

would have nothing to do with the "half-breed" child of her sister and wouldn't be caught dead near him. Evy had shamed the family, and Ella called him a bastard every chance she got. Daniel was an embarrassment and she wouldn't bring her friends to the farm. She was beginning to sound like her mother, and Evy was relieved when she stopped coming to the farm altogether.

Because of the war all of the farm had to be producing—and not just wheat. Huge gardens—Victory Gardens—were planned for spring and summer with a few back acres nearest the creek given up to corn. Kaffir-corn, animal feed, was planted for the stock, which now numbered several head of cattle, as well as, chickens, geese and a handful of ducks.

Canning was an all-day, several day affair in the fall. The cellar was filled with gems—reminders of a fruitful summer. The strawberry preserves alone made canning worth it when eaten mid-winter. They were self-sufficient and had to be.

By the end of the summer in 1945, the United States had dropped two atomic bombs on Japan. That August the war was officially declared over. The German madman had committed suicide and the world was ready to move out of chaos and return to normal. But what was this new *normal*? The world had changed forever.

The postmistress lamented the fact that she would be out of a job soon—men were returning and taking back the positions they had left. It would be back to having babies and taking care of a home. For many women, just not Evy.

Edward was nineteen and Daniel was nine. Daniel had discovered baseball—thanks to Walt's suggestion. From morning to night all summer long, he and a half dozen friends would play. He'd begged for use of the land behind the barn where a "real" diamond could be set up. Clemetts even found some used wooden planks and cobbled together a rough set of bleachers.

It was fun. Floodlights were added using electricity from the barn. Long extension cords, piggy-backed together, snaked across the grass and through the double doors. Many an evening, teams from town played double-headers in front of parents and friends.

Edward was the one who worried her. He graduated high school with a C average, not because he couldn't have done better, but between illnesses and apathy, he was lucky to graduate at all. He didn't seem to have a purpose—nothing that interested him that Evy could see.

It certainly wasn't baseball. He didn't even go to a game to cheer a team on—let alone support his cousin. He seemed preoccupied with how Daniel fit into the scheme of things—if he was his sister's child. He wanted to know whether Daniel was in line to inherit anything. Did he have any rights? It was all Evy could do to just tell the truth. Yes, Daniel had rights; the same rights that he did … but she didn't know that for certain. At least she had the proof, the birth certificate that she now kept safe with her own belongings. Still, it was all pretty much a muddle and wouldn't be sorted easily once the truth were known.

Edward had no interest in the farm, other than money, and begged her for an advance on his inheritance in order to buy a car. He was almost twenty and the trust would pay a sizeable first installment on his twenty-first birthday. A few months couldn't make much of a difference. She did it; but later questioned her decision.

He took to driving his new Oldsmobile coupe to Kansas City with friends—young men that Mattie called "pretty boys." He even took an apartment there, but that didn't seem to pan out and he moved back to the farm. Had he been thrown out? Evy thought so.

He brought a *friend* with him—Derek, a young man of eighteen with curly blond hair and a penchant for colorful clothing. Actually, women's clothing. Mattie showed her the lace bra and panties she'd found in the laundry basket.

After three months of drinking, allowing Derek to wreck his car twice, and parties in town that involved the police, Evy put her foot down. No one lived on the farm and enjoyed its largess without working for it. She needed help putting in a field of strawberries and both young men could help her.

But no, without so much as a good-bye, Edward moved to Wichita, taking Derek with him. Good riddance. Evy couldn't think of one person who would miss them.

Troop trains began rolling through town that year. The platform and the Harvey House teemed with young men in uniform. As a thank-you, a number of churches set up coffee and doughnut stands—several card tables pushed together covered with white cloths—manned by young women from town.

Perhaps, the most auspicious event of that year was her mother's death. Not even sixty. And in the end Constance had starved herself—refused all food and drink. The doctor had requested that she be fed intravenously, but even without speech, her mother made her wishes known. She'd simply had enough.

Evy placed Constance to the right of her father and had a headstone carved out of granite to match the other two. The plot was away from the house, down by the river—far from the broken ruins of Harold's mausoleum. Mattie confided where she thought Da and May's remains ended up, and Evy had the outhouse privy plowed under and the privacy structure removed. An ignoble ending at best. And Evy still wasn't sure she cared.

The service for her mother was brief. Several people from the church came and there was a cold buffet of ham, fried chicken, warm croissants, fruit salad and deviled eggs. An array of pies covered all of one table in the dining room.

Reverend Schmidt, now too infirm to attend, sent his regards and a written piece extolling her mother's virtues—a woman who was forced to face life's adversities and overcome them. A paragon of faith and righteousness. All of this because her mother had given the church and its missions a few hundred thousand? Evy thought so. And even though she had sent a note, Edward did not attend.

The following Wednesday she was upstairs when she heard the front door open.

"I'm home."

The voice was familiar but who was here? Evy walked to the top of the stairs and looked down. There was Ella standing beside a bulging valise and behind her were two trunks on the porch. For all the world she looked like a younger version of her mother—thin, rangy-tall, wispy dishwater blond hair stuffed under a scarf. Sensible shoes, a black and white herringbone tweed coat that reached mid-calf, and an expression of smugness—a barely concealed 'I'm here, you have to take me in' attitude.

"Ella. What a surprise."

"I realize that you need help with the farm now that

Mother's gone. And this *is* my home."

Was it Evy's imagination or was this last said as a challenge? She wasn't biting. Of course, Ella could stay even though it was the last thing on earth that Evy wanted. The two of them running the farm? This would not be easy.

After the shock wore off, everyone seemed to settle into a routine. Ella took her old bedroom and other than *managing* the kitchen, much to Mattie's dismay, Ella stayed out of Evy's way.

Evy was free to continue making farm decisions in general. She tried to keep fresh flowers in the heavy blown glass vase in a wrought-iron stand in the middle of her mother's grave, but after awhile she stopped walking the mile from the house to the grassy knoll. Life was for the living and she wasn't taking any joy in honoring a woman who had been so very different than she and had lacked so much compassion. Even though there was a certain sadness to her ending, it was more the passing of an era.

Edward, in five years, had never visited his mother. Not one time. Before she died, he'd even asked if he could move his bedroom downstairs. Now, still in Wichita, Evy was relieved that he hadn't wanted to move back to the farm. His latent anger at being coddled and emotionally suffocated by an overly solicitous mother left him scarred. Yet, he was family. When the new pastor at their church inquired about his going on a mission to New Delhi en route to Borneo, Evy enthusiastically gave her consent. Apparently, Edward had inquired about lending a hand to the establishment of new missions. She almost couldn't believe it. A true calling? Had she sold him far short? This was simply perfect—he was putting some direction into his life. Of course, she was asked for a "suitable" donation but she was glad to do it. He would be gone from Kansas in a month. The car, the pretty boys, the apartment in Wichita ... Derek ... all would be left behind. Perhaps all that had just been the foolhardiness of youth and all along Edward had been searching for a reason for being—a vision or a commitment.

The donation had been promised when Ella confronted her about its amount. She hadn't been consulted; she was the oldest; they simply couldn't be handing out money to anyone and everyone who asked. And, by the way, it was high time that her name be placed on all the accounts. Did she know whether or not Evy was even being fair? The money offered to assure Edward's new vocation ... was there an equal amount set aside for each of them? Did she, Ella, have a safe inheritance, earning interest in an account somewhere?

Evy probably needed to have been more careful. She was the one who stayed on the farm taking care of her mother—no one else had wanted that duty. She had chosen duty over what could have been happiness ... at the very least, an escape. But separate accounts? No. There were none, and only Edward's inheritance had been spelled out. Again, it had been assumed that girls would have husbands to take care of them. Assuring Ella's portion of the farm was probably long overdue. A trip to the bank and a meeting with a lawyer soothed ruffled feathers.

Life was beginning to take on a shape. Fewer players, fewer familiar faces but a shape—until one Thursday morning toward the end of the month. Just when life promised routine without surprises, it lied ... again.

Evy volunteered at the coffee and doughnuts table at

the railway station on Thursday mornings. It was the least she could do for returning soldiers. This morning in early September, the weather had turned chilly. Definitely, fall was in the air. The two girls who usually helped her didn't show, and Evy was on her own. She pulled her sweater closer and arranged a plate of chocolate doughnuts, then opened a box of yellow cake ones—some frosted, some not. The coffee had just finished perking in the big urn borrowed from the church. Cups were in a row, napkins, spoons—

"Any law against taking one of each?"

Before Evy even turned around, she knew that voice. Five years wasn't long enough to forget—maybe she never would have.

When she turned it was as though time rushed backwards—some twisted retrograde motion that brought a wave of feeling ... and apprehension. But she knew she was looking at one of the most handsome men she had ever known ... had ever been married to ... however briefly.

"Oh, Walt, I thought you were dead."

"*I* thought I was dead." The familiar grin, the same shock of dark brown hair that fell over his left eye, and she could have told someone he'd toss his head to get it back into place. Could have put money on it as she watched the quick jerk of his head to the right. And the lock of hair fell neatly in place as if trained. "Any chance I could get a kiss at this doughnut table? Hell, if you're selling 'em, I'll pay."

"I think I could manage a free one." She walked around the table and into his arms—only it was just one arm. She hadn't seen his sleeve pinned up. "Your arm?"

"There's a little bit less of me. But the donation was to

a good cause."

He traced her lips with his index finger, then slipped his right hand to the middle of her back gently bringing her closer. "You are so beautiful. I've thought of you every day."

His breath was coming quicker now and Evy reached up on tiptoe, put her arms around his neck and sought his lips, pulling his head downward to meet hers. There was a hint of aftershave, tangy, not unpleasant. His lips were warm and slightly parted and the kiss was one of promise but not necessarily chaste. Her first inclination was to push herself against him and just hold him as tightly as she could, burying her face in his chest and murmuring the words that were right there on the tip of her tongue. Instead she pulled back and looked up. He was real. This was happening. She might blink but he wasn't going away.

"Speaking of a good cause, I heard you could use a good man—one armed, or two." His arm was still around her; he seemed reluctant to let her go.

"On the farm?"

"Unless you're recruiting for something else? I've asked around and I don't see a ring there." He pulled up her left hand and played at inspecting her ring finger.

The grin was mischievous and she noticed his eyelashes almost touched his cheek. She blushed but wasn't really sure why. Call it shock, or the fact that kissing him had left her knees knocking, she was tongue-tied. This was something she had wished for, no, prayed for, and felt devastated when she thought he would never come back—so why couldn't she think of one interesting or clever thing to say?

"Hey, cat got your tongue? How 'bout we spring this joint and go get some breakfast. Hungry?"

Actually, she was. The Harvey House was full to the gills with customers waiting for a table to free up, but you could count on the best food in town. It was worth the wait. She put a note on the doughnut box telling people to help themselves and they went inside. The wait wasn't long. Another passenger train wasn't due for an hour and the crowd from the eight a.m. eastbound was thinning.

The high-backed booth offered privacy and comfort. The cracked leather upholstery somehow reassuring. She leaned back and took him all in. Breathed in the air around him. Her world had never felt so right. She knew the feeling was love before she could acknowledge the word.

She had loved Da and May, and always there would be love for Daniel, but this was different. If she looked into Walt's eyes, she could see her own life reflected. The happiness, the sadness, but above all else the promise and hope.

The bacon and eggs and biscuits disappeared and they lingered over coffee. His was a war story. There was a hole in his side that had healed haphazardly and stories of hospitals and operations and almost dying twice. Then when he could at least hobble around, the self-doubt crept in. He was less than whole, less than a man—wouldn't it be better if she just continued to think he was dead?

She reached out then and took his hand. "Never. You don't know what not hearing from you did to me."

"I was selfish. I was hurt, angry, and wallowed in it. It took me a long time to get up the courage to be here. I should have stood by you. I can't believe that I let money turn my head—let me use you and not even recognize the best thing that ever happened to me."

The house was quiet when they got home. Daniel was

at a baseball camp for the weekend, Edward had just left on mission to Borneo, and Mattie and Clemetts now in their fifties had taken a day to drive into Wichita—shopping and a movie was a recreational favorite. And mercifully Ella was visiting a friend from school and wouldn't be back until Monday.

* * *

He wanted to walk out back—look in the barns. She mentioned a new combine and tractor. Then, if she was up to it, maybe they could drive out and see the fields. The sun had burned off any early morning condensation and the day was perfect—clear, warm but not muggy, and without a hint of rain.

"I'd like to stay and help Clemetts. Think that could be arranged?" They'd walked the length of the field closest to the creek.

"I don't see why not. We are hiring help for putting in the winter wheat." Of course she wanted him to stay—needed him to stay. Why would he think otherwise? She wanted this to be his home.

He nodded and picked up a clod of dirt and crumbled it—commenting on its black color. "The soil is in good shape. I'm assuming you've rotated a crop or two of alfalfa." He brought the last bit of earth to his nose and breathed deeply. "I've missed this. Don't get me wrong, I liked the ocean but this is where my heart is." He looked off into the distance.

She waited for something more. If he loved the land, did he love her? Funny, but after their kiss earlier, he seemed shy—reluctant to even do it again—reluctant to commit.

He wanted to sit for awhile and a centuries-old cottonwood afforded just the spot. But once he'd leaned back against the tree, he fell asleep. She studied him. He looked older than his twenty-nine years. And gaunt. Mattie would say he needed some fattening up. But she liked being beside him. It felt right. For the first time in maybe forever, she didn't feel alone, without help and without understanding.

She let him sleep, even dozing herself. He must have needed the rest because he didn't move for three hours then startled awake, more than a little chagrined.

"My apologies for being bad company. You're going to send me back where I came from at this rate."

"Probably not. But I am hoping you're ready for a late lunch." She didn't have to suggest twice about going back to the house. He admitted to being starved and not having had home-cooking for a long time.

He helped her in the kitchen, set the table and poured two glasses of iced tea. Then sat down and waited for her to join him. She felt his eyes on her as she cooked and it didn't make her feel uncomfortable. She knew what he wanted to ask. Probably why he seemed quiet and withdrawn. But he was a man and he had to be wanting to ask if things had changed? Physically, could she have intercourse? But she let him stew.

After the second helping of potato salad and the last piece of fried chicken had disappeared, she continued to fill him in on the last five years. She kept the conversation on farm topics—last year's yield, the new dam and reservoir over by Marion, Daniel's grades, his love of baseball and the diamond out back. She touched upon Edward; she hadn't heard from him, but no news was good news ... she hoped. She saved the topic of Ella till last but then shared her surprise return the week they'd buried her mother.

She got up to clear the table but instead walked over to stand behind him, her arms around his neck. She laughed and leaned over his shoulder nuzzling his neck then bringing his head back to rest against her breasts as she whispered, "I have something in mind that you might like to do this afternoon."

Walt waved aside peach cobbler and a second cup of coffee and sat looking at her. Suspecting something was up? She certainly had his attention, but before he could answer she stood back, took him by the hand and led him through the kitchen, across the foyer and up the stairs.

Her bedroom faced east with a window seat surrounded by tall glass windows with leaded panels across the top. Her bed was a four-poster monstrosity inherited from her mother, the coverlet, shams and pillow cases hand-embroidered white eyelet. A little pristine and thoroughly feminine, but she was going to love sharing it.

Now all she needed was to keep her courage up. She wanted this man—all of him. She had no doubt that at twenty-nine he'd had other women. Would she measure up? Now that her doctor had assured her that there should be no reason to keep her from enjoying an adult relationship, as he called it. Psychosomatic muscle spasms.

Her fear that her secret would be discovered had kept her from being receptive—another one of her doctor's words. But he'd given her a pamphlet—Positions For Painless Entry was the title of one chapter and she was more than ready to test her newfound knowledge.

She willed herself not to shake as she slipped off her slacks and sweater, then panties and bra. She untied the scarf at the base of her neck and shook her hair loose to tumble around her shoulders. She turned to face him squarely.

"Clothing not allowed—I need you to get rid of these." She motioned in the general direction of his shirt and slacks. "Wait, I'll help."

She walked toward him aware that her nipples were hard points and that his eyes were taking in every inch of her nakedness.

She gently pushed his hand back and unbuttoned his shirt by herself. When it fell back, the concave, fist-sized scar on his side looked like an angry red welt. She touched it with her fingertips hoping her cold hands wouldn't be noticed; then, she leaned in and kissed it—close enough for her breasts to briefly brush his chest. He caught his breath but left his right hand down at his side. Her eyes met his and she saw what she needed to see—a silent plea for acceptance. There was none of his usual cockiness. He needed to know that he was okay. That *she* thought he was okay.

She tried not to stare at the stump—rounded flesh below the elbow of his left arm. Again she touched it, explored the feel of the puckered seam across the end. And it slowly dawned on her that this moment was important to both of them—there could be no secrets, no embarrassment, no holding back and not trusting. Literally the symbolism of them both facing each other naked wasn't lost on her.

She put a hand on his erection and quickly looked up to catch the hint of a smile followed by a nod. "It will be easier for me if you sit up—lean against the headboard." If he was surprised, he quickly covered it up and put two pillows against the headboard, sat on the edge of the bed then moved to the right and leaned back.

The jar of Vaseline seemed terribly unromantic but necessary. She was determined that she was going to give this every chance to be successful. The pamphlet insisted lubrication meant the difference between success and failure.

"Need help with that?" He was watching her intently. It was true that other than the fateful time five years ago she'd never even seen a man's penis—erect or otherwise. But, no, she didn't need help. She had to do this. She couldn't fail. This was her second chance.

"No, unless I'm not doing something right?"

"Oh, baby, you're perfect; just keep doing what you're doing."

He'd been circumcised; the hospital had insisted she have the same done to Daniel but she wasn't exactly sure why. Such an odd organ. Certainly not one that she could attribute beauty to—just the power it commanded. It helped if she stayed matter-of-fact, didn't give into the fright that threatened to immobilize her. But wasn't that the problem? Too much thought and not just going with the moment.

She took a breath and met his stare. Then locking her eyes on his, she traced the edge of the head with her index finger. Breaking eye contact, she dipped the finger into the Vaseline. She lightly applied a coating in downward motions around the head itself, stroking it between her thumb and forefinger. Then a thin coating of lubricant on the palm of her hand and she softly grasped the shaft and slipped her hand up and down coating its entirety.

Finally, she rocked back on her knees and surveyed her handiwork before straddling him and slowly lowering herself. She guided the head to just touch her opening and leaned in to kiss him. Feeling him so close, his mouth on hers, she couldn't deny an excitement that was overriding any rational thought—or fear of pain. She wanted him. She pushed downward and took all of him into her. No screaming, no jolting muscle spasms, just an exquisite pleasure that she could have never dreamed possible.

This time her hips moved rhythmically, hypnotically ... automatically. He leaned close and took a nipple into his mouth, sucking gently before tensing and crying out. She leaned forward and buried her face in his chest and didn't even try to stop the tears. She was whole. She could be a partner now and not have any worries.

"Hey, why tears?" He'd tipped her head back.

"I was afraid this wouldn't work and I wanted it to so much—needed it to."

"Oh baby, it works just fine. But now it's your turn." He gently pushed her onto her back and kissed and explored every inch of exposed skin. She felt her body flush warm, then tingle, then a feeling not unlike the exploding of a thousand tiny roman candles coursed through her body in a moment of blinding release. It took her breath away and she clung to him until she could stop trembling.

"I love you." He tucked a strand of hair behind her ear and traced the outline of her lips with his finger. "I've been an ass—thinking you wouldn't want me ... after the war and all. And I wouldn't have blamed you. It was shameful to take the money your mother offered—to pretend that I loved you. It took me awhile to realize I wasn't pretending. I don't want to live without you."

"So, it wouldn't upset you too much to know you're probably still married?"

"What do you mean?"

"I didn't get the papers until after I'd stopped hearing from you. I didn't see a reason to sign them and get them recorded then."

He propped himself up on his elbow and looked down at her and started to laugh. "You know, I think that's just dandy. I'm a married man. A very satisfied, married man. And my wife is the most beautiful woman in the world. Only a fool would be upset with this arrangement."

* * *

Emma May Schuler came kicking and screaming into the world nine months later—June 1, 1947. She was a fussy baby at first—demanding, finicky, prone to colic—but Evy loved her unconditionally from her headful of curly dark hair and long eyelashes to her dimpled knees. And Walt was besotted. He carried her everywhere, reluctantly sharing her with Daniel, her number one baby sitter.

Ella ignored the baby as much as she could but complained about the crying, the loads of wash, the special foods and the extra money it was taking to feed yet another mouth. As Evy pointed out, it was all something that their grandfather had not made a provision for.

But the farm was beginning to flourish again, get back on its feet after the war. With raising so much of their food, it wasn't a strain to support this new family.

Life settled into routine. On the national front—Rosie the Riveter was out of a job; nylons were back on the market; you could buy a set of decent rubber tires, and women were ogling colored kitchen appliances.

On the farm it was baseball, baseball and more baseball.

Walt took Daniel to see major league games whenever he could get away—mostly in Kansas City but once they took the train as far away as Chicago. He volunteered as a scout master and built the troop to twenty-four, ten- and eleven-year-olds. Every single boy that summer worked on a sports badge, which meant each had to be a participating member of a sports team. Of course, the sport of choice was baseball and the highlight of the summer was refurbishing the baseball diamond behind the barn.

Walt, with the help of Clemetts, worked tirelessly to make the area a real event-quality venue—new bleachers, hot dog stand, pillow and chairback rental, cold drinks and concessions. Even Ella made cookies, each wrapped individually and sold them for a nickel each. That summer was bliss.

Somewhere in her life Evy should have learned to be suspect that if things were too quiet, too easy, and without crisis, she should be wary. As her mother would say, "The other shoe is about to drop." And usually that other shoe was a big one.

She and Walt had spent an afternoon in Wichita looking at farm equipment. Two tractors needed replacing and with lunch out, they'd made a day of it. As they turned up the long front drive late that afternoon, they could see two men on the porch—both wearing suits on what was a very hot Kansas day.

Solicitors. Walt guessed their occupation before he'd even brought the car to a full stop. Each man was nursing a glass of iced tea— condensation from the glass having dripped onto impeccably pressed black trousers. So, they'd been there for awhile. Evy got out of the car with Emma sound asleep over her shoulder.

"Can I help you?"

Both men came forward. The taller and older of the two held out his hand. "I'm Nat Isley and this is Willard Cronin. We're with Cronin, Cronin and Myers, Esquires. Miss Everett, I presume?"

"Mrs. Schuler now."

"Ah, yes, of course, our client wasn't aware …"

"Client?"

"Yes, Mr. Edward Galen Everett—your brother. We are solicitors on Mr. Everett's behalf. Would it be possible to find someplace more comfortable to talk?"

"What is this concerning?" She wasn't going to waste time on some frivolous whim of Edward's.

He hadn't been home in a year and hadn't kept in touch. She knew he was living "on the continent" as he liked to say. His Christmas card mentioned touring Germany, France and England—with a friend. Nothing was said about his living arrangements, let alone his "friend." Mission work in Borneo hadn't agreed with him. Evy wondered at the time who had come to that conclusion. It had lasted less than six months. Had he been asked to leave?

Once he had turned twenty-one, Evy made certain his allowance was available. He would be twenty-two in February and eligible for larger sums, only the farm hadn't been able to provide such during the war—they were just now getting back on their feet.

There had been one request for an amount outside the agreed one thousand dollars a month. He had asked for a full ten thousand to be wired immediately—something about a car accident and there had been injuries. Against her better judgment, she did as he asked. That was over nine months ago. What in the world was it this time?

"I'd prefer to preface our discussion with a quick look at the papers I've drawn up. Maybe someplace where we could spread out a bit?"

She handed Emma to Mattie and asked Mr. Isley and Mr. Cronin to follow her to her father's study. Funny, she still called it that—after all the years.

"Ask Walt to join us after he puts the car away." Mattie nodded and took the sleeping Emma into the house.

The room was stuffy and Evy opened two windows in order to get a cross-breeze before sitting on the edge of the couch. Walt joined her and they both waited until Mr. Isley had finished placing various papers in neat stacks on the desk top.

"I'll get right to the point. Young Mr. Everett made a somewhat rash decision recently." He paused to wipe his forehead with a large white handkerchief, which he refolded and placed back in his briefcase. "He lost a rather large wager in a professional game of poker."

"*Professional* game? What does that mean?" Evy was at a loss.

"That only means that he was playing with people who have the wherewithal to collect a debt. These are not people who forgive a large sum of money."

"How much was lost?"

"Two hundred and fifty thousand dollars. And there's another twenty-five thousand in legal fees."

"I don't see what this has to do with us?"

"Mr. Everett used the farm as collateral."

"It's not his to do that with. It belongs to the children and grandchild—the issue of the original owner, my grandfather."

"I understand that but a portion, a percentage, does

belong to him. It's this that he's given up."

"And in plain English?" Walt stood up and took a step forward.

"Now, now, there's no need to overreact here. It simply means that you will have a partner in owning and running the farm. A managing majority, I might add. The will is worded so that the first, direct male offspring will have a bigger share in the farm, hence, this larger interest will simply mean that someone else will be making the decisions."

"Can he do this?" Evy's voice sounded small.

"I assure you he can and has. This is a debt fast becoming past-due. I know you don't want to see harm come to your brother."

Evy bit her tongue. Right about now boiling him in oil would be too kind. "Just how much time do we have?"

"For?"

"Buying out his share. Paying cash for your fees and the gambling debt."

"Well, well … I had no idea that a buy-out would be possible. I drew up papers for joint ownership—"

"I would need a week to access the funds." Evy chose to ignore Walt's look of utter disbelief. He shook his head and started to say something, but she put her hand up to shush him.

"Of course, I'm sure that would not be a problem." Again, looks of skepticism.

"I want some assurance that it wouldn't be and that such an offer would be accepted. I also want Edward bought out of the will. Times have changed; the basic requirements of the will have been met. There was no language in the will about the consequences of buy-outs or sell-outs. I will have our lawyer draw up the appropriate papers representing our side. This money will be Edward's share; he will not be entitled to more. He will always have a home here, but he cannot expect any further monetary supplements. That includes the current allowance he is receiving. There will be no more support. Is that clear?"

"This might be very difficult—"

"I don't believe he thought of us when he was gambling away our very livelihood and family home. He's an adult now. He needs to live with his decisions. He'll manage." She stood, "I'll have Mattie show you out. I want papers outlining my requests in my possession no later than two days from today. We should easily have this wrapped up by a week from Friday."

Walt waited until he heard the front door close. "You've never lied. What do you hope to gain by doing so now?"

"I have something to share."

The tale of the gold ingots found in Da's safe sounded surreal. Sewing them into the lining of the crib's blankets, traveling with all that money across an ocean … And they had been sitting in a safe deposit box in a New York bank for eleven years. Appreciating, she might add. If her knowledge of the market was correct, there might be enough to buy out Ella, too. The farm would then be theirs—Daniel's, Emma's and the two of them.

"Damn, lady, you are something else. And I do think you just saved the day."

"Actually Da did and I believe May. I can't think of anything they'd want more than to safeguard the farm for their son and us. It's been almost thirty years. All the major players are dead now—my grandfather, father and mother … Arthur Lloyd. The church has changed. Can you imagine anyone today trying to put Emma May into a women's religious order? If we did have to go to court, I don't think there would have been a problem overturning the will—not after we've met the original criteria."

* * *

All went according to plan. They made a holiday out of a trip to New York. Daniel, baby Emma, Walt, and Mattie came with her. Daniel was in heaven—a train ride half way across the United States. He was old enough to enjoy the city—museums, ferry rides, a ball game in the biggest park in this country. An autographed ball by Joe DiMaggio. This was a trip he'd never forget.

She converted some of the gold to currency and wired the required amount to the law offices representing Edward. The papers had been in order, and the farm no longer would pass down to the first male heir brought into this world by her mother. There was another two hundred thousand for Ella if she was willing to relinquish her part of the farm, and there was an ample amount left to invest in machinery and upgrades and put away for a rainy day.

Would her mother have approved? Of course not. Had Constance been well, it would have been interesting to see how she would have handled Edward's flagrant misuse of his inheritance—the long sought-after, much revered male heir who didn't give a fig about the farm or his siblings.

Other than a screaming, profanity-laced phone call from Edward, all went quickly and well. Somehow, he assumed that he could gamble away a fifty-one percent interest in the farm, watch it change caretakers and still draw his allowance.

When the screaming had subsided into sobs, it seemed not having a job and a place to live terrified him. Evy calmly pointed out that he should have thought of those things before and hung up.

She only felt relief—Edward had chosen his lot in life. She couldn't pretend to be concerned. Would she offer him a home if he showed up on her doorstep? She'd just have to consider that—if it happened. At the moment the answer was no.

For now, the players left were her family. She even included her sister and felt a burst of pride in a darkly handsome Daniel with smoldering eyes and her own baby Emma, again with the dark good looks that seemed above all else Da's gift to each of them. The caddis man's legacy. And there was a new baby. Just big enough for her to feel the first kick. Her life was complete.

Was that why she was blind-sided? She'd slipped into complacency? She'd asked Ella to join her in the study. Under Ella's definition of fairness, if she had bought out Edward, she should make the same offer to Ella.

She explained the circumstances—the gambling debt, Edward's compromising the farm—and how she'd paid off the debt and bought out Edward's interest. Ella asked the amount and sat back, pursing her lips.

"Tell me again just where this money came from?"

"I didn't tell you the first time."

"Well, maybe you better tell me now. You're looking to give away almost half a million dollars. Money that comes from some hidden account? You sold off my and Edward's stocks? Or something else? Land, perhaps? Did you coerce our poor dear ill mother to sell off land?"

Ella was standing, holding onto the back of a straight-backed chair. "Isn't that *our* money? After you've obviously compromised the farm? I'm seeing a lawyer. I will sue you for what you've done—stealing from family interests—interests tied up by the will of our grandfather."

"No, Ella. Not *our* money. Daniel's money. Money that Daniel's father had set aside for the safe-keeping of his son."

"You expect me to believe that some heathen, some illiterate man from the bush who knocked you up at the age of fifteen, had a half a million dollars?"

"No, I don't. Daniel's father is our father. His mother was our father's second wife." She said it quietly but opened the large manila envelope on the desk and arranged its contents in several neat piles. "I have the birth certificate and marriage license of our father and a May Smythe-Nelson Nutanda Everett, and several pictures."

"Our father *was* married."

"It seemed to slip his mind. He also converted to Catholicism. The money came from his wife's family—the elder Nutanda was a Congolese diplomat—elderly when Daniel was born, patriarch of an extensive rubber plantation that did rather well. I did as I was told and invested the money in Daniel's name. His grandfather was adamant that Daniel have a good life in America. I believe that everyone concerned would agree with how I've handled Daniel's inheritance."

A couple little lies, Evy thought, but it had the ring of truth. She didn't have proof that the gold *hadn't* come from May and her father. Evy watched as Ella walked to the desk and picked up Daniel's birth certificate, then Da and May's wedding picture.

"Were you aware that Mother was planning on taking

Edward and going to stay at the mission for awhile?"

"She told me."

"Did she know?" Ella pointed at the picture of a smiling Da and the beautiful May.

"Yes."

"And that's what killed her." Ella said it matter-of-factly, without feeling. "I secretly felt there was something—something more than your shame."

If Evy had thought that Ella would acknowledge that she had tried to save the family from what would have been a far more dire situation—would even offer a thank you—she would be disappointed. There was no acknowledging that Evy had sacrificed immensely to save reputations.

"Land, as well as investments, were sold in the '30s to save the farm during the Depression and then the drought. You're correct, there wouldn't have been enough liquid assets to bail out Edward. Daniel's inheritance saved us. But I want to offer you the same opportunity. The only thing I ask is that you don't tell Daniel about Da. I want him to be more mature, more able to understand the love a man can have for a woman ... I would like him to think kindly on his parents, to respect them."

"And you don't think it's a little late for that?"

"No, I've grown to forgive my father. I'd like to think you could, too."

"My mother married beneath herself. This is the result. I've always been relieved that I don't look like him." Ella toyed with a button on her blouse. "Suppose I take you up on your offer and relinquish my part of the farm—whatever I would have inherited—but want to stay on here?"

Evy tried not to show her surprise. "I don't have a

problem with that. This is your home."

* * *

Life was strained with Ella living there. She simply wasn't any help with the children. Harry Wayne Schuler was a big baby—healthy and robust. The apple of his father's eye. But with two babies in diapers, any help was appreciated—even if Ella still seemed to think the kitchen was her domain, Evy thought a little help with the laundry wasn't asking too much. But her pleading fell on deaf ears.

There were no servants now. Only Mattie and Clemetts, and they were slowing down. Even one-armed, Walt did the bulk of the work in the fields, hiring help as needed. So it was her turn. She needed an extra set of hands.

When the church bulletin printed a plea for foster families to take in young women from other countries so that they could pursue their education in the United States in exchange for light housework, she showed the article to Walt.

"It would be perfect. We have the room."

"I'm not keen on it but I would like you to have help."

"What could possibly go wrong? I'm sure the church checks the girls very carefully."

"I guess we'll see, won't we?"

Part Three

DANIEL (1950-1960)

CHAPTER FIFTEEN

I was fourteen before I found out my mother was really my half-sister, her sister was another half-sister, and the old woman who died was no relative at all. There was even a half-brother, but he was gone—lived someplace else. I was happy about having a family. Sort of.

But I had a father I'd never know and a mother who would never know me. My parents were dead. My father died after a number of deceits and my mother at my birth. I'd been cheated. Knowing them seemed so important. Would they have liked me? Would they have been proud? Would I have had other brothers and sisters?

There would never be any knowing now. I felt alone. But strangely enough I had a heritage and that was comforting. I wasn't just a mixed-race kid in America—an outcast in a small rural town—a kid everyone could bully because I was different and black.

The man I now know was my father had been an itinerant salesman. A caddis man. Riding the rails and scamming the unsuspecting—at least that was the town gossip. Now, the whispers, the insults they called me—nigger, scum—it was bastard *that hurt the worst. But nobody called me names when I played baseball. I wanted to play in the professional leagues—Sam Jethroe had just joined the Boston Braves. It was happening. Men of color were becoming heroes. Cheered on by people who heretofore thought they were only good enough to collect garbage or dig ditches.*

You can imagine what it was like to find that I came from a line of warriors and statesmen—leaders in my country. Yes, my country. My mother's gift to me. I rose above the pettiness of the small town, my now home.

I wasn't just different any more—I was better! And it wasn't just on a baseball diamond. I felt a pull to go back to my real origins, the place where I was born. My real home. But in all truthfulness? I needed to leave because of what happened.

There could be no staying after the threats, the name-calling, the bitterness. And maybe I could plead being too young, too stupid to have understood the consequences—how smart can a sixteen-year-old be with raging hormones and temptation under his nose?

* * *

The days were lazy, simmering from dawn to well past dusk in torpidity with air that was heavy, not oppressive but dead-still, filled with moisture and the scents of honeysuckle and climbing roses. Each day a hot, muggy testament to the Midwest's extreme seasons.

Edges of lawns were overripe with drooping heads of seeding grasses readying for the release of next year's cover crop of unwanted vagrants. Fields would soon be filled with the stubble of harvest. Long days in the hot July sun harvesting wheat. But the work was never done. The fields would need to be turned under; the ground leveled in preparation for the fall planting. Farming. Hard work … a hard way of life.

Yet, the verdant lushness languished that late June—a portent of things to come? A summer that would prolong itself—dog days promising to slip into Indian summer and Inge hesitated, her spirit and very being hung suspended, mind and body sucked into a lassitude that seemed almost an illness. To bend an arm, to wave, took an energy she couldn't summon, call upon to follow through her bidding. "The calm before the storm." Where had she heard that? It did seem apt. There was a certain waiting quality to her life.

She would turn eighteen on Monday, already old without a future. A high school diploma handed out to one in a long black line of gowned recipients was tacked on the wall of her attic bedroom. But there were no prospects, no young men driving by, honking for her to run out and go for a ride.

But they were so silly. Would she have wanted one had they stopped? She didn't think so. And college was out of the question. How could she be so certain? Simple. It was 1952. Girls were beginning to go on to school, but not that many. Still, to be a teacher she needed two years after high school. Her grades were good. She could qualify as an exchange student. She wished her parents in Germany didn't expect her to find a husband in this new country. And if she didn't, they would send for her. Was she already running out of time?

She watched the haze of early morning burn off of the fields. A canopy of condensation held hovering before it vanished, dissipated by a relentless sun. She pushed the swing outward and back, lulled by the steady to-and-fro. There was not one thing as far as her eye could see that belonged to her—not one section of fence, not one barn, not one living being. If a plant could prosper without roots, then that was what she was doing.

And prosper wasn't really the right word.

"Inge?" The voice rang out from the kitchen.

Oddly, Ella gave her name a drawn-out, two syllable twist that accented the last, lifting the *uh* sound to an aspirated grunt. Inge pushed off of the swing and walked barefoot across the porch. All the downstairs rooms opened onto that big wide, wrap-around white wooden circle—kitchen, living room, formal dining area, the small music cubicle at the corner with a turret, which was now a sewing room littered with quilt pieces. All rooms she had to dust and keep tidy. Only the study was at the back and not open to the porch. But it was kept locked and didn't need her attention.

The bedrooms were upstairs, four in all, with dormers and an attic. One long room held three beds and had been a sort of nursery, she thought. The top of the house was her room—the attic. A bed beside the only window, a desk, and bookshelves. The radio was her prized possession, a graduation present. She shared a bathroom but that was all right. The house had been built in the 1800s, maybe more modern than most older Victorians because it had two bathrooms, both added later. One up and one down. Just more to clean.

And changing the linens on the porch beds was her job, too—a part of the porch off the kitchen, screened-in along the back of the house to catch the breezes from the south and west, doubled as a sleeping porch when the heat-laden upstairs rooms were deathly still and sickeningly humid.

Daniel slept on the porch now. And it wouldn't have been thought correct for her to join him, no matter how hot her room became. Sometimes she would creep out her window and lie on the roof tiles. Spread-eagled on her back to let every part of her body enjoy a breeze. Only her fear of heights kept her from sleeping out there. To have shared the sleeping porch would have been heaven, but to join a sixteen-year-old who already stared holes in her chest as it was? No, that was not possible.

She opened the screen door and didn't try to stop it as it banged shut behind her, automatically catching on the rubber stopper on the door's wooden frame. Her bare feet squeaked across the shiny linoleum—the product of two hours' work yesterday afternoon.

Ella clucked her disapproval. "I'd like to think you'd want to earn your keep. That you wouldn't take constant reminding." Ella barely turned from the sink, overflowing with the tops of muddy onions, and simply spoke above the running tap. "God's mercy allowed you to come to this house. Not one other thing. I've thought of telling Mr. Schuler to make other arrangements. I don't think he thought he'd put a roof over the head of someone so slothful as to be absolutely worthless to me."

Inge didn't comment. None was expected. She'd been brought over as an exchange student to help Mrs. Schuler with the two babies. Help at the house and go to school. Constantly being yelled at by this strange woman hadn't been part of the bargain. Nor had working in the kitchen.

Yet, Ella was a presence and usually got her way. Not with bulk or bullying but with an assumed authority that was underlined by the starched stiffness of her apron over the cotton, much-washed softness of a print dress. Her no-nonsense oxfords, white for summer, black for winter, resoled each year in that pair's off season never carried a smudge or even dust. Tidiness was an obsession.

Ella was somewhere in her early thirties, but had looked the same at fifteen, Inge was certain ... thin, gaunt, non-descript with stringy, blond hair pulled back away from her face and braided to form a coil at her neck. A mole, dark reddish-brown, situated exactly in the crease of where the corner of her nose met the slope of her upper lip. Everything about her screamed "spinster" and there were no men. No one called.

"There's enough work here for ten of us. It's bad enough when my sister's husband lets that boy run wild." Ella stopped topping the onions, dried her hands and walked to the pantry. "I never agreed with that. Unsupervised play. It's time for work. He's not too young. Lots of young men work in filling stations or deliver papers at his age. All this baseball. False hopes, that's what I call it. Making that poor darkie think he could play professionally."

She returned with a heavy blue crock bowl and set it on the sideboard next to two-dozen hardboiled eggs. "I need those eggs peeled and chopped, Inge. Then change the beds on the porch."

It was never necessary to answer Ella. Answers weren't what her world was all about. Obsequious to Mr. Schuler and a tyrant in her own domain, she didn't need the opinions of others that she considered beneath her. So she would talk, going on and on, oblivious of her audience, but yet demanding her due—someone to listen. It was Ella's own little drama, acted out in quiet desperation in a sunny kitchen with a single person in her audience.

As much as she would allow herself, there were theatrics, a knowing look when she settled into the gossip of the day. A death or a marriage brought the appropriate sounds of approval or dismay. The daughter of a prominent family ran off with a Mexican—a man working in the railroad yards. It just about ruined the girl's mother. Lines weren't meant to be crossed. God would punish those who did.

Inge didn't mind the stories about people she'd never meet. She'd listen. More and more Ella's verbal wanderings included the past, when she and the boy's mother grew up on the farm, this farm.

"My mother was raised with servants but I can't imagine her lazing around half the day." Her eyes darted to the sleeping porch, then back—a reminder that Inge had work left to do. "Her father married at a young age, not much older than you are. Married, took over a five hundred acre farm and built this house."

"When he was eighteen?" Inge's w's had that unmistakable v-sound of the foreigner. But the accent was muted, not nearly so pronounced as it had been two years ago. A stack of Berlitz records, 78s, resided in boxes under her bed. Some of the grooves worn smooth enough to skate the phonograph needle across a half inch of slate.

"Boys matured in those days. Became men when they had to. Look at the War. No, my grandfather was not quite twenty-one when he married. Older than a lot of his friends."

"And he went to war?"

"No, silly girl, your people hadn't started any when he was young. No, both of my grandparents died just after we entered the Great War."

Inge tuned out. The Great War, the Only War—and then there had been another, number two great war—another world war ... both involving her ancestors. Even when she'd gotten her diploma, two classmates had hissed "Kraut" when she walked across the stage. The girl next to her whispered, "murderer."

CHAPTER SIXTEEN

Did your mother make the appointment to see me?" The man behind the desk peered through pince-nez at the paperwork in front of him. At least that's what Daniel thought they were called. Some sort of fold-out glasses on a stick. The man flipped them open to read. And he was old; they looked natural, like they belonged and didn't appear to be an affectation.

"My mother is dead. My sister—that is, half-sister—phoned."

"And your father?"

"Dead. I live with my half-sister and her husband and their two children."

"A copy of your high school transcript shows all A's. Very good grades—very high GPA. And you've been offered several sports scholarships? Baseball, isn't it?"

Daniel nodded. The man behind the desk continued to leaf through the papers in front of him.

"My high school took the state championship this year."

"I see. You are a pitcher?"

"And I've played some first base." Daniel waited. Did he expect him to say more?

"I see." More peering at notes, then a glance up. "Let us start then with why you think you are here. Why would your half-sister have made an appointment?"

"Because of the incident. Because my seeing you is court-ordered. I have to be evaluated."

"Yes, I see that here. And what was this incident?"

"Inge's death. Was it a suicide or … something else? There's an investigation."

"Inge?"

"The exchange student who lived with us."

More shuffling of papers. "Why don't you tell me about this Inge?" An almost smile, closed-lips, barely showing the tips of yellow teeth before the doctor leaned against the back of his chair. "Breathe deeply. Relax. We are not here to judge, but to listen. When you are ready."

Daniel took a deep breath. "You know how an event can make an impact? Color all else for the rest of your life? No matter what comes or goes, you know … rather you remember exactly where you were standing, what you were saying, the color of the sky …?"

His lankiness spilled over the straight-backed chair; he needed to tilt it backward to rest on two legs just to have room to stretch out. He'd inherited his father's sultry, good looks, but he'd shot up this last year to over six foot. He'd inherited the tall, willowy frame of his grandfather. Evy showed him pictures of this African family. Even he, trying to be objective, could see his mother's head-turning beauty.

He was a composite but now he had to prove himself. He had to clear his name, appear sane and level-headed in front of this doctor. So, there was no mistaking his earnestness, the urgency in his voice, hands leaving his lap to punctuate a shrug, belie a nervousness that couldn't be hidden. Daniel wasn't comfortable and so much was riding on his answers.

"Go on."

"That's how it was last summer. Only it wasn't just one thing. It wasn't like 'Where were you when the war ended?' That's one event, one day; it was more, it was like the whole summer ..."

A pause, some self-conscious picking at a loose thread escaping around a button-hole. The tie, which seemed an afterthought, Evy's idea, flung on, knotted haphazardly, was pushed aside ... a wry, absent smile. "You could say that summer grabbed my life and threw it away ... laughed even ..."

"Who laughed?" A creak of the chair as the doctor leaned forward, upper torso on elbows rooted solidly across from him on the desk's blotter, hands clasped, a calculated move showing rapt attention, directly in front of him, but Daniel hardly noticed.

"Doesn't matter. It's the 'why' I need your help with. Why did it happen? So much was going on. If we had known that Ella had a brain tumor ... could we have turned things around? Stopped the chain reaction of events? But what if they were unrelated? Something predestined, out of anyone's control?"

"Is that what you believe?"

More fiddling with the fractious buttonhole, then Daniel shrugged.

"Do you know one of the last things I remember her saying to me?"

"Who was this?"

"Ella, my half-sister. The old maid."

"And what did she say?"

"I'd run home for lunch when there was a break in ball practice. I slammed the screen door coming in, accidentally, but nobody noticed. That was odd because that usually brought Ella's fury. I walked over to the table. My uncle was already seated, so was Evy—she's the one who raised me—and their two children. I asked Ella if my friend, Joey, could eat with us. God, I can still remember, no, *feel* her fury. She whirled on me and actually sprayed spit all over trying to get the words out."

"Do you remember what she said?"

"'I won't have cat-lickers at my table.' Just like that. It was a term I didn't know so I stood there dumbfounded. Visions of Joey leaping the Spirea to chase his old mangy Persian down the alley … maybe corner it against the garage for a quick once over with his tongue … well, that brought me to my knees giggling."

"Then what happened?"

"She struck me. The palm of her hand against the side of my head with enough force to send me sprawling sideways into the table. 'You will not make light of heathens in my house.' That's what she said."

"What was your uncle's reaction?"

"Walt was the one who jumped up, grabbed her arm, threatened her, told her that if she ever did that again, he'd break it. Then he just righted the salt shaker and threw a pinch over his left shoulder."

"Was that a superstition?"

"I suppose so. I never thought of it, but that fits. Just in case, never take a chance."

"Ella lived with you?"

"Yes. She'd moved in with us sometime back. It wasn't her house—not any more hers than the rest of us. She was the eldest of my father's five children. Her twin died as a child, her brother had left home a couple years earlier, Evy was the younger—but I was the one she hated. I was proof of her father's infidelities. So, it was her God-fearing duty, or so she saw it that way, to keep the family together. Give them moral strength because her father had failed to do so."

"She was religious?"

"Mennonite. Strict. Old World narrow."

"But your family wasn't Mennonite? Or isn't now?"

"No, not any more. They were, or pretended to be, before. My father went to Africa for the church—missions in the Congo. But, I guess, he converted to Catholicism before I was born. My father and mother were married by a Catholic priest—my father married while still being married to Ella's mother."

"I see. Her own father ... So Ella would have had strong feelings about Catholics? That, perhaps, was behind her striking you for wanting to bring your Catholic friend home?"

"Maybe. But she did crazy, demanding things all the time."

"Things like?"

"Stripping all the upstairs beds and throwing towels and bedding and rugs down the stairs to lie in a heap. Said she was getting eaten alive by bugs … maybe bed bugs or fleas. Then she threw everything out of the freezer."

"Why?"

"Said she knew that some of the packages contained road kill that the "R" marked with a grease pen didn't mean 'roast.'"

"And this odd behavior was the first indication that something was wrong?"

More reading of the notes in front of him. "You didn't, in fact, know that this Ella, was dying?"

"No. She didn't die until October."

"And this was …?"

"Early summer. She had always been one of those pinched-faced, severe sorts—punitive instead of caring. It was difficult to say when her personality changed … and then, maybe, I wouldn't have noticed anyway."

"Do you think your uncle noticed?"

"If he did, he wouldn't have said anything. Quiet suffering was something I was raised to aspire to, a part of manliness—even godliness. He was a wounded war vet. Stoic. He even lost an arm."

"That could greatly impact a man's outlook on life, wouldn't you say?"

Daniel shrugged.

"What was your sister's reaction?"

"She's the one who took Ella to a specialist."

A pause, the turning of a page. "Let's move on. You said there was more than one event that summer?"

"Yes."

"We have time to talk about another one today. You can stretch, walk around if you like."

Daniel unfolded his length from the chair and stood.

If he'd hoped they were about finished, he didn't say anything. The air in the room was close and smelled of aftershave, light and tangy with a clean hint of citrus, odd coming from the old man behind the desk. He would have more expected a strong odor of mothballs.

Daniel stretched, walked to a window and leaned against the casement. The fourth story office overlooked a park. The tops of sycamore and locust and mulberry rolled with the wind of the early afternoon in an ocean of green. It was quieting. Soothing to just stand there and watch.

"Take your time. You've earned a break." That thin-lipped smile again.

Daniel turned back. "About a month later … It was late morning. I was still in bed with a summer cold. One of those that settles on the chest and makes you wheeze when you talk. Emma, my five-year-old niece, would try to get me to whistle because I sounded like bellows. Anyway, after I got up, I poured a glass of milk and went out on the porch to sit in the swing. And I was just sitting there, rocking, thinking how pissed I was to be missing ball practice … and fishing."

"And Ella by now was ill? But was still at home?"

"Yes. We didn't know how sick she was. Signs of the illness came and went. Evy knew. But it was still a secret from the rest of us." Daniel paused.

"Go on."

A deep breath. "Our house was about three blocks from the creek and Joey had tried to get me to go fishing that morning but I wasn't up for it. So I just sat rocking and thinking and when old Mrs. Bayliss ran up the walk yelling 'Come quick, there's been an accident at the swimming hole,' my first thought was Joey.

"I knew it was something to do with Joey before I ever left the porch. He hated the water—only went because he loved to fish. I got up running, barefoot, no shirt, just flew off that porch and ran those three blocks ..." Daniel took another deep breath, turned back to the window and again watched the pitch and ripple of the green below him. A dog, unattended, had wandered onto the lawn and was busy marking his territory before trotting down the street.

"What did you find?"

Gentle urging. The voice was kind. Another deep breath. Daniel ran his hand through his hair, fingers stiff, slightly curved to glide across a temple, and pushed the dark brown hair up and over his ears. He spoke without turning around.

"Joey had gone fishing with two other kids. I think he'd have rather gone with me but anyone would do. He lived to fish. I saw them standing on the edge of the place where we went swimming, just screaming that he was in there, screaming and pointing to the deepest part under the bridge ..."

"What did you do?"

"I don't think I stopped running. I just saw those kids and ran right past them into the water. I dove and surfaced and dove, but the water was murky, too much sediment. The silt was awful, got between your toes; you sank in it— couldn't open your eyes underwater, it got stirred up so bad. I was the best swimmer of any of our friends but I never even touched him. I broke the surface and went into a coughing spasm. I'd taken in water and couldn't get my breath and I couldn't get my footing."

"You were, in effect, drowning, too?"

There was a nod as he let the quiet settle around them.

Drops of rain hit the window, comingled and slid into tiny streams that branched, then slipped silently over the bricked ledge to disappear. The room had gotten dark.

Then softly, "I felt her arms come around me, from the back, keeping me from flailing, pulling me toward shore with long, strong strokes." His voice was quiet, halting, as if the memory was being tugged from him. "When we got to the shallows, she left me to go back in. I crawled up the bank and laid in the grass and watched. It took her maybe ten minutes to find Joey. She brought him in, too, just like me but he wasn't struggling, wasn't moving at all. And then I realized something incredible. She was naked. I guess not entirely, but she had taken her dress off and her slip was molded to her body and she didn't have on any underwear, no bra or panties, just this short slip that showed every curve, her pubic hair, just a dark mound between her legs ... nipples pushing against the fabric..."

"Who was this woman?"

"The exchange student who lived with us, Inge."

"What happened next?"

"The fire department came. They worked over Joey until I wanted to scream that it was no use. I knew he wouldn't come back. His father was there. Someone had called him at work." A glance at the man behind the desk, then a drop of the chin. "I saw his father cry."

"What were you doing?"

"She came to sit by me. She was so beautiful. Blond, large-boned but not fat. She could have been a model, I think, but everything about her exuded strength and life ... that's why ... that's why ..." He swallowed. "... it's so hard now." Daniel stopped, took a breath. "She had thick hair past the middle of her back, tied at the neck, hands as big

as mine with long tapered fingers. She played the piano."
He glanced up as if this last had special significance. The
man behind the desk waited but Daniel didn't go on.

"So this Inge—"

"Actually, Summer, she wanted us to call her 'Summer.'
Anyway, she put her arm around me and hugged me close
and all I could think about were her breasts, right there
under my chin, a naked leg next to mine ..."

"This happened last summer so you were sixteen?"

"Almost seventeen."

"And this woman, the student?"

"Eighteen. I couldn't move because I was getting a
hard-on. My best friend was lying dead not twenty feet
away, and I couldn't keep thoughts of sex out of my mind.
Was that some sort of cover-up for not facing what had
really happened? Do you think that could be a part of the
problem now? Why we got in trouble?" Agitation leaked
into his voice. Wasn't this why he was here?

"We'll see. Go on."

"I couldn't stand to see his father cry. Joey was the
oldest. He was his father's favorite. That night, the night
of the drowning, was the first night we slept together."

"You and Inge, or Summer?"

"Yes. I slept on the porch in the summer and she
sneaked down. We made love. Do you think I did it to
forget?"

"Did it work?"

"Yes and no."

CHAPTER SEVENTEEN

Inge wadded the letter but didn't throw it away. She put the other mail on the hall table and walked back out onto the porch. It was what she feared, but also what she expected. Her parents were demanding her return to the small town outside Frankfurt where she grew up. Home, but not the home she wanted.

Now, she had seen the world. And she was educated but without prospects. There had been no scholarships, and the church had awarded their two stipends to young men from Kenya. It was time to return home. The last straw? Her mother hinted of a "match" back home. A family friend had lost his wife and needed a caretaker for his growing family—and someone to help in his butcher business.

In her mother's no-nonsense way, she had ended, "You could do worse. You would make your family proud. I will send money for a ticket."

But maybe, just maybe she could do better. She wouldn't be the first to trick a man—well, a young one in this case—into marrying. She would get pregnant. He would have to marry her. She would live in this country and the baby would be a citizen.

They could live here on the farm. It could be her home, too. Ella would have to show her deference—she would be family. She would have money. There would be no punitive father who would take a strap to her for wearing lipstick and call her 'whore.' And a mother who pretended she didn't see.

The more she thought about it, the more the plan seemed to be the right one. Fool-proof. Her ticket to, if not riches, then stability and she wouldn't have to scrub down blood-stained counters and floors, or scrape offal off the utensils. And she would never have to see her father again.

What she was doing didn't seem wrong. She cared for Daniel. She didn't have a hang-up like others just because he was a negro. She would not be able to go to school but that was not as important as having a home and staying in this country. Daniel could help his uncle. Mr. Walt needed good help. The family would thank her.

She wrote back to her mother, saying that because of the harvest next month she would not be able to return home until late August. Would that be enough time? Yes, if God willed it.

She knew from being raised on a farm that animals that were free to breed on their own, as many times as nature dictated, became impregnated quicker, with stronger calves and foals. Or so it seemed. Certainly on the farm artificial insemination was at best iffy and carried no guarantees. Only a few practiced it.

No, she must couple with Daniel as many times for as many days as she could. Only then would success be guaranteed.

There was only one tiny obstacle. After that first night, Daniel had started wearing condoms. As far as she could tell, there was always a rolled-up Trojan in his billfold. But one morning while changing the sheets on the porch bed, she found the entire package securely tucked between mattress and box spring. Twenty-five altogether. Would a tiny imperceptible pinprick to each one be enough?

* * *

Evy cleaned up the broken tea cup and saucer. Ella's tantrums were coming on with some regularity now. The X-ray of her brain showed the tumor to be inoperable. A twisted mass hugging the brain stem with tendrils poking outward into areas that governed personality and motor control. Her temper was dangerous but Evy was adamant. She would not put her in a home.

She would enlist Inge's help, write to her mother and ask to have her stay. She even offered to pay for beginning college courses at the Mennonite college in town. And of course, she would pay Inge a salary. Perhaps she shouldn't have mentioned the salary. Evy had the distinct feeling that Inge's parents would demand the money be sent home.

When Evy approached Inge with the offer, her reaction seemed hesitant. She accepted but there was no excited thank you, no ready eagerness to stay. Perhaps, the child wanted to go home? But when questioned, Inge seemed adamant that she did not.

So, did she think nursing Ella would be a burden … an unpleasant one? Yes, but she was willing to help. So, what was it? Evy was left in the dark. Inge was not going to divulge more. But she had the help she would need, and Evy put it out of her mind. Maybe it had only been her imagination.

* * *

Yes, yes, yes. She had missed her period last month and there had not been one this month. She was pregnant. She knew it. But Evy had offered her a job—a paying job. And a way to go to school. She only had to help with Ella. If she'd known, she wouldn't have had to trick Daniel … she wouldn't have to tell him he had to marry her. She wouldn't be having a baby out of deceit and manipulation.

That night she suggested a swim. It didn't take a second invitation—the evening was stifling. Late July and the oppressive weather had simply settled over the land—a perfect blanket of heat lifted occasionally by an afternoon shower, but even those respites were fewer and farther between.

The harvest had been successful and the farm seemed to take a collective deep breath before fall preparation of the fields would begin. If there were any lazy days on a working farm, these would qualify.

The creek at the edge of the property had been dammed up to hold water—part of a new irrigation system put in last year. It wasn't deep, maybe only six feet in the middle, but it was cool and refreshing, the water kept clear with a rock bottom. They dove and splashed water on each other and, finally spent from the horseplay, both crawled onto the dock. Daniel flopped out full length on his back, arms above his head, fingers laced together making a pillow.

"You are quiet." Inge sat beside him.

"I leave in two weeks."

"Leave to where?" Inge felt a coldness and she shivered.

"College. Early because of baseball tryouts."

"Where is this?

"California."

"I will come with you."

"Inge, after Ella dies, you'll be going home."

"You and me, we have—"

"Nothing. A summer of fun. That's all."

"And a baby." Silence. She stared out over the water. And waited.

Daniel propped himself up on one elbow then pushed to a sitting position, leaned over, took her chin in his hand and turned her face toward him. His voice was deadly calm. "No, that can't happen. I've been careful. I don't appreciate lies. If you want to stay in this country, figure out another way to do it instead of trying to ruin my life by tricking me."

"It's true. I don't lie."

"Then I'll pay for the abortion."

"Abortion? Never. My religion, my God, would never permit ..." She pulled away and stood.

"So, what are you going to do?"

"We have to get married."

"Oh no, we do not. We don't love each other."

"I love you."

"And I don't love you." Daniel stood now, too, started to say something, anger showing in a clenched jaw. Then thinking better of it, he dove into the water and in strong strokes, reached the bank and didn't turn back. He slipped on his jeans and tennis shoes, gathered up a towel and strode off toward the house.

Inge could hear the loud voices even before she reached the porch. Daniel and Walt. Had he told his uncle? It would seem so. She crept around to the dining room window and slipped to the porch floor. A perfect vantage point.

"Stupid. You ever hear of protection?"

"Yeah, and I took precautions."

"Well, if she's telling the truth, it wasn't enough. I can't believe that you'd throw away college, a baseball scholarship for a piece of ass … Do you know how many boys would envy your position? Give just about anything to have the chances you've been given?"

"I haven't thrown away college. How will this affect my going?"

"Because you'll do the right thing. You'll stay here and support your family whether you like it or not. I won't have any part of someone in this house shirking his duty. I'll tell you this. You'll lose your scholarship. A young man with a family isn't the kind of freshman they're looking to recruit into college today. You'll be on that baby's birth certificate and you'll never be able to get away."

"You're not my father. You aren't any relative. You can't tell me what to do."

"I agree." Inge peeked around the casement to see Evy enter the room. "I wouldn't take direction from someone who accepted money to marry a girl with a baby, only to make promises that he never intended to keep. Took off at the first opportunity. How is this that much different?"

"I'm here now, aren't I?"

"That's not the point. We're talking about when you were just a couple years older than Daniel. Were you all hot to take on responsibility? Or was money the motivator?"

"I was in love with you."

"Oh? It took you five years to figure that out."

"This is no place to talk about our life."

"Really? I think it's a perfect place. I will not stand by and let you attack him just because he won't be able to fulfill *your* dream ... yes, your dream. Daniel is a terrific athlete but be honest with yourself, baseball was going to be *your* life. Until that." Evy gestured toward his amputation. "You can't live through him. You have to let him decide for himself. I will never force someone to marry against his will—baby or not. Two people have to be in love. It wouldn't be fair to anyone—least of all a child."

Inge sat back. What was she saying? That she wouldn't make Daniel marry her? That the baby wouldn't have a father? Would they send her home? Her father would kill her. He would, at the very least, throw her out. No, no, no. This could not be happening.

She was shaking but pulled herself up to lean against the porch wall. *Think.* She needed to think. She opened the front door and walked across the foyer, then up the stairs. Even when Daniel called out, she didn't stop until she reached her room, slammed the door shut and turned the dead bolt. But he pounded on her door, demanded that she open it. It would only be minutes before he'd get a key from the hall closet. She hesitated then ran to the window and stepped out onto the slate roof just as she heard the key turn in the lock.

She couldn't talk to him. She wouldn't. What was there to say? He was demanding she come back in, talk to him.

He was holding out his hand, stepping through the window trying to grab her. She backed away, screamed at him to let her go as his hands clasped her arms. She twisted, putting all her weight into pulling back.

To Walt and Evy in the dining room, it sounded like a sack of flour had been tossed off the roof to careen over the edge of the second story, breaking the gutter and several branches of the sycamore. She wasn't breathing when they rushed outside to see her broken body crumpled on the steps. Walt checked for a pulse and administered CPR. But neither one of them held out hope. Evy rushed back inside to the hall phone and dialed the police and asked them to send an ambulance. Then she looked up to see Daniel just standing at the bottom of the stairs.

CHAPTER EIGHTEEN

The police took Daniel in for questioning. They told Evy and Walt that they wouldn't book him unless they thought they had something—a reason to do so. They assured her they would get to the bottom of things. If it was manslaughter and not murder, well, that too, would be dealt with. Evy was beside herself and insisted on following the police to the station.

For all intents and purposes, Daniel seemed in shock. He answered questions but only in a monotone while staring at the floor. The police seemed to have already judged him—last to see the victim, both on the roof, fighting … Yet, Evy couldn't help but wonder if Daniel were white and not one of a handful of negroes in a small, Midwest town, would they handle things differently? She thought so.

Inge had lost the baby due to the fall, and her condition was apparent to the emergency room medical team. Armed with motive, the police were relentless.

Daniel was adamant—he reached for her, she pulled away and fell. Over and over. That was his answer. Was he getting married? No. Was the child his? Yes. Was he prepared to provide for it? Yes. How? Money from his trust. Was she going to be sent home? No idea. Or was she going to stay on at his sister's house? No idea. Would he have gotten a scholarship if he were married? Don't know because he wouldn't have been. Did being cornered like that make him angry? No, because he didn't feel cornered. Had he worried about her trying to trick him into marriage? No. Did he think of himself as honest and upstanding—a good citizen? Of course. Did upstanding, honest young men take advantage of young girls?

He countered, did young girls take advantage of young men? That answer made them angry. They took another tactic. What kind of grades did he make? All A's. So, he thought he was better than everyone else? No. Did someone help him in school—'cause he was from Africa. No. Was he sure about that? Yeah, he was sure.

Would he agree to see someone who could attest to his being of sound mind? A professional who would be able to tell if he were lying. Maybe take a polygraph test? Yes. He would welcome it.

* * *

"And so, here you are."

"Yes." Daniel sat back down in the chair across from the doctor.

"What do you think should happen now?"

"I want to go home."

"You will. All in good time; our session is almost over."

"No, not my home here; my home in Africa. My mother's home—where my parents died."

"And your scholarships here? To play ball?"

"Three have been rescinded."

"You passed the polygraph. You are not charged, and with my recommendation all this will be put to rest."

"I think the greater crime was a man of color getting a white girl pregnant. The newspapers weren't kind."

The doctor just nodded. "This will not be the only time in your life that you will encounter narrow minds."

"I want to live where there aren't so many."

* * *

Evy had talked it over with Walt. Daniel's preoccupation with his birth parents seemed over the top—a fixation, obsession, actually—and she wasn't sure it was healthy. Couldn't it mean just more disappointment?

At eighteen he seemed to be pulling away from her and Walt and six-year-old Emma, and her baby brother— from his current family. His only family. They would be able to live down the Inge tragedy. Their lawyer settled for a discreet amount with her parents. They shouldn't hear any more. And people's attention span was notoriously short—who would remember in a few years?

But Daniel didn't seem to hear any of this. He'd come to her about how he could find members of his *real* family. He hadn't meant to hurt her feelings and was beside himself when she burst into tears. She had never told him about how she'd put her own life on hold to give him one—to save him needless ridicule and anger. To protect him from her mother. At sixteen she was willing to sacrifice to make certain he had a share of what was owed to him as Da's child—only, at the time, no one could know the truth.

She'd tried to explain why she'd needed to appear as his mother and not be honest about really being his half-sister. Didn't he understand? Didn't he know the cost? How could she give him up? Send him to strangers? People who had disowned his grandmother and never, as far as she knew, ever even met his mother. Why did he expect to be any different? Be met with any less animosity and hatred?

Daniel had no comeback. He just kept saying that he needed to connect—to find out who he was. She gave up trying to talk him out of searching for May's family. But Evy wasn't of much help. She felt that his grandfather was dead—his mother's father. He was elderly and ill when Daniel was born. And the Smythe-Nelsons? English, but where in England? She had no idea, only that they had disinherited their daughter when she had married Nutanda. Would there be a record of the marriage or the fact that May's mother died in childbirth? Were any of these people still alive?

Daniel was tenacious. He held out hope that there might have been children by another marriage on his grandfather's side, giving Daniel more half-brothers and -sisters. Or maybe his mother's mother or father had brothers or sisters, leaving him with uncles or aunts? Evy honestly had to admit she was curious but didn't want Daniel to be hurt if his inquiries fell on deaf ears.

"I guess I wouldn't want you to give up baseball." Walt joined in the dinner conversation one night. A night like a hundred others. More and more, discussion centered around Daniel's quest for these people who seemed to be the ghosts in the room. The ghosts in his life. "You're good enough to go pro now. You don't need college. In fact, the longer you put the big leagues off, the more opportunity there is for you to get hurt … an injury could ruin your chances for all time."

"I know that." As always, supper was strained. Usually an evening meal meant Daniel wolfing down his food and bolting for the door before he might have to face any scrutiny. "But I think I know how to find these people."

"How's that?" Evy was curious.

"The new church minister is going to help. He thinks the Catholic Church in the region has kept pretty good records. They easily go back eighteen years. He's sent some letters on my behalf."

"What does he hope to find? Records of what?" Evy brought the coffee pot to the table and placed it on a trivet before sitting down. This was the first she'd heard of any help. She was more than vaguely upset that he hadn't confided in her.

"New members, baptisms, births and deaths. If my father joined the church as an adult, he would have had to have been baptized. There's no record that he was baptized in the Mennonite Church here. Certainly my mother was baptized there as a baby and there would be a record of her mother's death. And probably addresses, names of towns, at least."

"Perhaps." Would this just be more disappointment, Evy wondered.

Walt pushed back from the table. "I've written letters, made some calls. I wanted this to be a surprise but you'll be contacted by two scouts. What are you going to do about them? They're going to want to set up tryouts. Are you just going to walk away?"

Evy put a hand on Walt's arm but he stepped out of reach. This had become a major rift between them.

"Maybe." The belligerent edge was unmistakable. Emma asked to leave the room. Evy motioned for one of the girls in the kitchen to take Harry Wayne, too. "I appreciate your help but I never asked for it."

"What will you do when you find these people? People, who in eighteen years haven't bothered to find you." Walt had a point but Evy hated to see the hurt on Daniel's face.

"Maybe they don't know I exist." Defiance … challenging the living and the ghosts. Did her father ever imagine this for his son? Of course not. How very like Da Daniel was—alike in looks, alike in tenacity—the need to get his way.

"I have to try. Can't you understand that?"

"Okay, I'll make a deal." Evy looked over at Walt. They hadn't discussed any deals. "Give me this next year. Nine months. That's all I'm asking. Go to camp in the spring. There are tryouts in Kansas City in August. Let the big boys look you over. It's my guess they'll want to tie you up—send you to a farm team for basics. By then you'll know what to do—go to school, join the major leagues, or walk away from both and seek your family."

"Serious?"

"I'll pay for a trip to England or Africa. Your choice."

"Thank you." Daniel held out his hand and the two shook on it.

In a way Evy was relieved. Happy that a family crisis had been averted. This was the right answer and let Daniel stay in control, make his own decisions without feeling controlled or forced. Evy caught Walt's eye and smiled. It was a good bargain. And she wouldn't be saying good-bye anytime soon.

* * *

It had been a rainy spring—excessively cool—and followed a decidedly bitter winter. Temperatures in January had hovered around minus five during the day and plummeted at night. She had no idea whether it was the truth or not, but the Comptons, her neighbors to the right, swore three of their hogs froze standing up. Found them on a Saturday morning just leaning against the corn crib like they were having a chat about farm futures.

The cows started calving in January and had to be kept warm. She even had to put a warming bulb in the chicken house. They brought on an extra hand to live in the barn and tend to the animals overnight. Daniel had raised rabbits since he was ten—a 4-H project that was fun and profitable. Emma inherited the colony of some fifty, and one afternoon Evy returned from town to find twenty-five newly weaned kits hopping around the kitchen floor—with Emma sitting cross-legged in the middle, three more in her lap and Harry holding a doe.

"It was cold, Mommy. Can they stay inside?" So the screened-in area of the back porch was turned into a warren.

"You spoil her silly."

"She has a point about the rabbits—it's cold out there."

"For God's sake, Walt, they have fur."

He just smiled at her and went back to reading the paper.

If they thought the winter would never end, it really didn't. It simply got marginally warmer but stayed overcast, blustery and wet. Just when people were longing for sunshine and warmth, they woke up to day after day of gray monotonous dreariness. Many an afternoon she'd curl up with a good book in the window seat in the dining room and cope with the weather by ignoring it.

On this particular afternoon she had a good book, a cup of tea, and the house to herself—Walt working in the barn, Emma in school, Daniel running errands, getting ready to leave for spring camp. Walt had been right—Daniel was picked up by a major league team. And scouted by the All Negro Team. There seemed to be lots of opportunities and baseball seemed to have won out over school. She wasn't thrilled with this decision but kept it to herself. Peace in the family and Daniel's happiness meant everything.

This afternoon was hers. She cherished this time to herself. But today it didn't last long. She watched a cab approach the house. A yellow cab doing ten miles an hour up the long drive. How unusual. Hillsboro didn't have a cab company. Unless this was some new addition, the cab was probably from Kansas City or Wichita—an expensive trip.

She grabbed a sweater and walked out onto the porch. They weren't expecting anyone; this must be some mistake. She watched as the driver hopped out and held the back passenger-side door open. An older man in a perfectly tailored navy suit, white shirt, polished black shoes and a rather dapper gray felt, narrow-brimmed hat emerged. He was somewhat small in stature and it was difficult to determine his age. He seemed to be sizing up the house, gazing up at the second story, then backing up to take it all in.

"Can I help you?" He started like he hadn't seen her.

"Why, yes, you can. My name is Sterling Abbott, I'm looking for young Mister Everett. Daniel, I believe is the first name."

"And this is concerning …?"

"I represent the family of his mother, May Smythe-Nelson Everett. Recently they were contacted by the parish priest where Ms. Everett had lived. An African mission in the Congo, I believe. This inquiry was on behalf of her son, the young man, Daniel."

"I am aware that Daniel had made inquiries some time back. Who exactly has sent you?"

"Oh, forgive me, it wasn't my intention to be vague. Daniel's great-aunt, his grandmother's sister, Doreen Ward, is holding out an olive branch, if you will."

"An olive branch?"

"Well, not a secret that Ms. Ward's niece, May, was never acknowledged—her mother was disinherited. Ms. Ward would like to atone for all that. After the war and all, Daniel is the only direct male descendent on his mother's side of the family."

Evy took a deep breath. How interesting. "Would you like a cup of tea?"

There was no point in continuing to stand out in the cold. Yet dread seemed to almost render her immobile. Spasms of fear upset her stomach. She just wasn't ready for this—whatever it was, she didn't want it. She didn't want to lose Daniel to strangers—strangers half a world away.

"Oh my, yes, tea sounds wonderful—if it wouldn't be too much trouble."

She waited a moment while he dismissed the cab then

motioned for him to follow her through the front door. "We won't be disturbed in the kitchen."

She arranged cups and spoons alongside a small pitcher of milk and matching sugar bowl. The plate of chocolate chip cookies was fresh. Mattie wasn't as active in the kitchen as she once was but cookies were still her domain, and Daniel almost always had a jar of his favorites in the pantry.

"Here's a letter to the family. That would be you and your husband. Another here is for young Mr. Everett."

She waited to open the letter until after the tea was steeping, then she pulled back a chair and sat down. Still something kept her from just ripping it open, olive branch or not. What could Ms. Ward want now after eighteen years?

Finally she slipped a finger under the flap, tore it open and pulled out a letter. After a quick scan, it was apparent what she wanted—Daniel. She was offering him four years of schooling at Oxford. Oxford? England? Evy's brain was taking its own sweet time digesting this offer.

"How can Ms. Ward assure Daniel that he would be accepted at Oxford?"

"Ah, for starters, she's made inquiries. Daniel is quite an accomplished student. Fluent in German, three years of advanced Latin, chemistry, advanced math including calculus—"

"She was able to obtain his records?"

"Why, yes, as a relative and potential patron. His mother, of course, maintained dual citizenship which extends to Daniel."

Dual citizenship? She had no idea. But patron? Why did the word have such a stilted, archaic sound? Did Daniel need a patron? No, he did not. There was ample money to send him to any school he wanted. Didn't they know that?

"I don't think you understand. My husband and I are quite capable of sending Daniel to any school he chooses."

"And that's not the point, is it?" The little man with just the hint of a conciliatory smile—or was that just smugness—leaned across the table. "May I remind you that I am here, sent by his great aunt because *he* inquired about his family. I don't think it's up to what you or I might want but rather what Daniel wants."

She didn't want to concede this point, even though it was valid. Daniel had been on a quest to find his roots. And she was looking at the result.

"Then we'll just have to see what he decides."

Daniel would be home any minute so she left Mr. Abbott nursing a second cup of tea and ran to the barn to have Clemetts find Walt—letting him know that they had a visitor for lunch.

With all the parties assembled, lunch was a somewhat awkward affair. Luckily, there was cold pork tenderloin from the night before and it didn't take long to whip together potato salad and put out fresh crescent rolls. Dessert was berry tarts—freshly canned strawberries from last season.

Daniel's excitement was barely controlled. Evy requested any "business" be discussed over dessert and not during the meal. She could see that it was tough for Daniel to respect her wishes. But finally with tea or coffee in hand, they retired to the study.

"What's she like? Was she close to my grandmother? Did she ever visit Africa? For her sister to be disowned, it must—"

"One question at a time young man. And we don't mention your grandmother's … um … indiscretion."

"Then I can't understand why she is interested in me. Does she know I'm of color?"

"She does. The minister from your church sent several pictures—ones from the summer camp last year. May had sent her a picture of her wedding—her marriage to your father. You look very much like him."

"What do you think she wants of Daniel?"

Evy almost laughed. That was so very much like Walt to just cut to the chase.

"She wants to assure him of a good life."

"I can do that here."

"No one is doubting that, Mr. Schuler. No one. But this is an elderly woman—seventy-years-old this year—who in her remaining time on this earth wants to be assured her family will continue. There's a fair amount of property, I might add. The Smythe-Nelsons were quite … comfortable."

"She would expect me to enter school this fall?"

"She would like you to return with me now. She doesn't want to lose a minute of time in getting to know you and sharing your heritage with you."

"Return with you … when?"

"I will be leaving at the end of the week."

Four days. Evy almost cried out. How could she bear this? So sudden … so permanent.

"I can't leave until the end of spring. I've made a pact. I have three more months." Daniel didn't look at Walt but the inference was clear. And he had made a pact.

"I think that particular contract is negotiable. Under the circumstances, if this is what you feel you must do, your sister and I will support you in every way that we can."

She could have hugged him. Walked across the room and simply threw her arms around Walt's neck and thanked him. It would be difficult. Walt would miss Daniel terribly. He'd made an investment in another's life but knew when to step aside. She would always love Walt for that. And baseball might remain a dream. A disappointment. But can one ever choose another's path in life? Wasn't it better not to question but just go with Daniel's decision?

And if it's meant to be, it will happen. Baseball. School. Whatever would be, would be. There, she was beginning to sound like Walt. Or, maybe her father.

EPILOGUE

Daniel left that Friday to go by train halfway across the United States to New York and from there a plane to London. Four trunks would follow. He promised pictures and phone calls and letters. I didn't really expect he'd remember his promises in the excitement of exploring a new world. But he did.

That first summer, a two-month African Safari held him spellbound. And how truly thoughtful of his great aunt to provide this sort of treat. A side trip from Kenya to the Congo to look for family connections was the highlight.

May's father had died sixteen years ago but two male children from Mr. Nutanda's first marriage welcomed Daniel into their homes. Both had political standing in the community and pressured Daniel to pursue studies in international trade. What an eye-opener for a young man who had never traveled. He started school that fall with purpose and a direction.

Walt and I would visit Daniel years later, but he would never return to the States. He excelled in his studies, married and rose in his country's politics. Da would have been proud. I, along with my children, inherited the farm—more than meeting any stipulation put in place by a narrow-minded grandfather so many years before.

And my mother? Constance would have agreed with Emma May and Harry Wayne being the final recipients of what she held so dear. Her love, her obsession, Edward, was not the son who would carry on, but he did return. His remains were sent by a friend—ashes in a brightly decorated, lidded pot with the request that I place him beside his mother.

So, in retrospect? I couldn't shake the feeling that I'd lost a child. That always I'd have an aching hole in my heart for the caddis man's son, Daniel. The baby who shaped me as a person. Made me know what I was capable of. Made me understand conviction and right from wrong.

Most say that I should hate my father. Every shrink I've ever seen starts there—assumes some festering latent anger. But I didn't have to do what I did. No one made me. Da was dead by the time I decided. It was my decision at a time in my life when the nuances of being an adult were new and fragile.

Yet, can one ever overcome one's history? Or perhaps, I should say destiny. Be better or worse or more than? For those of us who try, the struggle can be challenging. How different would things have been if I hadn't lied? Hadn't changed the course of my family forever? And only now with a sense of my own mortality can I look back and say I'd do the same thing again.

Caddis Man – Book Club Discussion Questions

- Constance, at the beginning, comes across as a sympathetic character who has been dealt a bad hand in life. Later, we see a much harder edge to her. Do you think that's because she changes, or was she always somewhat rigid in her ways? How much of our perception comes from the point-of-view character (Constance presenting herself one way, her children seeing another side)?

- Harold Everett/Harry Evans, the caddis man – was he a con man all along or did her just fall into a situation beyond his control when he married Constance but later found himself in love with someone else?

- Evy has a difficult position as the "middle child" between the twins and the only son. Did you admire her, or did she become as controlling as her mother?

- How did you feel about Constance's generosity toward the church and community versus her stingy nature with her children? Was she teaching them values by her actions?

- The working farm – how much did its atmosphere play a role in the story? Can you imagine the setting for this saga taking place anywhere else?

- The mission location in the Congo – same question as above – could those events have taken place anywhere else, or was the remote mission crucial as a locale?

- At some moment did you stop feeling sympathy toward the sickly Edward and begin to dislike him? Did he have a flawed character all along or did Constance's mothering cause it?

- Was Harold's decision to stay in the Congo with May because he genuinely loved her or because he couldn't face Kansas and the family again? Did you feel sympathy/empathy for him or not?

- Which characters got their "just deserts" in the end, and which didn't?

- Were you curious about where this family's story would go in the future or did their saga end at exactly the right place?

Thank you for taking the time to read *The Caddis Man*. If you enjoyed it, please consider telling your friends, introducing it to your book club, or posting a short review. Word of mouth is an author's best friend and is much appreciated.

Thank you,

Susan Slater

What's next up from Susan Slater?

Susan brings us the next in her exciting Dan Mahoney mystery series, with *Widow's Walk*.

A St Augustine ship's captain has retired to run a tourist attraction—a fleet of four schooners that take water tours along the Intracoastal and Atlantic. The business is insured with Dan's company—United Life and Casualty. The story opens when the owner's wife falls to her death from the widow's walk tower on their home. Come to find out the Captain has insured her for two million. Is he the killer? He's having money problems. But then one of his schooners catches fire and sinks—another million in insurance from Dan's company.

Now, a finger is directly pointed at the Captain—only Dan believes he's innocent. Could a rival tour company be involved? Or the Captain's new wife, twenty years his junior, who married him one month after he buried his wife of thirty years? The suspects abound, as always, in this highly anticipated new book from award-winning author Susan Slater, coming in spring of 2022.

Books by Susan Slater

The Ben Pecos Mystery Series
The Pumpkin Seed Massacre
Yellow Lies
Thunderbird
Fire Dancer
Under A Mulberry Moon
The Thaw
Ghost Dust
Paper Arrows
A Way to the Manger (a Christmas novella)

The Dan Mahoney Mystery Series
Flash Flood
Rollover
Hair of the Dog
Epiphany

Standalone Novels
0-60 – contemporary romance
The Caddis Man – historical fiction
Five O'Clock Shadow – mystery-thriller

Visit Susan's website at susansslater.com where you can sign up for her free newsletter and a chance to win some very cool stuff.

Contact Susan: susan@susansslater.com
Follow Susan on Facebook